THE FEDSEX MAN

SCOTT HILDRETH

To my only sister, Amy.

We talked more than usual while I wrote this book. For that, I'll be forever grateful. While I struggled with the final touches, you died a tragic and very untimely death. As you floated to the heavens above, my mind seemed to blossom. I then made some changes, added a few things, and ended up with what I believe to be my best book to date.

Hope you and Pop enjoy it.
Kick his ass in Scrabble, will you?
I doubt (short of God) there's anyone
up there to challenge him.
As God's undoubtedly busy,
I know you're just the one to do it.

Love you, Sis.
Hoot

AUTHOR'S NOTE

The acts and actions depicted in the book are fictitious, as are the characters.
Every sexual partner in the book is over the age of 18. Please, if you intend to read further than this comment, be over the age of 18 to enjoy this novel.

This book is a work of fiction. Names, characters, places, and incidents are the product of the author's imagination or are used fictitiously. Any resemblances to actual events, locales, or persons living or dead, are coincidental.

Cover design by Jessica Hildreth

Follow me on Facebook at: www.facebook.com/sd.hildreth

Like me on Facebook at: www.facebook.com/ScottDHildreth

Follow me on Twitter at: @ScottDHildreth

PROLOGUE

THE HELICOPTER'S crew chief adjusted the spotlight, shining it directly onto the frantic scene below. Littered about the officer's feet, numerous brass shell casings glistened, giving indication of the utter hell that had been unleashed mere seconds before.

Standing nervously beside the bullet-ridden silver sports coupe, the officer stretched a rubber glove over his left hand, tearing it in the process.

"Son-of-a-bitch," he exclaimed, tossing the shredded rubber onto the ground at his side.

He anxiously rifled through the back pocket of his trousers for another. Simultaneously, his right hand blindly searched for the microphone that was clipped to his uniform's lapel. Upon finding it, he pressed the button on the side of the newly-issued device.

"Four-Twelve-Bravo to dispatch, shots fired! Shots fired! North Central Expressway and East Park. Eastbound off-ramp. Requesting ambulance. Possible airlift. White male. Mid-thirties. Multiple gunshot wounds."

"Roger, Four-Twelve-Bravo," the dispatch operator said, confirming the officer's request. "North Central Expressway and East Park. Do officers need assistance?"

The officer pulled his bare hand from his empty pocket, hesitated, and then placed his index and middle fingers against the blood-soaked neck of the man slumped in the driver's seat of the car. A pulse, albeit faint, provided a glimmer of hope.

Please. Let this man live, the officer prayed.

"Dispatch to Four-Twelve-Bravo," the operator called out. "I repeat, do officers need assistance?"

The officer's eyes met the crying passenger's tear-filled gaze. *It's going to be just fine,* the officer thought. *Don't worry, help is on the way.*

He gazed blankly at his bloody hand. *How did things go to hell so quickly,* he thought?

"Four-Twelve-Bravo, can you confirm officer casualties?" the operator asked. "Confirm by keying your mic, Four-Twelve-Bravo."

"Negative, dispatch." The officer traced his bloody fingertips along the side of the man's neck once again, hoping the pulse hadn't faded.

"We're code two on that bus, dispatch!" the officer shouted. "What's the ETA?"

"Ambulance en route, Four-Twelve-Bravo. ETA eleven minutes."

Despite the young officer's lack of experience, he knew one thing for certain.

Eleven minutes was too long.

1

JO

A WELL-WRITTEN BOOK allowed me to experience the character's hardships, joy, and pain no differently than if I was at their side. When I read, I was transported out of Allen, Texas, and into the book's setting. Depending on the author's ability to craft an artistic tale, my thoughts often remained with the book's characters until long after I'd finished reading.

With my focus being independently published romance novels, I opened a small bookstore after graduating college. The location was in a run-down strip mall flanked by a cut-rate hair salon on one side and a seedy massage parlor on the other.

Hoping to share my passion of reading with others, I filled the shelves with books written by the industry's most colorful authors. I developed a stream of loyal customers, most of which – at least initially – came from the hair salon.

The massage parlor offered no walk-in business from the unhappily married men who snuck in through the back door, but late afternoon entertainment seeped through the paper-thin walls that separated *Cum-N-Go Massage* from the bookstore.

My income wasn't much at first, but the satisfaction I received from being surrounded by something I was passionate about was priceless. Two years later, my growing success demanded that I hire a co-worker to aid me with my endeavors. After a painstaking process of interviewing two-dozen well-qualified housewives and one twenty-three-year-old high school dropout, I chose the high school dropout, Jenny.

Hoping the distance between her birthplace and her new home would be enough to deter her overbearing parents from monitoring her every move, she relocated to Texas from Phoenix, Arizona.

She was young, passionate about reading, and provided all-day entertainment by voicing her opinions without filter or fear of repercussion.

"BB Easton is a badass." She carefully placed BB's newest book, *Star*, at the top of the four-book display. "I would love to be her for a day. Not now. But, like, when she was in school. When she was with Knight. If we had guys like that in my high school, I would have stayed."

"I didn't like that guy at first" I admitted. "He was the first anti-hero that I warmed up to."

"Anti-hero?" Her nose wrinkled in opposition to my statement. "He wasn't an anti-hero, he was a man who was misunderstood and under-loved."

"In the end, I really liked him." I added, gesturing to the book in question. "Getting to that point wasn't easy, though. A wannabe skinhead with a penchant for kicking guys in the kidneys with his steel-toed boots isn't my typical hero."

"I like the thought of a guy who's willing to stand up for himself much more than a guy without a backbone." She twisted her long blonde hair into a quick bun, revealing her underlying brunette roots in the process. "Nothing turns me away quicker than a man who isn't willing to protect what he loves."

"There's a big difference between protecting what one loves and blindly beating anyone who opposes you," I quipped.

"Whether we feel threatened or not," she traced her fingertip along the cover of the book on BB Easton's display. "Women find value in hiding under the umbrella of belief that our man can protect us from the demons that wander this earth."

Jenny had a strikingly beautiful face and an equally gorgeous body. Her personality was magnetic, and she was easy to talk to. Discussing matters with her never turned into an argument, leaving the conversations enlightening and fun.

The resting bitch face she often wore was enough to ward off many potential beaus. The few that remained were often turned away by her foul mouth and unfiltered manner of spewing out her beliefs.

Wearing a denim skirt, embroidered cowgirl boots, and a sleeveless white *Chris Stapleton* concert tee, she looked the way she always did.

Cute.

"If you found a guy who was protective and handsome would you date him?" I asked.

She thought for a moment, and then shrugged as she turned away. "I doubt it."

I giggled. "Why not?"

She faced me. "You asked me if I'd date him. I might fuck him, but I wouldn't necessarily *date* him. For me to date someone, I'd have to be interested in him. For me to be truly interested in a man, he has to have three things."

"Just three?" I leaned against the book shelf and gave her a curious look. "What are they?"

She extended her index finger. "One. He's got to be sexy."

"What's your definition of sexy?"

"Not what you'd think. Sexy can be the way he walks, carries himself, or if he's a really good storyteller."

"A storyteller?" I'd never thought of a good storyteller as sexy. "You think that's sexy?"

"You know the kind of guy that uses his hands when he talks?" she asked, waving her hands as she spoke. "I think it's sexy when they wave their hands around to make a point."

I didn't find hand waving sexy. In fact, I found hand-talkers to be annoying. "That drives me nuts," I said. "What are the other two?"

"Number two." She extended her middle finger. "He's got to

be gifted in the dick department." She raised her eyebrows and ring finger at the same time. "And, number three, he's got to be loyal."

"It's that easy, huh?"

"Easy?" She laughed. "Guys who tell good stories never have big dicks, and from what I can tell, nobody in this state is loyal to anything other than football."

I had no experience with big-dicked storytellers, but I couldn't argue the loyalty issue. During football season, the only thing that mattered to the citizens of Allen, Texas was football. It consumed my father entirely from August until February, leaving only a small window of time for him to pay attention to me during my childhood.

I had a great relationship with my father, but because of what I felt I forfeited so he could enjoy the sport, I detested football and those who devoted any measurable portion of their life to it.

"Those are tough shoes to fill," I said. "Football is all people seem think about."

"*Here?*" she said. "Yeah, you're right."

"You mean in Allen?"

"In Texas." She pursed her lips and looked away, but quickly returned her gaze to meet mine. "Not in other places, though. Arizona wasn't like this, I can tell you that much. I think the men here have shriveled hearts, great big egos, and little bitty dicks."

"Is that statement made based on experience?" I asked with a laugh.

"It is," she responded. "I've had two sexual experiences since I moved here. Both guys had tiny cocks and huge attitudes."

"So, everything's *not* big in Texas?"

"The first guy?" She held her thumb and index finger about two inches apart. "It was the size of one of those weird-shaped tomatoes."

I laughed out loud. "A Roma?"

"Yeah. A freaking Roma. Or an egg. It could have passed for either." She shook her head in clear disgust. "Second guy was just as bad, but his wasn't as thick as the other guy. His was the size of my thumb. I think I hate this state. If I didn't like working here so much, I'd probably go to Alabama or Arkansas."

"Arkansas and Alabama?" I gave her a crazy-eyed look. "What's there?"

"Nothing. But, I'm guessing if the arrogant egomaniacs in Texas have small dicks, the hillbillies in either of those states have got to be hung like horses. Humble and hung, that's what I'm thinking."

I mentally laughed at her theory but couldn't help but agree with her logic. "You know what? You're probably right."

She adjusted her bun and grinned. "I'd take a well-hung hillbilly in a twenty-year-old Mustang over one of these cowboy hat wearing egg-dicked jerks in a new pickup truck any day."

"Just because he's hung doesn't mean—"

"A big cock is a prerequisite," she insisted. "A guy with a little dick and a great personality will never do it for me. Ever."

Although I'd read enough to qualify for having a lifetime of relationships, I had minimal real-world experience with men. Through reading, I'd deduced that well-endowed men came with no guarantees, other than an assurance of multiple orgasms and earth-shattering sex.

"You don't think that's shallow?" I asked.

"Shallow?" She laughed. "Not at all. Being boned by a guy who's packing a pencil is like being finger-banged, only there's some idiot on top of you breathing heavily. I can finger myself, I don't need someone to do it with his dick."

Any dick was a good dick, as far as I was concerned. I was a book nerd in high school and remained a book nerd. Men's lack of interest in women like me made sure my dick well was constantly dry. I'd take any dick I could get my eager hands on, big or small.

"So, if you met the perfect guy, but he had the Roma tomato thing going on, you wouldn't give him a chance?" I asked. "You couldn't love him?"

"Nope."

"Even if he was perfect?"

"If he had a little dick, he wouldn't be *perfect*," she insisted. "He'd be a guy with a fabulous personality and a little dick."

The various shapes, length and girth of a man's penis fascinated me. I'd spent countless hours looking at them on the internet. I couldn't help but wonder what it would feel like to be impaled by one of the record-breaking schlongs of the porn industry's leading men. Nonetheless, I stood firm in the position I'd taken in our dick-debate.

"So, what happens to all the guys with little dicks?" I asked with a laugh. "Do they wander the earth aimlessly looking for women they'll never satisfy?"

"They end up with women who have miniature vaginas," she said matter-of-factly. "Either that, or they stay single forever. Single and searching for that girl with the little va-jay-jay. One that fits their tiny wiener like a fleshy little glove."

I choked on a laugh. "This conversation is ridiculous."

She curtsied and turned away. "Glad I can entertain you."

After unlocking the front door, she propped it open. A hint of freshly cut grass and the sweet smell of honeysuckle replaced the lingering smell of coconut-scented massage oil that permeated through the ventilation system. I closed my eyes and let the aroma of early spring find its way to my nostrils.

"Oh. My God," Jenny squealed. "He's coming around the corner."

My eyes sprung open. "Who?"

"That guy," she said.

I peered through the window but saw nothing more than a few passing vehicles. "What guy?"

"The one I told you about last week." She glanced over her shoulder. "The FedEx man."

Her earlier description of the new driver left little to the imagination. I felt she'd embellished the portrayal of him she'd given, as no delivery driver had ever captured my interest in the manner that she claimed he'd garnered hers.

A handsome man with massive biceps and a million-dollar smile definitely wasn't the typical hiring requirement for the Allen, Texas FedEx drivers. Repulsive looking men who were six inches shorter than me with sparse beards and bulging calf muscles seemed more the norm.

I nudged my way between her and the doorframe. As I gazed toward the street, his truck came to a stop at the curb in front of us. A quick glimpse of the driver's profile before he disappeared into the back of the truck was enough to make me feel like a nervous high schooler.

Jenny's description of him was spot-on. He was handsome, athletic, and filled out his two-tone blue uniform completely.

"Are we expecting something?" I whispered.

"I don't know," she breathed. "I hope so."

I turned away, hoping to seem less interested than Jenny, who was standing in the doorway with her mouth wide open and eyes bulging.

"Don't look so eager." I grabbed one of LJ Shen's books from the display and began pacing the floor as I flipped through the pages. "You'll freak him out."

She laughed. "You look guilty as fuck."

I lowered the book and glared at her. "Of what?"

"Of wanting to get on his dick," she whispered.

"I don't want to *get on his dick*," I said, even though the thought entered my mind for a fleeting moment. "I was just trying to see what he looked like."

She gave me a quick look and then shifted her eyes right back to the FedEx truck. "You're pacing the floor like you're guilty of *something*."

In school, while the other girls dreamed about boys, I spent my spare time in the library fantasizing about faraway lands, alternate forms of life, and escaping Allen, Texas.

I'd since exchanged my pressed button-down blouses for more modern tops, replaced my pleated skirts with a wider variety of options, and wore low heels instead of Oxfords. Nothing changed, though. Since college, I'd become more transparent than when I was in school.

A transparent and everlastingly single nerd.

I still favored reading, but thanks to CD Reiss, LJ Shen, Vi

Keeland, and Penelope Ward, my dreams were now filled with being sexually ravished by billionaires, bikers, and badasses. Sadly, my sexual encounters were limited to dreams.

Wild dreams but dreams nonetheless.

When the driver stepped through the truck's open door and onto the sidewalk, I stopped breathing.

Completely.

I lifted my gaze the length of his lean muscular frame. The company-issued polo he wore clung to his wide chest. Mid-stride on his way to the door, the Texas wind blew the fabric tight against his flat stomach. The outline of a rippled torso was overshadowed by the bulging biceps that flexed when he handed Jenny two small cardboard boxes.

She smiled and took them from his grasp. "Thanks."

"I'll need a signature," he said, revealing an envious set of perfectly straight teeth. They were a shade of white reserved for Crest commercials and internet ads for cosmetic dental surgery.

No one with a smile so charming could be a bad person.

He scanned the boxes and then handed her the device. Wearing a guilt-ridden smirk, she signed the screen with the stylus and returned the scanner. He clipped it to his belt and took a precursory glance around the store. While he did, Jenny's gaze fell to his crotch.

Naturally, mine followed.

My heart began to beat so rapidly I feared he might hear it. I pressed my palm to my chest and stood statue-still, hoping he didn't notice me gawking at his noteworthy nether region.

Along the inner side of his upper right thigh was the outline of what God had graced him with. He'd been blessed with far more than a remarkable body and an infectious smile.

Incapable of ripping my eyes away what was hanging heavily inside the leg of his shorts, I stared as if it were a ten-car pileup on highway 75.

My thoughts drifted from the incredible chunk of flesh to him tossing me onto the mountain of boxes in the back of his truck and forcing every thick inch of his manhood beyond my deprived folds and deep inside my soaking wet warmth.

The sound of the paperback's spine hitting the floor brought me back to reality. Embarrassed, I bent down and picked it up, hoping he didn't notice. As I straightened my stance, his curious stare pinned me to the bookshelf I'd been using as shelter.

He held my gaze with hazel eyes unlike any I'd ever seen. Green with flicks of translucent brown sprinkled throughout the iris, they were fascinating to look at. Frozen in place like a deer in the headlights of an oncoming truck, I stared back at him feeling as if he was peering into my very soul.

He grinned. "I like your shirt."

I melted into a puddle. Hypnotized by his presence and incapable of something as simple as formulating a response, I swallowed heavily and parted my drying lips.

Hi, my name's Jo.

I'm single. Would you mind showing me your dick? I'm fascinated by them in general, and yours seems to be quite a specimen.

Please?

"Huh?" I murmured.

"Your shirt," he said with a nod. "I like it."

I was far too young for hot flashes, but one shot through me nonetheless. Uncertain of what shirt I had chosen, I brushed the wrinkles from the weathered fabric and glanced down.

girl

gərl/

noun

1. an attitude with boobs

It was one of my favorite shirts, but not at all what I would expect someone to compliment me on. As all the blood in my body rushed to my face, I pushed my glasses up the bridge of my nose and returned a crooked smile. "Thank you."

He undressed me with his eyes and turned away. As he walked to his truck I braced myself against the bookcase and swam in the compliment he'd given regarding my choice of attire.

"Ho-Lee-Shit." Jenny spun around. "Did you see that?"

Still mesmerized, I stared blankly as he drove away. "See what?"

"The package he *didn't* drop off." She let out a long breath. "Jesus. H. Christ. That thing was huge."

I feigned innocence. "Huh?"

She gestured toward the empty street. "He was hung like a freaking mule."

I desperately needed time to recover. My skin was on fire and my pussy was throbbing. The look he gave me pushed me over the edge of reality and right into a pool of lustful thoughts.

On the surface, I remained calm. On the inside, I was being pressed against the bookshelf and shoved full of the world's newfound eighth wonder.

"I didn't notice," I lied.

"It looked like he had a can of Red Bull stuffed in the leg of his shorts," she said excitedly.

I maintained my look of innocence. "A what?"

"His dick was the size of a can of freaking Red Bull." She raised her hands and held them a foot from one another. "Not the little one that sells for a dollar ninety-nine, either. The big one. The five-dollar can."

"Oh." Still blushing from his remark, I turned toward my desk, hoping Jenny didn't notice my level of embarrassment. "I'll take your word for it."

"I can't believe he made that comment about your shirt. Look at what I'm wearing." She brushed her hands over her ample chest and then tugged at the hem of her shirt. "I've got Chris fucking Stapleton and titties hanging out my non-existent sleeves. He didn't even take a second glance."

I sat down and fanned my face with the book. "Maybe he did, and you didn't notice. Sounds like you were pretty busy checking out his energy drink."

She tossed the boxes on the floor at my side. "Well, if he noticed, he sure as fuck didn't say anything."

After a moment, the blood drained from my face, leaving me disappointed that he'd managed to escape. I wondered when – or if

– he'd ever return. Then, I realized I held his fate in my shaking hands.

Most of what was delivered to the store was through the US Postal Service's media mail program. I had the freedom, however, of choosing the carrier for non-book related freight. As Jenny mumbled obscenities and tidied up the book shelves, I ordered a new pair of shoes from *Zappos*.

Next-day FedEx delivery with a signature required, of course.

2

TYSON

"THE BOX you left last week was upside down." Her voice was edgy, like that of a smoker. "Everything was all jostled around," she continued.

Miss Everly was new to the neighborhood. In the past six days I'd made six deliveries to her home, but I had yet to catch a glimpse of her. I preferred associating a face to a name, so I turned toward the raspy voice without hesitation.

Athletic legs sprouted from fuzzy slippers and seemed to go on for miles. They disappeared beneath the hem of a monogrammed terrycloth robe that was far too short to be wearing anywhere but in the privacy of one's home.

She flipped her platinum blond hair over her shoulders. The edges of her full lips curled into a slight smile. She looked as if she'd stepped off the set of a centerfold shoot for *Playboy* magazine.

I smiled in return. "Sorry about that, but I don't pack the boxes or label them. I place them on your porch with the printed address facing up. If someone put the label on the bottom of the box, it would end up upside down."

Box in hand, she took a step in my direction. When she did, her robe fell open, revealing much more than a glimpse of her disproportionately large boobs. "Well, it's not a big deal," she said, making no effort to cover herself. "I just thought I'd say something."

"You might mention it to whoever packed the box." I lowered my gaze from her bulging breasts to the box she held. I gave a half-hearted wave. "Have a nice day."

"Would you like a glass of tea?" She asked. "It's terribly hot out here."

She was right. It was early spring, and over hundred degrees. Nonetheless, I knew myself well enough to realize a glass of tea with a half-dressed wannabe supermodel wouldn't be limited to a glass of tea. I had somewhere else I was anxious to go and didn't need – or want – the distraction.

At least not at that moment.

"Sorry," I said. "I've got a full truck. I'll have to take a rain check."

She shifted her gaze to the sky. "One glass of tea won't hurt."

While she ogled the cloudless sky, I stared at her tanned mounds of buttery smooth flesh for long enough to memorize the location of each freckle. With reluctance, I tore my eyes away from the scantily dressed temptress and cleared my throat.

"I'm on a tight schedule," I said, forcing the words past my lips. "Thanks for the offer."

"That's a shame." She cocked her hip slightly and threw me a hopeful smile. "Tomorrow?"

"Tomorrow's Saturday," I said with a smile and a wave. "Maybe some other time. Thank you."

With a half-stiff dick and a mind reeling with ideas of what to do with it, I left Miss Everly's home and completed my residential deliveries, finishing before nine am. An hour later I was on my commercial route, delivering a next-day package to a local book store.

The book store's owner was the newfound object of my sexual desires, and my reason for putting Miss Everly on the back burner. Jo Watson was a mirror image of the sexiest woman I'd ever seen. She also shared the last name of one of my idols.

I had plans to seduce her.

She was the twin to Miss Garber, my high school librarian. The subject of daily lunchroom conversations between every boy in school, Garber was thin with curves in all the right places. Her high cheeks, long legs, and pouty lips attracted the attention of every male within eyeshot and garnered the envy of the entire female population of Plano, Texas.

Wearing form-fitting skirts and button-down blouses, she defined all that was sexy throughout my formative years. With horn-rimmed glasses perched low on the bridge of her nose she strode through the library, leaving a room of raging hard-ons in her wake. I ached to fuck her for four years and continued to fantasize about her long after graduating. I now had the opportunity to screw her doppelganger, and I intended to take advantage of fulfilling that fantasy.

Eagerly, I grabbed the Zappos box and hopped out of my truck.

Wearing a pair of cut-off jean shorts, boots, and a Johnny Cash tee shirt, her well-endowed co-worker stood with her nose pressed against the glass door. I flashed a quick smile and gazed at the bookshelf beyond her, where Miss Garber's look-alike adjusted a row of books.

Jo Watson's ass was shaped like the waning crescent moon, perfect in size and as round as the glass sphere paperweight that sat atop the desk behind her. The pair of black-framed Rayban glasses she wore were in complete contrast to her pale skin, and her hair was in a braided messy bun that rested against the back of her bare neck.

I reached for the door handle, paused, and took every inch of her into view. Dressed in a sleeveless black dress and black low-heeled shoes, she looked remarkable. While I revered her every feature, my cock acknowledged her beauty by stiffening a little more with each beat of my heart.

Emotionally committed to delivering the package, and far too confident in my manhood to allow a stiff dick to embarrass me, I pushed the door open and stepped in front of the large-breasted cowgirl.

"Good morning." I glanced at the label on the box. "I need a signature from Jo Watson."

The cowgirl's gaze was fixed on the growing bulge in my shorts. "Jo," she said without looking away from the outline of my cock. "He's got a package for you."

Jo looked up. When our eyes met, she grinned. I watched admiringly as she approached, all the while feeling the cowgirl's breath against my neck.

"Can I sign for it?" Cowgirl asked.

"No," I lied. "I've got to have the signature of the recipient."

Jo stepped to the cowgirl's side. "Hi." She removed her glasses. "How can I help you?"

"Well, for starters," I began. "You can put those glasses back on."

A confused look washed over her. "Pardon me?"

"The glasses," I explained. "I like it better when you're wearing them."

"These?" Holding the temple between her thumb and forefinger, she twirled the spectacles like a prison guard twirled his keys. "They make me look dumb."

If anything, they completed her ensemble. I shook my head lightly in disagreement. "I disagree."

"Really?" She swallowed heavily. "Why?"

I leaned close enough to smell her innocence. "Because, when you wear them." I paused for effect. "You're irresistible."

Her glasses hit the floor with a *clank*. While she stood in front of me with her mouth agape, I set the box at her feet and picked up the sexy frames.

She stood statue-still as I raised them to her face.

"Here." I said. "Let me help you."

I slid the temples over her ears and positioned them on her nose. The addition of the glasses changed her appearance from attractive to irresistibly sexy.

I crossed my arms and studied her. "Ir-re-sistable."

"Don't you have packages to deliver?" Cowgirl asked in a snide tone.

I gave her buxom coworker a lingering scowl, and then picked up the box. While Cowgirl's attitude-infused glare burned holes into the flesh of my back, I sauntered toward the desk in the distance.

I set the box beside the paperweight, and then scanned it. "Miss Watson?" I asked over my shoulder. "Would you like to sign for this?"

She walked in my direction fluidly and precisely, like a lone soldier marching across a parade deck. I stole a few admiring looks of her rose-colored cheeks while she signed for the package, wondering if the color was natural or makeup.

She handed me the scanner. "Thank you."

Her voice was feather-soft. I gave her a quick once-over, and then grinned. "What time do you close?"

"Close? We uhhm," she stammered. "We close at seven."

"Do you have plans after work?"

Her brows knitted together. "Plans?"

"Yes," I said. "Do you have plans? After you get off work?"

"I uhhm." She folded her arms over her chest. "No. Not really."

"Care to grab something to eat?"

"With you?"

"Yes." I struggled to remain straight-faced. "You and me. Together."

Her cheeks flushed from pink to red. "Oh, I uhhm," she stammered. "Thank you, but I don't think so."

Her cowgirl counterpart stepped to her side. "She'd love to."

"No," Jo insisted. "It's probably not a good idea. I've got to get—"

Her coworker led her away by the wrist. After a moment of inaudible whispering, the look on Jo's face softened.

Cowgirl shifted her gaze to meet mine. "She'd love to."

"Sooo." I leaned to the side, looking beyond the cowgirl, who now stood between Jo and me. When Jo met my gaze, I raised my brows. "Which is it?"

Jo's face remained ruby red. Nonetheless, standing before me in her sleeveless black dress with her hair pulled into a perfectly imperfect bun, she was strikingly beautiful.

"I uhhm…sure…" She adjusted her glasses. "We can get something to eat."

Cowgirl struggled to keep her shallow grin from morphing into a toothy smile.

"I'll see you at seven," I said.

The corners of her mouth turned up ever so slightly. "Okay."

I offered a smile, nodded, and then turned away. Just before I reached the door, Cowgirl stepped in front of me and pulled it open.

"If you do anything to hurt her," she said under her breath. "I'll dig your eyes out with a fucking spoon."

I stutter-stepped and grabbed the door's frame to stabilize myself. "Excuse me?"

"I'm not joking," she said dryly. "Not even a little bit. I'll dig 'em out and flush 'em down the freaking toilet."

I gave her a quick look-over, waiting for her to laugh. The laughter never came. Nervously, I broke her glare and turned toward my truck.

The last thing I needed in my life was vengeance-seeking spoon-wielding maniac.

3

JO

I LIVED in a bubble of well-being, limiting my outreach to family members and a handful of girlfriends I'd befriended over the years. Despite my social anxiety, it was easy for me to talk to women.

Men were a different story. Men made me nervous.

Once I was comfortable around a man, I became my outgoing and obnoxious self. Reaching that point either required that I expose myself to him until I was comfortable, that I was drunk, or sex. Sadly, expressing my willingness to have sex required that I be drunk or comfortable. Being comfortable took time. Men were impatient creatures, which normally meant they gave up before I relaxed enough to be myself.

The anxiety created by my social inadequacies wreaked havoc on my sex life.

"What do you feel like eating?" he asked.

Making decisions wasn't one of my strong suits. To maximize my social skills and minimize the awkwardness between us, I drank two glasses of wine before he arrived. Even so, he was still a man, and I was a few drinks away from being my outgoing self. If he wanted me to be at ease in his presence, he needed to pour half a bottle of wine down my throat, park the car, and fuck me.

I wished I had the ability to tell him it was that easy.

"I'll eat anything." I offered a grin of reassurance. "Really."

"I want to eat somewhere that's got something you like. Something you enjoy. What's your favorite food?"

We were parked at the curb in front of the bookstore. His right hand clutched the steering wheel tightly, which caused his muscles to flex. I hoped he and his bicep would decide where we were going to eat without any input from me.

"I don't really have favorites." I shifted my gaze to meet his. "I like everything."

While he focused on jockeying through Allen's evening traffic, I thanked the tee shirt gods for crafting a garment that fit him like a thin layer of powder blue paint.

He glanced in my direction. "How does seafood sound?"

It sounded hideous. Eating seafood often made me sick. It happened more often than often. Always was more like it. Seafood was nasty, and my digestive system knew it.

My stomach churned in disapproval of his suggestion. I forced myself to smile. "Sounds great."

I didn't want to give him a reason to reject me. Choking down a piece of fish was the least I could contribute in exchange for a date with him. An evening filled with muscles, pearly white teeth, and a mile of dick were well worth vomiting in a restaurant bathroom.

"There's this place called *Rockfish* over on Park Boulevard." He checked for traffic before changing lanes. "It looks like a shitty little dive and they serve the food on plastic plates that don't match, but it's really good."

Men who looked like he did asked girls like me on dates for one reason, and one reason only.

Sex.

Some girls were able to measure their successes by counting the months they'd been in a relationship. I wasn't so fortunate. My relationships simply didn't last. Having sex was my means of measuring success, and I was hoping for a successful night.

There was no doubt that vomiting during our dinner date would end the possibility of a post-meal sexual romp. Frustrated at the thought of getting sick, I gazed out the car's side window.

Changing his seafood plans was paramount to our night's successes. Sucking his dick while he drove should make him forfeit the dinner plans, leaving us with nothing to do for the evening but have sex.

Introducing the idea of an in-car blowjob would require that I consume at least two of the miniature-sized bottles of Apple Crown Royal that were rattling around in the bottom of my purse. Sneaking them in the confines of his car would be impossible.

There was no way around it. Seafood was on the horizon.

"Sounds great," I said cheerily.

"How long has the bookstore been there?" he asked.

Shifting the subject matter from fish to books was a nice change of pace. I decided to sprinkle clues of my willingness to have sex throughout our conversation – Hansel and Gretel style.

"Five years. I opened it right after I graduated college. Romance novels are the store's specialty." I gave him my best sultry look. "Steamy contemporary romance novels."

I hoped *steamy contemporary* was suggestive enough to spark his interest. I braced myself for the onslaught of sexual innuendos that he was sure to make.

"Out of school for five years, huh? I thought you were older. Not that you look older, it's just…" He glanced over his right shoulder. "I think it's the glasses. They make you look distinguished."

I was disappointed that he didn't bite on the romance novel lure but was flattered about the distinguished comment. The remark regarding my youthful appearance edged its way beneath my skin. After a lingering moment, I began to itch.

Outside the confines of the bookstore, I felt young and unaccomplished. As one might imagine, I hoped I didn't appear that way.

"I'm probably older than you think," I said. "It took me a while to get through college. Allen Eagles class of 2007. I graduated college in 2013."

He gave a shallow nod as he maneuvered through traffic. I

waited for him to acknowledge what I'd said or continue the conversation, but he said nothing. After a few moments, I broke the awkward silence.

"How about you?" I asked.

"How about me, what?"

"Where did you go to school?"

"Plano Senior High," he said.

"When did you graduate?"

"A few years before you."

His face was free of any wrinkles, whatsoever. I expected he was a few years younger than me. I really didn't care how old he was. Eventually, curiosity got the best of me.

"What year?" I asked.

He drew a long, slow breath. "2000."

"Oh," I said. "I would have guessed you were younger than that."

I no more than spoke and wished I could take it back. He did look young, but I didn't want him to think I took exception to him being a few years older than me. Truth be told, I was attracted to older men.

"But I'm glad you're not," I added. "I prefer guys who are older than me."

He flashed a smile that could have melted steel. "I'm thirty-five."

I grinned. "Twenty-nine."

He shrugged playfully. "What's age, anyway?"

"Nothing but a number."

"Exactly."

The novels about men who were fractionally older than the respective women they dated all eluded to the same thing. Older men were more capable – and willing – to take care of their female counterparts than men who were lesser in age than the women they courted.

I wanted to ask how someone like him could be single but was one glass of wine short of being courageous. Bravery came with wine or with time, and there hadn't been enough of either. At least not yet.

Following the failed erotica discussion, I opted to bring up a subject that all men seemed eager to discuss. Talking, regardless of the subject matter, would ease my state of mind.

"I like your car," I said.

I knew nothing about cars, other than that my father and brother were infatuated with them. They talked about them for hours on end, leaving my mother and I to talk about reading, our fingernails, and bargains. Men's attachments to cars, I'd learned, could be life-long. Cars were to men what shopping was to women.

An obsession.

"Thanks," he replied. "It's been a project."

The car was perfect in appearance and didn't appear to be any sort of a project. I wrinkled my nose in opposition to his claim.

"Project?" I asked. "What do you mean?"

"It had been wrecked, and there was significant interior damage. It was a declared a total loss from the insurance company. I rebuilt it with my bare hands. I replaced the damaged interior, added a supercharger, headers, high performance exhaust, bigger intake, a closer ratio…"

He continued to speak, but the words stopped registering. He sounded like my brother. I waited until his mouth stopped moving and then I smiled. Close ratio widgets and bigger thingamajigs did little to stimulate me. I wanted to devise a way to discuss above average penis sizes and the advantage of having a friend with benefits.

"Oh wow," I said, beaming with false excitement. "That's awesome."

He smiled a lip-thinning grin, revealing his incredibly perfect teeth. I admired him longer than I probably should have, enjoying the minute details of his handsome facial features.

While I was deep in admiration, his smile twisted into a sly grin. "Watch. This."

Dripping with intention, the two words hung in the air like a heavy fog. I craned my neck in anticipation, mentally prepared for him to pull out his cock. Believing the sight of it alone might fuel me to eat fish with vigor, I fixed my eyes on his torso and prepared for the show.

He met my wondrous stare. "Ready?"

I parted my dry lips. "Uh huh."

His right hand reached for the gear shifter. He downshifted. A horrendous whining sound came from under the hood, and the car shot forward with so much force that it plastered my stomach against my spine.

I wanted to scream and laugh and vomit all at the same time, but the force of the car's acceleration prevented me from doing any of them.

The rear tires screeched. The car shot forward at the pace of Mars-bound rocket. Incapable of doing something as natural as drawing a breath, I sat with my mouth agape and gawked through the windshield with bulging eyes. A quick glance at the speedometer revealed a 125 mile-an-hour – and still rapidly increasing – speed.

While my thrashing heart reminded me of the dangers associated with triple-digit speeds along a city street, my eyes tried to make sense of the objects as they sped past. Apart from what was inside the car, everything became a blur. Everything except for the flashing lights on the six police cars that blocked the road ahead.

I desperately needed to shout out a warning, but the words didn't come.

Upon seeing the roadblock, he slammed on the brakes. "Those motherfuckers!"

The car slowed from warp speed to a crawl in an instant, slamming my chest against the seatbelt's strap in the process. The force sent a shockwave of pain across my shoulder and along my spine.

I surveyed the roadblock. The police officers were carrying assault rifles, which wasn't typical – even in Texas. I envisioned being yanked from the car, patted down for weapons, and handcuffed. I'd never been arrested and wondered if the experience was anything like what I'd read.

While an officer approached the car, I swallowed what felt like a throat full of sand and looked in my nameless date's direction.

"What's your name?" I squeaked. "I don't even know your name."

"Sorry," he said. "It's Tyson. Tyson Neese."

I mentally prepared for being made the bitch of Collin County jail's lesbian shot caller. "Are we going to jail, Tyson?"

"As long as you don't say anything, we'll be fine."

"Say anything?" I stammered. "To who?"

"The cops," he replied. "Don't say anything when they start asking questions. Not a word."

I swallowed heavily. "About what?"

"Anything," he said through clenched teeth.

My mind went in a thousand different directions. Flashing lights. Speeding cars. Heavily armed cops. Maintaining silence. Spending a night – or more – in jail. While my perfect little world began to spiral down the drain of life, the officer rapped his knuckles against Tyson's window. Beyond him, flashing lights and uniformed cops filled the street.

Tyson cracked the window no more than an inch.

"License and registration," the officer said, his tone muffled by the car's nearly shut window.

"Why am I being stopped?" Tyson asked.

"We're searching for someone," the officer responded. "License and registration, please."

"A specific someone?" Tyson asked. "Do I fit the description?"

"License and registration, please," the officer said.

"Is the individual you're seeking driving a 2004 Mustang Cobra?" Tyson asked in a snide tone. "Silver in color?"

"License. And. Registration." The officer cocked his head. "Please."

The *please* was in the most sarcastic of sarcastic tones. It was just my luck. My first date since my junior year in college, and it was going to end with Tyson and I being hauled to jail before I got a chance to show off my mad blowjob skills.

While I prepared for the car doors to fly open and the cuffs to be snapped in place, Tyson explained his position further.

"Under the Fourth Amendment of the United States

Constitution, I'm protected against illegal search and seizure. *Lujan versus State* made it clear that the state of Texas has deemed random checkpoints contrary to the Fourth Amendment," Tyson said in a stern, but respectful, tone. "There's no specific reason for stopping me, therefore this is an unwarranted stop."

The officer stared blankly.

"Am I being detained?" Tyson asked.

The officer leaned away from the window. His eyes thinned to slits. His right hand hovered over the holstered pistol that was secured to his belt.

Oh. My God.

We're going to be shot.

Tyson and the police officer glared at one another. After what seemed like an eternity, the officer broke Tyson's gaze.

"Sarge!" the officer shouted. "You're going to need to come over here."

The sergeant meandered to the officer's side. He looked at the window, and then at Tyson. "Roll the window down," he demanded.

Tyson shook his head. "I can hear you just fine."

The sergeant lowered his mouth to the opening. "License and registration, please."

"Under what grounds am I being stopped?" Tyson asked.

His voice was expressing the irritation that was obviously building within him. I had no idea why he was so frustrated and wondered why he didn't simply comply with the officer's demands.

"We're looking for someone," the sergeant said.

"Do I fit the description?" Tyson asked. "Was he driving a silver Ford?"

"I'm not at liberty to say," the sergeant responded.

"Am I free to go?" Tyson asked.

The sergeant motioned beside the police cars that were parked in front of us. "Pull over and shut off the car, Sir."

"Am I free to go?"

No, you're not. He just told you to pull over.

"Pull over and shut off the car, Sir?"

There, see? He wants you to pull over.

"Am I free to go?"

I was on a date with big-dicked cop-hater. I was headed to jail for sure, and I was wearing a crappy outfit.

Beads of sweat burst from my body's every pore. I glanced around the interior of the car, looking for something to shield the hail of bullets that was sure to come, but found the car's cabin meticulously spotless.

Then, it caught my eye. Wedged between the edge of Tyson's seat and the car's center console, was a pistol.

Oh. My. God.

Upon seeing the gun, my heart lurched into my throat, blocking me from taking another breath. I glanced up, wishing someone could answer the thousand questions that were rattling around in my head.

"Do you have any weapons in the vehicle?" The officer asked in perfect timing with my discovery.

We did have weapons in the car. At least one, anyway. It was hidden from the sergeant's view by Tyson's well-toned thighs.

My future was clear. We were a modern-day Bonnie and Clyde. The possibility of pre-dinner sex evaporated. My feeble life flashed before my eyes. I filled with regret at my lack of accomplishments. At minimum, I was going to jail.

If I survived the gunfight, that is.

The search of my personal belongings would reveal six mini bottles of liquor, one of Jenny's Xanax, my vibrator, and a bottle of CBD oil that I thought was legal but wasn't quite sure. My contraband-stuffed purse was pale in comparison to the firearm that Tyson's was shielding from view.

I wanted to bid farewell to my parents but knew reaching for my phone would end disastrously. Texas cops who were armed with machineguns shot anyone who reached for anything.

It happened at least once a week. Watching the evening news was proof.

"I have a license to carry," Tyson said in a matter-of-fact tone. "My permitted firearm is at my side, officer."

My entire body tensed in anticipation of the officer's reaction.

"If you don't touch yours, I won't touch mine," the police sergeant said.

"Barring a threat on my or my passenger's life," Tyson said. "It will remain in its holster."

The sergeant's glare bore through the window and warmed my pale flesh. As still as a stone and fearing for my life, I waited for him to shout things like *keep your hands where I can see them*, or *no sudden movements*.

Instead, he waved his hand toward the four police cars that were ahead of us. "You're free to go."

Tyson gave a nod. "Have a nice evening, officers."

The air shot from my lungs. I looked at Tyson. Although my heart was beating as if I'd just completed running a marathon while breathing through a soda straw, he seemed calm and without an ounce of concern. I wanted to be angry with him. To scream and kick and demand that he let me out of the car, but that wasn't at all how I felt.

Narrowly escaping the grip of death was oddly exciting. I hadn't been pulled over by the police in years, but recalling the event wasn't difficult. I followed the officer's demands, had no weapons in the car, and received an expensive traffic citation in reward for my compliance.

Tyson, on the other hand, had been driving one hundred miles an hour over the speed limit, was armed and noncompliant. In exchange for his argumentative nature, he was released without so much as the speeding ticket he deserved.

I glanced at the pistol and then at Tyson. "Can I talk now?"

He maneuvered through the makeshift roadblock, waving at the officers as he drove past. "Sure."

"Are you always like that with police officers?" I asked.

"Like what?"

"Refusing their demands? Not following directions? Being argumentative?"

"He had no right to ask me to do *anything*," he explained. "Contrary to common belief, police officers often lure unsuspecting civilians into incriminating themselves. They hide behind their shields and use deceit to lure those foolish enough to trust them into believing the lies they tell."

"You don't trust cops?"

"I did. I don't now."

My fear of being shot was replaced by a fascination with Tyson's bold attitude regarding law enforcement officials. "So, you did at one point, but you don't anymore?"

"That's right." He gave me a serious look. "I learned the hard way."

"The hard way?" My eyes narrowed. "Were you wrongfully accused, or something?"

"*Something*," he snapped back.

The tone of his response let me know I was headed down the wrong path. I promptly changed directions.

"Why do you carry a gun?"

"Because, in this state almost everyone carries a gun. The few who don't are at a clear disadvantage when faced by those who do. Personally, I prefer to have the upper hand."

"You've got a permit to carry it, though? Right?"

"I do."

He was a handsome older man armed with a big dick, a pistol, and a vast understanding of law. One he learned the *hard way*. Tyson was becoming sexier by the minute.

I wanted to know more but knew better than to inundate him with questions. Small talk in the restaurant would be better received. I relaxed in the comfort of the car's plush leather interior, thinking of what I might ask during dinner. If I talked more than I ate, I might make it through the meal without spewing chunks of fish out my nostrils.

The car came to a stop, jolting me from my dreamlike state. I looked up. A hand-written sign – one that appeared to have been crafted with crayons by a mildly artistic child – was taped to the restaurant's window. It announced the night's special.

All-you-can-eat crayfish $13.99

"Oh, wow." He shut off the car. "They've got all you can eat crayfish tonight."

The taste of bile crept up the back of my tongue. I swallowed heavily. "They sure do."

Giddy with excitement, he looked right at me. "Are you ready to do this?"

I wasn't, nor would I ever be.

Nonetheless, I nodded. "I can't wait."

I reached for my door handle. My future with Tyson would be determined in the restaurant. Inside Rockfish we'd tell stories of our careers, somehow manage to introduce sex into the conversation, and eventually leave with the promise of bumping uglies as soon as we reached his bachelor pad.

I sharpened my blank stare. Seated just inside the restaurant, a man was elbow-deep into what appeared to be a bottomless bowl of bright red sea-spiders. Methodically, he plucked the creatures from the bowl, broke them in half, and shoved their mutilated bodies into his mouth.

Mesmerized, I stared at the repulsive sight.

After witnessing him gobble down two fistfuls of the vile creatures in a split-second, I barfed into my mouth just a little bit.

Excited to talk to Tyson, but not-so-excited to be amongst crayfish starved Texans, I stepped out of the car and paused. Eager to get started on the all-you-can-eat shellfish-fest, Tyson peered over the top of the car and grinned. I tried to smile in return, but the mouthful of pre-vomit substance I was trying to swallow prevented it.

Having him realize the state of my digestive system would undoubtedly put an end to our night together. I shifted my eyes toward the restaurant. The sign's cartoon crayfish figures taunted me to come inside. Beside the sign, mister elbows-deep ate crustaceans at a record-setting pace.

I barfed in my mouth again.

The day, in its entirety, proved to be too much. Having Tyson pick me up. Angry police officers. A date with a handsome stranger. The anticipation of sex. Speeding down a major roadway at breakneck speeds. A hidden gun. The glass of wine I drank to calm my nerves. A police roadblock. The second glass of wine I drank in hope of gaining courage. The sight of an all-you-can-eat crayfish lover eating all he could eat.

Everything began to spin.

I closed my eyes.

You can do this. He's handsome, older, and has a big dick. You can do this. He's handsome, older, and has a big dick. You can do this...

I opened my eyes.

"Are you okay?" Tyson asked.

I wasn't.

I shook my head.

Tyson's face washed with worry. "What's wrong?"

I didn't tell him. I showed him. By vomiting. This time, however, it wasn't into the back of my mouth.

4

TYSON

EVERYONE KNOWS someone who keeps their car so impeccably clean that there's never so much as a fingerprint on it. They'll often carry a lint-free rag inside the car, using it to wipe off a smudge left by a person simply touching the car's surface with their hands.

I was that someone.

I was an anal retentive neat freak. At least when it came to my car.

Resembling the scene from *The Exorcist*, vomit shot from Jo's mouth and splattered onto the top of my car. Shocked beyond belief, I stared beyond the pool of wine-colored substance and into Jo's troubled brown eyes. A few troublesome seconds passed. I'd never seen anyone throw up, and I can't say I cared to ever see it happen again. Especially in the violent manner that she'd done so.

Clearly embarrassed, she leaned against the car window and began fumbling through her purse. Confident that she was done spewing the vile substance, I rushed to her side.

"Are you okay?"

Still conducting a frantic search of her purse, she looked up. The color of her skin had vanished completely, leaving her complexion stark white.

"I'm so sorry," she said.

I tilted my head toward the restaurant's entrance. "We can use the restroom inside to clean up."

"I fine right here," she blurted. "I just need to find something to wipe my mouth off with."

I felt terrible for her. After mentally fumbling with what to do, I removed a clean rag from the car's glovebox and offered it to her. "This is brand new. It's all I've got."

She chuckled as she took it from my grasp. "You probably keep clean ones in your car to wipe off fingerprints, don't you?"

I hated to admit it, so I shrugged instead of responding.

"My brother's the same way," she said, seeming to shake off a little of the embarrassment that she was feeling. "He wipes off the door handles after I get out of the car."

I looked at my vomit splattered car, and then at her. "So, what happened?"

"I get really nervous around guys. I'm sorry. I'm just a dork."

"*That* was nerves?" I asked, trying to make light of the situation.

"Pretty much, yeah. Well, nerves and being grossed out. I'm sorry, but I'm not a big seafood person. I should have said something, but I didn't want to disappoint you. Then, we got here, and…" She gestured toward the restaurant. "I saw a guy in there munching on lobster-ettes and it was just too much. You can take me home now. Sorry about your car."

"Do you want to go home?"

"Not if you don't want me to," she responded. "I'd prefer a toothbrush from CVS and some *Lockhart's* barbeque."

Given an opportunity to eat without repercussion, a man's choice will be meat. Eating barbequed meat allowed that same man to enjoy a delicate smoky tenderness that couldn't be obtained at home, regardless of the hours of time spent slaving over the grille. Barbequing meat was a skill understood by a select few and envied by all others.

Women, on the other hand, preferred salads and seafood. Or, so I thought.

"You like Lockhart's?" I asked, my tone filled with doubt.

"I love it. Their brisket is the best."

"It's right up West Park Boulevard," I said. "There's a CVS on the way. We can stop and get a toothbrush."

"Only after you wash your car."

As the acid from her vomit etched its way through the clearcoat and into the paint of my beloved Cobra, I responded in a manner that was contrary to my beliefs.

"I don't need to wash my car."

Spending Saturday morning buffing the imperfections from my paint was far better than having our night together end before it ever started. I needed to make measurable progress toward fucking her into oblivion.

Taking her home was counterproductive.

"Your car is just like my brother's car. Spotless." She waved her hand toward the vomit-covered windshield. "Or, at least it *was*. I'll agree to Lockhart's, but only if you promise to wash your car on the way there."

I wouldn't have guessed she could become any more attractive to me, but with that demand, she certainly did.

"Fine." I huffed as if I'd been coerced to do something I didn't want to. "We'll wash the car first."

Twenty minutes later, we were both standing in Lockhart's with clean teeth and a plate filled with barbeque. We found our way to a remote table in the rear of the restaurant and sat down across from one another.

After the embarrassing events in Rockfish's parking lot, I wanted to make her feel as comfortable as I could. I picked up a rib and paused before biting into it.

"So, what exactly is a steamy romance novel?" I asked.

Her face lit up. "They're romance novels for adults. Not like what your mother used to read, that's for sure. They're descriptive, sexy, and fun."

"Descriptive and sexy romance novels for adults? Like that Fifty Shades book?"

"*That* wasn't contemporary romance." She peered over the top of her glasses. "It was erotica."

"What's the difference?"

"If the story drives the sex, it's contemporary romance. If sex drives the story, it's erotica."

I took a bite of my rib. Her line of work allowed me to introduce sex into the conversation without seeming like a pervert. I took advantage of the situation and lobbed her an underhanded pitch.

"Give me an example of each," I said. "Can you?"

Her eyes narrowed. After a moment's thought, she set her fork aside and clasped her hands together.

"I'll use your example, *Fifty Shades of Grey*, by E.L. James, and another, *Cocky Bastard*, by Vi Keeland and Penelope Ward. In Fifty Shades, Christian, the hero, is a Dom who encounters a naturally submissive woman, Anna. Their relationship quickly turns to sex. That sex is instrumental in telling their story. In fact, without it, there's not much left. The story's development can be measured by the progression of the sex."

"So, there wasn't much of a story?"

"The story was great," she argued. "But, it required sex to tell it. Cocky Bastard was just the opposite. A girl named Aubrey meets a smart-ass named Chance while she's running from the memories of her cheating ex. She's driving across country and he needs a ride. Together, they take a journey that's hilarious, sexy, and fun. Take the sex out of the book, and there's plenty of humor, growth, and plot to tell the story. Take the sex out of Fifty Shades, and there is no growth."

She left the sexual door wide open. Considering my intentions, I stepped right through it. "So, some stories are just like relationships, they're sex-driven. Others, on the other hand, aren't."

"Exactly."

"Which one are you?" I asked. "Fifty Shades or Cocky Bastard?"

She pierced a slice of brisket with the tines of her fork and raised it to her mouth. "Which book did I prefer?"

"No. Which relationship do you prefer? Sex-driven or otherwise?"

She choked on her food, turning beet red in the process. After a few gulps of water and a minute or two of fanning her face with her hand, she let out a long sigh.

"Sorry, I choked on that meat at the exact same time you asked that question," she said. "Which what? Where were we?"

"Are your relationships sex driven or otherwise?"

She barked out a laugh.

"What?" I asked.

She adjusted her glasses with nervous hands. "I've never been in a relationship."

That tidbit of information could have been the introduction to a blessing or a curse. She was either a sexual free spirit, or she was a sexual prude who lived vicariously through the characters in the romance novels she read. I needed to know which.

"You've had sex before, right?" I asked jokingly.

"Seriously?" She coughed. "Did you just ask me that?"

I arched an eyebrow. "Did you just answer me without answering me?"

"Yes," she said. "I've experienced it a time or two."

"Was it sex driven or otherwise?"

She blinked a few times. "The sex?"

"Yes."

"Definitely sex driven." She laughed. "Sex driven sex is the best."

"I prefer sex driven sex, too," I said straight-faced.

"What was option two? 'Otherwise sex'? *Otherwise sex* might be good stuff, who knows?" she said, looking away as she spoke. "It leaves quite a bit to the imagination."

"'Otherwise sex' might be great," I agreed.

She looked right at me. "Do you have a vivid imagination?"

"Sexually?"

"Sure." She relaxed against the back of her seat. "Sexually, how's your sexual imagination? On a sexual level?"

She covered her mouth with her hand and waited for me to respond. A slight smirk stretched beyond the tips of her fingers, giving away the fact that she was enjoying the conversation more than she wanted me to know.

"Mine's pretty vivid," I responded. "How about you?"

"Vivid."

I wrung my hands together and studied her. With her hair up and glasses on, she looked just like Garber. A few seconds into my admiring stare, my cock began to rise. When it reached a point that it was painfully erect, I looked away.

"What are you thinking about?" she asked.

"Truthfully?" I shifted my gaze to meet hers. "I'm wondering if being around guys makes you so nervous that you puke, how it is that we can have this conversation without you barfing all over the place. You went from nervous to bold pretty damned quick."

"Once the ice is broken, I do pretty good," she responded.

"Did we break the ice already?"

She chuckled. "It was fractured when the cops pulled us over. I think it cracked pretty good when I hurled on your car. Then, it pretty much shattered when we started talking about sex."

"Talking about sex doesn't bother you?"

"Not so much." She said with a shrug. "Should it?"

"Most women aren't willing talking about it openly. I guess depends on the person. I wouldn't have guessed you'd be comfortable with it."

In clear opposition to my statement, she folded her arms over her chest. "Why not?"

"You seem pretty reserved."

Her eyebrows raised. "I've got social anxiety."

"What does that mean?"

"I'm much more comfortable alone than I am in the presence of people I don't know. When I'm around strangers, I've got this constant fear that they're judging me. When I puked on your car and you didn't ask me to go home, I knew you weren't the judgmental type. Instantly, I felt comfortable. Once I'm comfortable, I'm pretty outgoing. It might seem weird but barfing on your car made me comfortable."

"Comfortable enough to talk about sex?"

"I don't think there's anything wrong with thinking about it or talking about it."

"What would it take to embarrass you?" I asked.

She shifted her gaze toward her purse, which was in the seat beside her. "If my purse tipped over and everything fell out."

Naturally, I glanced at it, wishing I could see inside. "What's in it?"

She chuckled. "What isn't?"

"You can't give a response like 'I'd be embarrassed if my purse spilled', and then not tell me what's in it. What's in it?"

"Things that would embarrass me? Or everything?"

"Embarrass you."

"Six little bottles of Apple Crown, a remote controlled mini-egg, a random Xanax that wasn't prescribed to me, a rag with barf on it, and a little Ziploc bag that's filled with fingernail clippings. Oh, and my driver's license. The picture's pretty awful."

"Is a mini-egg what I think it is?"

"Probably."

"A dildo?"

"It's not a dildo. It's a vibrator."

"What's the difference?"

"Roughly the same as the difference between a goat and a cup of coffee."

"A goat and a cup of coffee?" A laugh escaped me. "There's no similarities there."

"There is, too," she argued.

"What are they?"

"They both taste good."

"You've eaten a goat?"

"Every chance I get," she replied. "Goat tacos are the best. Have you ever been to Mexico?"

I shook my head. "We'll come back to the goat later. Let's discuss the vibrator. What's the difference between a dildo and a vibrator? I'm serious."

The thought of her carrying a dildo in her purse, regardless of what she called it, was a huge turn-on. Visions of her diddling herself at a traffic light or while sitting in a Carl's Jr. drive-thru rattled around in my head while I waited for her to respond.

"For future reference, a dildo," she explained. "Is an object shaped like a dick that is used to simulate sex. A vibrator may or may not look like a dick, but it always vibrates. A dildo may or may not vibrate, but it will always resemble a penis. Mine doesn't look like a penis, so it's a vibrator."

"Why's it in your purse?" I asked.

She rested her forearms on the edge of the table and looked me dead in the eyes. "Because if it was in the only other place it belongs, the buzzing sound would distract us while we're trying to eat."

I grinned at the thought. "Do you take it everywhere?"

"It and my American Express card," she said in a stolid tone. "I hate to leave home without either of them."

I rested my chin in my hands. An admiring look followed. "You're funny."

"Acting this way masks my true feelings." She grinned a clever grin. "It's a front. A façade."

"What are you truly feeling?"

"Right now?"

"Yes," I responded. "Right now."

She removed her glasses. "Tingly. I feel tingly. The all over kind of tingly."

Once she opened up, she was much different than I expected her to be. I suppose I could have perceived her bold attitude as meaning many things, but I saw it as flirtatious. Pleased beyond words, I studied her as she twisted a loose strand of hair with her index finger.

I pushed my plate to the side. "If they were going to make a book about your love life, would it be contemporary romance, or erotica? And, what would the name of it be?"

"Who are *they*?"

"I don't know." I shrugged. "Book people."

"It'd definitely be erotica," she replied. "There's been zero love in my life, so far."

"What about the name?"

"Give me a minute." Her eyes shifted to the ceiling. After a moment of aimlessly searching around, she met my gaze. "We're talking fiction, right?"

"Sure."

She grinned. "*The Cops, the Cock, and the Girl in Gym Socks.*"

I laughed so hard I snorted. "Why gym socks?"

"I love gym socks."

"What's the plot?"

"I can't answer that."

"Why not?"

"Because. Erotic Romance plots are driven by sex. So far, the only meat I've had is barbeque. I need fuel for thought."

My plan to get her undressed was coming along much better than I expected. I raised both brows and tilted my head toward the door. "Are you ready to get out of here?"

"I'm enjoying myself, so I guess that depends. Where are we going?"

"My place."

"Let me grab my purse." She grinned and reached for it. "Hopefully without spilling it."

5

JO

I NODDED toward the bulge in Tyson's jeans and gave him my go-to introductory line. "I want to suck it."

He seemed confused. "You want to suck my dick?"

I guess it wasn't what he expected. I gave a reassuring nod. "I do."

His eyes gleamed with approval. "Will you leave your glasses on?"

I'd have worn a bunny suit if he asked me to. Sexual fetishes fascinated me as much as the men who harbored them. Refusing Tyson's desires would have required an extremely odd request on his part.

Wearing glasses during a blowjob wasn't it.

"I'll leave them on if you want me to." I gripped the frames and wagged them up and down playfully. "Sure."

His response came on the heels of an exhaled breath.

"Leave them on," he murmured.

The person who trained me in the art of oral pleasure lived with his parents at the time, just across the street from the home I grew up in. I was enamored by his wispy mustache, tight-fitting Levi's, and the ribbed white tank top that later became his trademark.

Bart told me that the way to a man's heart was not by feeding him, but by sucking his dick. We agreed that he would spend the summer teaching me how to give head. After the following school year started, we would go our separate ways.

Over the course of one summer, he taught me how to properly (his words, not mine) suck a dick. The "training" (again, his words, not mine) began in mid-May while our parents were at work. By the end of August, I'd sucked him off no less than a hundred times. During that time, my palate learned to accept the taste of a man's semen as being the reward for a job well done.

I envisioned going back to high school a more marketable – and much more desirable – young woman. Much to my surprise, a summer of having a dick shoved down my throat managed to boost my self-esteem.

It did nothing, however, to polish my social skills.

I went back to school versed in the art of giving head, but far too socially awkward to convey my newfound talent to any of my male classmates.

I lowered myself to my knees and stared with eager eyes while Tyson fumbled to free himself from his blue and white striped boxer shorts. After what seemed to be an eternal battle, his manhood sprung free.

"Holy crap!" I gasped.

He chuckled. "Sorry."

I studied his massive member for a moment. It was perfectly shaped, thick from base to tip, and as long as my forearm from wrist to elbow. A second job as a leading man in A-budget porn films was an attainable goal if he ever lost his FedEx job.

I pushed the glasses up the bridge of my nose and met his downward gaze.

"It's perfect," I breathed.

He huffed out an argumentative sigh. "It's a pain in the ass."

"Why would you say such a thing?"

"Walk around with this fucker between your legs for a day and see what you think," he replied.

"I'd love to."

"Love to what?"

I gripped it with both hands, only to find that I couldn't wrap either hand *completely* around it. Elated at the thought of having him force it into my willing folds, I looked up and smiled.

"I'd love to have it between my legs for a day."

He grinned a half-assed grin. It was the same odd smirk that preceded every blowjob I'd given. Male-speak, I guessed, for "suck my dick, please".

I accepted my cue and guided the tip of his cock in my mouth. Upon tasting his salty pre-ejaculatory fluid, my eyes fell closed. A few practice strokes followed. Then, I eagerly took half his length into my throat.

"Jesus. Fuck," he exclaimed. "Stop."

Reluctantly, I slid my mouth free of his rigid shaft and opened my eyes. A strand of saliva draped from the tip of his dick to my lower lip. I collected it with my index finger and then met his wide-eyed stare.

I sucked the mixture of pre-cum and saliva from my fingertip. "What's wrong?"

He pressed the heels of his palms against his temples. "I need to get ready."

"For what?"

"To have you suck me stupid, I guess."

Sucking a man's dick was like auditioning for the lead role in a Hollywood movie. If I played the role to a T, I'd get the part. If I faltered or didn't give it my best, I'd remain unemployed. I'd been out of a job long enough. I needed long-term employment.

"Would it be better if I let you drive?" I asked.

His eyes narrowed. "What do you mean?"

"You can fuck my mouth if you want," I deadpanned. "Just grab ahold of my head and pound away."

"Are you--" He wiped his brow with the web of his hand. "Are you serious?"

His cock swung from side to side as he spoke. A glistening droplet of pre-cum clung to the tip, threatening to drip free with every breath he took. I encompassed the swollen head with my lips and sucked it free of the bitterly sweet substance.

The head of his dick resting against the tip of my tongue. With an open mouth and inquisitive eyes, he waited for me to respond. Holding his gaze, I sucked the tip one more time for good measure and then flashed a smile.

"Yes," I responded. "I am."

He swallowed heavily. After a short pause, he gripped the sides of my head with his hands. "Tell me when you're ready."

"I'm on my knees with an open mouth," I said. "What do you want, a written invitation?"

Without further provocation, he rowed his hips back and forth slowly, forcing half of his rock-hard shaft into my mouth with each stroke. After receiving no complaints on my part, his thrusts became more aggressive.

Within a few seconds, he was engaged in a full-fledged face fucking.

The satisfaction of having a man's cock in my throat was difficult to explain. During the act, I felt helpless and at the mercy of my partner. Upon bringing my partner to climax, I felt powerful and in charge. The strange mixture of feelings made the act extremely satisfying.

I held his gaze as he pounded his thick length in and out of my throat. The smell of his sweet cologne merged with the musky odor of sweat and sex. Floating on a cloud of hope, I eagerly accepted the punishment, optimistic that I'd satisfy him enough to bring him to climax.

His eyes glistened with satisfaction, leaving little doubt that he was in heaven.

I, too, was lost in a blissful state. My nipples ached. My pussy throbbed. I hoped he wanted to have sex with me, but even more so, I wanted to please him with my oral abilities. I gripped his thighs tightly in my hands, knowing I was mere strokes away from needing to draw a breath.

His cock swelled.

The sound of his labored breathing gave hint to what was next.

I pressed my tongue against the base of his rigid shaft and lifted my chin slightly, allowing him free access to my willing throat. Several aggressive full-length strokes followed. Then, he paused, gazed into my eyes, and gave one last balls-deep thrust.

His demonic cry of pleasure echoed off the walls of his living room. His thick cock pulsed as the warm reward erupted in my throat. Satisfied beyond measure, I remained motionless, waiting for him to recover.

He released my head from his grasp and retracted his hips. "Holyfuckingshitthatwasawesome."

After sucking a breath, I wiped the corners of my mouth with the pad of my thumb.

His flaccid cock hung heavily between his legs – a reminder that our night's journey, sexually speaking, was over.

I looked up. His face was covered with his hands. While I caught my breath, I relished in the thought of satisfying him enough to bring him to climax.

He lowered his hands and met my gaze. "That was fucking amazing," he breathed.

"I thought so, too," I responded.

"Can we do this again?" he asked.

Bringing him to climax suggested that he was pleased with what I offered him. Having him verbally express his pleasure, however, made his thoughts crystal clear. Before I had a chance to respond, he continued.

"Not *this*," he stammered. "I mean see you again. I'd like to see you again."

With those spoken words, I received the part I'd auditioned for. Filled with pride, I stood and smiled. "I'd love to."

6

TYSON

SATURDAY MORNINGS WEREN'T SET ASIDE for the sole purpose of cleaning my car, but I often found myself in the driveway doing just that. After wiping the final drop of water from the hood, I stood back and surveyed the car for any areas that needed attention.

Shawn studied the top of my car for a moment, and then turned around. "Let me get this straight. This chick puked all over the top of your Cobra and wiped her mouth off on a microfiber towel. Then you let her suck your dick with her dirty puke-covered mouth? That's nastier than fuck."

"Her mouth was clean. She brushed her teeth after she puked."

"If she carries a toothbrush in her purse, that makes it even worse."

"She doesn't, but how the hell would that make things worse?" I asked.

"If she carries a toothbrush, she's a certified puker," he explained. "Pukers have issues deeper than puking, dude. That chick will end up keying your car when you dump her. Or, she might stab you in the eye with something. She might even cut off your dick while you're sleeping. Rest assured, motherfucker, she'll do *something*."

Completely paralyzed by his ridiculous warning, I stared at him with tired eyes and an open mouth.

"I'm tellin' ya, Gary was dating a puker," he continued. "Freaky bitch wore that dark purple lipstick all the time and had him whip her with a wire coat hanger while he was fucking her. When he broke up with her morbid ass, she drank a bottle of fuckin' Drano. Sucked it down like it was an ice-cold Budweiser. Her sister found her naked body in the bathroom with a note to Gary written on the wall in purple fuckin' lipstick. The nutty bitch ended up in the hospital for damned near a month. Spent a week or so in there to fix her burned up guts, and two more for a psyche eval. They figured out she was mentally bankrupt, and the cops hauled her crazy ass from the hospital to a nut house in Austin. Bitch is still there, wadded up in a straitjacket and suckin' her meals through a straw."

I was completely lost by his lipstick laden tale. "Who the fuck's Gary, and what's a *puker*?"

"Gary's a forklift driver from work." He poked his finger in his mouth and acted as if he was gagging. "A puker's a chick that pukes up her food after she eats."

I looked at him as if he were insane.

"Your chick's a puker," he insisted. "Did she run to the bathroom after you guys ate?"

"No. You're talking about bulimia. She's not bulimic."

"They never admit it."

"She's not bulimic, you idiot."

His eyes narrowed. "How do you know?"

"It was nerves. She's gets anxious in front of people she doesn't know, and she got really nervous. She just puked. After that, she was fine."

He arched an eyebrow in disbelief. "How big is she?"

I shrugged. "Average sized."

"Compared to who?"

"Compared to everyone."

"Compare her to someone." He put his hands on his hips and

cocked his head. "Give me an example. Compare her to someone in school."

Shawn was my closest friend and had been since we were kids. He was a running back on our high school football team, and never quite let go of the memories associated with that four-year chunk of his life.

The haircut he wore throughout high school – a faux hawk – was typically worn by gaunt-cheeked teens and douchebags who rested their white Oakley sunglasses on the backs of their heads. Nevertheless, Shawn still wore his hair in the same fashion.

My father had always referred to him as being an instigator, but I disagreed. He did, however, have an opinion about everything and seemed to enjoy voicing it through the dramatic stories he often told.

"I don't know." I rubbed a water spot from the passenger side window. "Karen Felper."

He threw his arms up in frustration. "Who the fuck's Karen Felper?"

"Blonde chick that was dating Chad when we were freshmen."

"I'm drawing a blank." He touched his product infused hair as if to make sure it was still there. "Compare her to one of our cheerleaders."

"A fucking cheerleader?" I glared at him. He should have known better. "Really?"

"Sorry, Bro. I wasn't thinking. Compare her to someone else."

"Cameron Diaz."

"The actress?"

"Yeah. She's tall-ish, and thin."

"Tall and thin? She's a puker for sure."

"She's not bulimic. She's naturally thin."

His brows raised. "Does she have wrinkled up titties? Pukers have shriveled up titties, that's one way you can tell."

"No, they're not wrinkled," I said. "They're just small."

"Describe 'em."

"Average sized. C-cup. A small C-cup."

He swung his right hand into a large arc. "Does she have a big fat ass?"

"No. She's pretty average in the ass department."

"Skinny chick with no tits, no ass, and she pukes a lot. I'd drop that bitch before this even gets off the ground."

"She puked once."

"Dude, you've only been on one fuckin' date," he complained. "Look at it this way, she's puked on one hundred percent of the dates you've been on. That's terrible odds."

"Whatever."

"Does she wear purple lipstick?"

I spit out a laugh. "No. It's normal colored. Lip colored. Pinkish-red."

He turned away in dramatic fashion, walked to the rear of the car, and paused. "What if that motherfucker puked every time you went out? From nerves or whatever the fuck she told you? Then what? Lipstick notes on the bathroom walls and straitjackets, I'm tellin' ya."

"Garber," I said.

His eyes widened. "What about her?"

"She looks like Garber."

He faced me. "The librarian?"

"Yep."

He strolled toward me, stopping no more than an arm's length away. "Looks like her a little bit, or looks like her a lot?"

I shrugged. "Could be her twin."

After studying me for a few seconds, he scoffed and turned away. "Bullshit."

"I'm serious. She could be her twin," I insisted. "She looks just like her."

"Dark hair?"

I nodded. "Yep."

"Thin, but curvy?"

"Yep."

"Big fat dick sucking lips?" he asked.

"Yep."

"Thin face with high cheeks that are accentuated with just the right amount of blush?"

"That's her."

"She doesn't wear those black cat-eyed glasses, does she?"

I grinned. "She sure does."

"Show me a picture of her." He pushed his hands into the pockets of his shorts. "Pic, or it didn't happen."

"I didn't take a fucking picture of her."

"Why not?"

"I didn't have an opportunity. That's fucking creepy, anyway."

He burst into laughter. "You're a creepy fucker. Creepy fuckers do creepy shit."

"I'm not creepy."

"You're creepy as fuck," he argued. "You're going to mess with this bitch until she gives up the pussy, and then you're going to fuck her a few times and move on to someone else. In your weird way of thinking, you'll have banged Garber, who you were infatuated with.

"Garber was every Plano Senior High graduate's dream." I spat. "I'm not creepy."

"You're creepy, and that's creepy."

"I asked her out because she's attractive. That, and, she's interesting."

"Interesting, huh?" He laughed. "That came into play in your decision making? You're moving on to the 'interesting chicks' now?"

"I'm not 'moving on' to anything. It just so happens that she's interesting."

"Interesting how? Does she dress really fashionable?"

I shrugged. "I don't know. She looks nice."

"You said she's *interesting*. Does she use big words? Carry a cat in her purse? Have a tattoo behind her ear of one of those infinity symbols or a flock of birds flying out of her armpit?"

"She owns a bookstore. She sells books like Fifty Shades of Grey, and stuff like that."

"No shit?" His gaze lowered. After staring blankly at the sidewalk for a moment, he looked up. "Maybe she's into being tied up and having shit poked up her butt."

"Might be."

"Jesus H. Christ. If she looks like Garber and likes having shit poked in her poop shoot or being slapped with a wooden paddle, she'd be a keeper. Possibilities are endless with a chick like that. I always wanted to hit someone with my cock." He made a swatting motion with his clenched fist. "If a chick like that let me slap her in the face with my cock, I'd be in fuckin' heaven."

"She swallowed my entire cock," I said. "I *was* in heaven."

"Now I *know* you're lying," he said with a laugh. "If anyone ever managed to choke that motherfucker down, you'd tell the world."

Every male student during my tenure at Plano High had either seen my cock in the locker room or heard a description of it from someone who had. The locker rooms were a torturous place for kids who were different than everyone else.

I was the equivalent of a walking carnival sideshow.

"The world doesn't care," I said. "So, I'm telling you."

"Are you serious? She deepthroated it?"

"Yep."

"All of it?"

"Yep."

"How far down did she get?"

"I already told you. All of it."

He lifted his chin slightly. "Did she touch her lips to your balls? It doesn't count as a deepthroat if she didn't. Balls-deep or it was a failed attempt."

"She smashed her lips against my nuts."

He spun in a circle, Justin Timberlake style, snapping his fingers as he came to a stop. "She's got lips like Garber's?" he asked excitedly. "Big thick fuckers? DSLs?"

"She does."

"I want to meet this chick," he blurted.

"Afraid not."

"Why not?"

"Why would I introduce you to her?"

"I'm your best friend. Best friends do shit like that for each other. Most of 'em, anyway. It's pretty standard stuff."

He was more than my best friend. He was as close to family as any man could ever be. Nonetheless, I shook my head. "When men introduce the woman they're fucking to their best friend, it sends a message to the woman. It says they're a part of that man's life. She's never going to be a permanent part of my life, so you're not going to meet her."

He exhaled a breath of frustration and crossed his arms. "Yeah, you've got a point."

"Maybe we could just happen to go by her bookstore one weekend," I said. "I might go by there today, but I don't need you tagging along."

"Why the fuck not?"

"Because. I'm planning on seeing if she wants to fuck tonight. I don't need a third wheel."

"Does she have any decent looking chicks working there?"

"As a matter of fact, she's got some chick that works with her that you need to meet. She's got huge titties."

His brows raised. "Considering your fucked-up opinion of what's *skinny*, I'll need a description of *huge*."

"The size of cantaloupes."

"Big ones, or those little fuckers that they sell at HEB in the winter?"

Using both hands, I made the shape of a large sphere. "They're between cantaloupes and soccer balls."

"Soccer balls?" He arched a brow. "How big is this chick?"

"She's skinny. A hundred and fifteen pounds, maybe one-twenty."

"And she's got tits the size of soccer balls?"

I shrugged. "Give or take."

"What's she look like? Medusa? Bitch better not have snakes growing out of her head or any kind of shit like that."

"She's got blond hair growing out of her head. Blond-ish. You know that kind of fade shit they do where it goes from brown to blond?"

He gave a nod. "She's got 'freak hair'."

"What?"

"Freak hair."

"What the fuck is 'freak hair'?"

"Chicks with hair like that are always freaks in bed, so I call it *freak hair*. She'll be a wild piece of ass, guaranteed."

I gave him a look of disbelief. "Because of her hair?"

"Precisely."

"So, all girls with dye-jobs are freaks?"

"If they have two-tone hair or if they've dyed it a weird color it's a guarantee, yeah."

"What's a weird color?"

"Blue, pink, purple, that weird red, and some of those orangey-blondes."

"Girls with those hair colors are freaks in bed?"

He gave a crisp nod. "Guaranteed."

I spit out a laugh. "You're an idiot."

"What's the big tittied freak look like? She better not look like a troll."

"She's cute. Kind of got a dirty-looking cowgirl thing going on."

"Dirty, like she didn't take a bath? Or, dirty like, 'damn, that's one sultry-looking bitch'?"

I chuckled. "Did you just say 'sultry'?"

"Yeah. Sultry. If you're gonna be fucking a book store owner, you should broaden your vocabulary."

"It's broad enough," I said with a laugh. "She's the nubile kind of dirty."

His eyes narrowed. "What the fuck's that mean?"

"She's *sultry*."

"I want to meet 'em both," he said. "Hell, we should just go over there now. You can use my introduction to the 'nubile cowgirl' as the reason for stopping by."

Once every few years, Shawn came up with a good idea. Convinced this was his shining moment for the next two or three years, I gave a nod of approval. "I'll introduce her to you, as long as you don't get in my way."

"What do you mean?"

"I'm planning on fucking Jo tonight, and I don't need you getting in my way."

"No need to worry about me getting in your way." He chuckled a dry laugh. "If anything, you'll need to stay out of *my* way. I'll be poking my thumb up that sultry cowgirl's ass before you get the first sentence out of your mouth."

Sadly, he was probably right.

7

JO

JENNY LAUGHED SO HARD she couldn't catch her breath. "I saw him pulling out of the alley when he came to pick you up. Anyone that drives a fifteen-year-old car that looks that nice is anal-retentive as hell. I bet he just about shit his pants, didn't he?"

"He really didn't seem to mind. I insisted he wash it before we ate, though."

She looked offended. "What? Why?"

"My brother is pretty anal about his car," I responded. "He always has been. I knew if I'd have thrown up on *his* car, he'd have washed it immediately. So, I insisted we got through the car wash before we ate."

"I've never thrown up on a date. There's a few assholes I'd like to have thrown up on, though. You've heard that saying, 'Who pissed in your Cheerios?', right?"

"I've heard people say it, yeah."

"Well, I kind of pseudo pissed in a guy's Cheerios once. That's as close as I've got to barfing on a date's car."

With Jenny, nothing shocked me. Even so, I needed to hear the story of how she peed in a guy's cereal. "Oh my God," I gasped. "What happened?"

She scrunched her nose. "Do you really want to hear it?"

"Sure."

"Short version, or long version?"

I looked at my watch. "You've got twenty minutes."

"Long version, it is." She plucked a copy of LJ Shen's *Scandalous* from the display rack. "Payne was his name. You know, in hindsight, I should have known he was going to be a douche just because of the name. You can tell a lot from a guy's name. Anyway, we were dating at the time. I kept hearing that he was cheating on me. People were telling me over and over that he was screwing my friend's sister. I was like, *whatever*. But people kept saying it. So, I got his phone and put one of those text trackers on it."

"What do you mean?"

"A text tracker. It's a program that lets you get online and see all the SMS messages on a phone. So, I put the program on his phone, tracked his messages, and in one freaking day I found out he was screwing Bryce's sister, Karen."

There would be no worse feeling than finding out the man you thought you were in love with was spending intimate time with another woman. A man capable of having sexual relations with two women wasn't deserving of either of them. If it happened to me, I'd probably curl up in a ball and die. I felt terrible for Jenny.

"Oh, wow, that's awful," I said. "Sorry isn't enough, but I'm sorry. Was Bryce a friend of yours?"

"He still is. He didn't know. His sister Karen is another freaking story. She was riding Payne's dick and talking shit on me while he and I were dating." She rolled the book into a tube. As she continued speaking, she twisted it tighter and tighter. "The skinny little whore knew we were seeing each other and did it anyway. I should have choked that fucking bitch."

"That's terrible."

"It's the worst feeling ever. He could have stuck his dick in her nasty twat before school, and then had me suck it after school. Thinking about it made me sick. So, anyway. I always carried a bottle of water in my backpack, and I'd squirt that stuff in it. That flavor stuff. You're supposed to use like three drops, but it takes half a bottle to make it taste good. You know what I'm talking about, right?"

"Yeah, the *MiO* drops or whatever?"

She nodded. "I knew because I always had a bottle of colored water in the little mesh pocket that no one would think anything. So, I peed in a cup, poured it into the bottle, and carried it to school in my backpack. My school was one of those that catered to the kids who are 'gifted' – the problem kids who are bored in regular schools. Anyway, the school served awesome breakfast, so everyone went into the cafeteria in the mornings. We hung out and ate breakfast until around nine, when school started."

She glanced at the book, only to find out that she'd all but ruined it. While she tried to flatten the twisted cover, she continued. "So, while he was eating his cereal, I sat beside him like I did every morning. Then, I motioned off in the distance and said, 'Oh my God, look at what she's wearing', and I pointed at some random girl. When he looked, I poured the bottle of piss into his cereal bowl. After he ate half of it, I said, 'Guess what, asshole?' He looked at me and said, 'Why'd you call me an asshole?'. I stood up and said, 'I know you've been fucking Karen, and by the way, I pissed in your Cheerios'. Looking at his cheating ass every day is part of the reason I dropped out."

"It sucks that he did that to you, but it sounds like you got even."

"I did. Not with the Cheerios." She laughed. "But with something else."

I winced at the thought of her doing anything more. "What did you do?"

"I don't know if you want to hear it. It's one of those things that sounded good at the time, but afterward, it seemed kind of psycho."

I looked at my watch. We didn't open for ten minutes. "I want to hear it."

"It's pretty psycho."

I grinned. "I *really* want to hear it, then."

She placed the tattered book at the top of the display. "When we were dating, he gave me keys to his house. His parents were never home, and my parents were never gone, so I'd go there most days after school while he was at football practice. That's how his sister and I got to be friends. Anyway, we broke up that morning at breakfast. That day, at lunch, he was sitting with Karen. Like nothing ever happened between us. I thought, 'You son-of-a-bitch'. You're not even going to let me mourn, are you?' So, that night I went to his house, like normal. On the way, I stopped at CVS and got a bottle of *Nair*. Oh, by the way, he had *really* nice hair."

"Holy crap. You didn't—"

"I did."

I gasped. "You put it in his shampoo?"

"I mixed it like, I don't know, half-and-half, yeah."

"What did it do?"

"Just what you'd think. His hair fell out in fist-sized clumps. His parents thought he had some anxiety disorder associated with our breakup. They had him taking all kinds of tests to try and find out what happened. They figured out later that it must have been a prank in gym class. He ended up shaving his head, which is what I wanted. Everyone laughed at him for a month. It's what he needed. When I left town, I told him I did it. I thought he needed to know, even if it was five years later."

"Because you felt guilty?"

She laughed. "No. I didn't feel guilty at all. He cheated on me. That's what he gets. He's lucky I didn't stab him."

"Oh."

"So, that's my story." She shrugged. "It's not barfing on top of a car, but it's close."

"Kind of. One was intentional, and one wasn't."

"You're telling me you barfed solely from the jitters?"

"My anxiety got the best of me."

"I'm glad I didn't make you barf during the job interview. That would have been awkward."

Jenny and I hit it off the instant we met. When she applied for the job, she told me she liked my outfit, commented on my glasses, and then told me she loved my hair. She talked a mile a minute, never shut up, and seemed sincere. I was comfortable around her from the moment we first spoke.

64

"I was comfortable around you," I assured her. "From the instant we met."

"That's funny. If anyone makes you nervous, you'd think that list would include me."

"Why?"

"Because I'm loud and obnoxious."

"I'm most comfortable around outspoken people," I admitted. "Quiet people make me itch. I never know what they're thinking."

"Uhhm." She gestured toward the door. "We probably ought to unlock the door. What time is it?"

I looked at my watch. "Crap!"

Each month, we held a contest. Every purchased book throughout the month counted as an entry. On the last Saturday we picked ten entrants at random, with each winner receiving a signed paperback from one well-known Indie author.

The participating authors were selected in advance. The entire month was spent promoting their social media accounts, most recent book, and backlist. The contest was a win-win, driving traffic to the bookstore, and to the author.

As soon as Jenny unlocked the door the women rushed past her and toward the corkboard. One of the women screamed. Another followed. A third shrieked, and then things went quiet.

"Sounds like there's only three winners," Jenny said. "I feel bad when the afternoon crowd doesn't have a chance."

"I like it when it's spread out throughout the day, too. It makes it more fun for everyone."

"Speaking of fun, you need to tell me what happened after you washed the car."

I hadn't told her about the blowjob yet, but I intended to. I'd never had a girlfriend I could talk to and doing so with her was therapeutic. As far as she knew, I barfed on Tyson's car and went home afterward.

"I will." I turned toward the box of signed books. "Actually, I've got a lot more to tell you about."

While I struggled to pull the signed books from the box they were tightly packed in, Jenny laughed.

I looked up. "What?"

"Maybe you could get the FedEx guy to tell me."

I gave her a look. "Why would I do that?"

"Because." She craned her neck and peered toward the door. "He just pulled up outside."

8

TYSON

I SCANNED her from head to toe. Her hair was up, and her glasses sat low on the bridge of her nose. Wearing a pair of black low-waisted dress pants and a matching tight-fitting sleeveless top, she seemed taller.

I normally found the type of pants she was wearing rather unflattering. That particular pair accentuated her perfectly round butt, leaving nothing to the imagination. With Shawn at my side and my eyes fixed on her ass, I sauntered in her direction.

"Jesus," Shawn said. "That cowgirl's sexy as fuck."

As always, Shawn's tone was three notches louder than it should be, leaving everyone within earshot aware of his intentions, regardless of how quietly he thought he was talking.

"Keep your thoughts to yourself," I whispered. "She'll hear you."

"She's a freak," he responded. "If she hears me it'll turn her on."

I covered my mouth with my hand and feigned a yawn. "You're an idiot."

"She's a freak. I'm tellin' ya, if she hears me, it'll make her clit tingle."

"If she hears you, she'll think you're a douchebag."

"Whatever." He glanced at the women. "Nerdy chick looks like Garber for sure. Sexy ass lips on that bitch, god dayum."

I turned toward the bookcase and plucked a book from the shelf.

"What are you doing?" Shawn asked.

I thumbed through the pages, stopping at a completely random section. "I'm going to need you to shut the fuck up," I whispered.

He stepped beside me and grabbed a book. "She can't hear me."

"*Everyone* can hear you."

"Fine," he huffed.

"So, you'll shut the fuck up?"

"I'll do my best."

I skimmed through a paragraph and chuckled at absolutely nothing. "Don't fuck this up," I said under my breath. "I mean it."

"Dude's got an ice cube in his mouth and he's sucking some chick's tits on the front porch," he said matter-of-factly. "He just dropped her dress to the floor. She's standing there, naked, *on the porch*."

I glared at the book he held. "What the fuck are you reading?"

He glanced at the cover. "*Submission*. I'm buying this fucker."

"You're not buying a book."

"The fuck I'm not. Chick's dig intellectual dudes."

"You're not intellectual."

He raised the book. "If I buy this, it'll look like I am."

Feeling regretful for having brought him, I shook my head. "Don't embarrass me."

"*Moi?*"

I closed my book in a dramatic fashion and put it back on the shelf. "I mean it."

"All I'm going to do is buy this book. If she goes gah-gah when I do, I can't help it."

I gestured toward Jo with my eyes. "Come on, Romeo."

Giggling and clutching books close to their chest, two women walked past us, toward the front door. Although one was an extremely attractive women, Shawn seemed unaffected. Surprised by his unwavering focus, I meandered to where Jo and the cowgirl were standing.

I looked at Jo and smiled. "Good morning."

She smiled in return. "What a surprise."

"'Mornin'." Cowgirl extended her hand in Shawn's direction. "I'm Jenny."

She was wearing a pair of tight-fitting jeans, boots, and an equally snug white tee shirt that appeared to have had the sleeves ripped off mere minutes prior to our arrival.

Stray threads dangled from the arm holes. The word *BITCH* was emblazoned across the front of the garment. I wondered how true the description was, and if she had another shirt that read *CRAZY*.

Shawn set the book in front of her and then shook her hand. "Nice to meet you, I'm Shawn."

She glanced at the book. "Do you read CD Reiss?"

"I haven't yet," he responded. "But that one looks good."

"Everything she writes is good."

Shawn chuckled. "I decided when he unzipped her dress and let it fall on the porch that I needed to read it."

Her gaze narrowed. "Are you a voyeur?"

"I wouldn't describe myself as one, no," he said. "But sexy is sexy, and that was sexy."

Jenny scanned the book and then handed it to Shawn. "That'll be $11.72. Do you drive a truck?"

"Say again?" Shawn stammered.

"Eleven. Seventy. Two. For. The. Book." She cocked her head to the side. "Do. You. Drive. A. Truck?"

Shawn handed her a twenty-dollar bill. "I. Do. Not."

"What. Do. You. Drive?"

"A. Mustang. Cobra."

She leaned to the side and looked beyond him. After satisfying herself that there was no one standing behind us, she folded her arms over her chest. "Tell me a story."

In a mimicking gesture, Shawn crossed his arms. "About what?"

"I'll let you pick."

Wearing a delicate smile, Jo looked at me and shrugged. At a complete loss as to what was going on, I returned an awkward grin and waited for Shawn to do what he did best.

"It was about two in the morning on a Wednesday night," Shawn began. "I was going home from the bar. Probably a little drunker than I should have been, but not so drunk that I couldn't recognize a hunger pang. One hit me in the ribs about halfway home, so I pulled into a Circle-K to get a chilidog."

He tapped his ribcage with the tip of his index finger and winced in mock pain.

"You're not going to tell *that* story, are you?" I asked.

He gave me a look. "I was planning on it, why?"

"I would have guessed you'd tell a different one. That one's a little, oh, I don't know. Harsh."

Jenny shot me a glare. "Let him tell his story."

"Where was I?" Shawn asked.

Jenny grinned. "You were getting a hotdog at Circle-K."

"Yeah. The hotdog." He glanced at each of the girls. "When I rolled into the parking lot, it was empty. Empty as in *empty*. I pulled in and parked at the side the building, so no late-night drunks that happened to stop in would ding my car doors. Half drunk and hungrier than fuck, I stumbled around the corner of the building and toward the door. As soon as I get to the front of the building, I see this crazy-acting fucker through the glass. It looks like he's arguing with the guy behind the counter. The guy behind the counter is facing me, and he notices me. So, the weirdo with his back to me spins around, and his eyes get as big as dinner plates. There's this big display of Cheetos beside him, so I can't see *everything*, but I noticed when he turned around he shoved his hands in his pockets really fast."

He looked at Jo, took a dramatic pause, and then looked at Jenny. After another long pause, he continued. "Now, remember, from inside the store a person couldn't see my car, because it was around the corner of the building. So, when I see this big-eyed weirdo, I didn't think too much of it. You know, just that he's shocked because I came walking up out of nowhere."

"He was robbing the place, wasn't he?" Jenny asked.

"You'll just have to wait and see what happens," Shawn said.

"Sorry, go ahead."

"Now this guy stands about six foot seven, weighs about a buck-fifty, and he's as white as a fuckin' ghost. The kind of white a guy gets when he's never been exposed to the sunlight. When I walk in, this ghastly-looking string bean motherfucker stops talking and starts pacing the floor. I give this weird fucker a glare and go back to the hotdog machine. While I'm getting my chilidog all doctored up, I notice he's scratching his arms like they're on fuckin' fire. I'm thinking 'this fucker's a meth-head', but I step beside this lanky prick to pay for my chilidog anyway. While I'm leaning against that oversized display of Cheetos and digging in my pocket for change, the guy behind the counter looks at me like, *help me*. I hand him a wad of change and give him a *what the fuck's going on?* Look. He opens the register and gives me that same *help me* look right back."

"What did you do?" Jenny asked.

"I was armed with a chilidog, a pocket full of change, and an empty wallet. I couldn't have been much help. So, I paid for my chilidog, took a big bite off the end of it, and walked back to my car."

"No, you didn't."

"I had to," Shawn said with a laugh. "To get my gun."

"He *was* robbing the place, wasn't he?" Jenny gasped.

"At that point, *no*," Shawn replied.

"Ohmygod." Jenny clasped her hands together excitedly. "Tell us the rest."

"I'd realized during this little hotdog getting venture that I was drunker than I'd originally thought, so I ate that chilidog on the way to the car. After washing it down with half a bottle of Coke, I popped my trunk and loaded my shotgun."

"Wait," Jenny spouted. "I've got two questions."

"Let's hear 'em."

"You got a bottle of Coke, not a can?"

"Always get a bottle. Cans taste like shit."

"Glass or plastic?"

"Glass. The ten-ounce Mexican bottle. If it ain't made in Mexico, I won't drink it. The Mexicans have got their shit together. They still use the original recipe. Circle-K keeps it in the side cooler by the *Jarritos* and that funky white cheese. They call it the 'Mexican Cooler'. What's the next question?"

"You carry a shotgun in your trunk?"

"I'm a Texan," Shawn replied. "I carry an arsenal in my trunk."

"Point taken," she said with a playful wave of her upturned hand. "Please continue."

Shawn positioned his hands as if he were carrying a shotgun. "This shotgun's one of those things like Arnold Schwarzenegger carried in *The Terminator*. Pistol grip, short barrel, extended magazine. An *assault shotgun*. Well, in my infinite wisdom, I decided to walk around the *other* side of the building, so I'd *really* sneak up on this fucker. So, I'm drunker'n a monkey stumbling around the backside of this dark as fuck building. When I came around the last corner, I see this lanky prick's got a pistol in his hand. He's robbing the guy, just like I thought he'd be."

Jenny's eyes went wide. "What did you do?"

"Remember, I'm walking on the other side of the building, in unchartered territory. And, I'm drunker'n fuck. So, I'm stumbling across this unfamiliar chunk of concrete, and my eyes are fixed on the weirdo's pistol. Guess what happens? I trip over an imperfection in the sidewalk."

"No, you didn't?"

"I sure as fuck did. Fell flat on my ass. When I hit the ground, the shotgun went off. Shattered the fucking window. Glass and Cheetos went *everywhere*. So, the meth-head came running out of there covered in orange dust, and when he did, I was trying to stand up."

He paused and glanced at each of us.

"Now, there's a part I haven't told you yet. When I was in there getting my chili dog, I got a little plastic baggy full of jalapenos and put 'em in my hoodie pocket, because I love those little fuckers on my chilidogs. It's the same baggie you slip the hot dog in if you're taking it home to eat it. The bag's open on one end, so if you tip it over, everything spills out. At this point, I haven't eaten any of 'em, because my drunken ass forgot I had 'em. So, back to the story. I'm on the sidewalk half-drunk and scared this wigged-out weirdo's gonna shoot me before I shoot him. When this crazy-eyed Cheeto-covered weirdo's running out the door, I'm trying to stand up. As soon as he sees me, naturally, he points his gun at me. I'm struggling to get up, and the barrel of his pistol's wobblin' all over the fuckin' place because this fucker's all strung out on whatever he's strung out on. For a minute, time kind of stands still. At that exact instant, when life was closing in on me, it dawns on me that the one who survives is the one who pulls the trigger first. I'm struggling to get up and he's trying to point his shaking pistol at me, and all of a sudden..."

He threw his arms high in the air and shouted, "*WHAM!*"

I'd heard the story a hundred times. Jo and Jenny, of course, hadn't. While they recovered from nearly jumping from their skin, Shawn continued.

"I slip on a pile of fuckin' jalapenos and fall flat on my ass. *Again.* When I hit the ground, the shotgun went off. *Again.* That time, the shot blew the meth-head's arm clean off right above the elbow. His fuckin' arm hit the ground with the pistol still clenched in his dead hand. This one-armed fucker looks at his arm, looks at me, and just stands there like, *did that really just happen?* I said, 'don't move, motherfucker, or I'll blow off the other one.' The clerk was so appreciative of me saving him that he gave me all the free chilidogs I could eat. By the time the cops got there, I'd sucked down four more of 'em, and was as sober as a nun."

"Ho-Lee-Shit," Jenny exclaimed.

Shawn grinned and nodded. "They labeled me a hero and put me on the morning news. Ends up the meth-head was on a three-day streak of robbing gas stations, banks, and grocery stores. They sent his one-armed ass to prison for twenty years."

A puzzled look washed over Jenny. "They didn't sew his arm back on?"

She'd asked exactly what Shawn was hoping for. While I waited for him to tell the rest of the story, I glanced at Jo.

Enthralled by Shawn's tale of the one-armed meth-head, she was waiting intently for him to continue. While her eyes were fixed on him, I allowed her flattering black outfit to hijack my thoughts.

Before Shawn finished his response to Jenny's question, my cock was at full attention. Slightly embarrassed, I pushed my hands into the pockets of my shorts and struggled to hide my satisfaction in how Jo's choice of clothing accentuated her body's perfect curves.

If things went the way I planned, I'd be balls-deep inside her in less than twelve hours. My stiffening cock tingled at the thought of it.

"What do you mean 'they never found it'?" Jenny asked. "It was a freaking *arm*. Where'd it go?"

Shawn shrugged. "It disappeared."

"An arm doesn't just disappear."

"Maybe someone took it," Shawn responded.

"Who would have taken it? There was the guy inside, the cops, the paramedics, you, and the ambulance attendants."

"Maybe some drunk who had chilidogs on his breath did something with it. Out of spite. Or boredom. Or, maybe he was just disgusted."

"Oh. Emm. Ghee. Tell me you didn't steal that guy's arm."

"I didn't *steal* it, I just put it somewhere."

"Tossed it on the roof?"

Shawn shook his head.

"In your trunk?"

"Nope."

"Dumpster?"

"Negative."

"Oh my God. Tell me."

"The one-armed dude was duct-taped to the light pole, and I was sitting on the curb eating chilidogs like a madman while I waited on the cops. I kept lookin' at that bloody stump, and it was creeping me out. The pasty white fucker was just lying there on the sidewalk gripping that pistol. So, knowin' the cops would want the pistol, I unhitched it from that clammy hand and set it on top of the bottled water display. Then, I tossed that nasty arm in a manhole beside the building. When the cops questioned me, I told 'em I didn't know where it was. They didn't believe me, so I let 'em search my car. After they didn't find it, they assumed someone took it. I figured they'd bust down my door down one day, saying they had me on film tossing it in the sewer."

"But they never did?"

"The Circle-K didn't have outside cameras. When I found out the guy had been robbing places for three or four days, I figured he got what he deserved. That bloody arm's floating around somewhere under Plano, Texas right now."

"The one-armed meth-head." Jenny chuckled. "That's one of the best stories I've ever heard."

"Pfft," Shawn said with flippant wave of his hand. "I've got a million of 'em."

Jenny smiled a genuine smile, which surprised me. What little I'd seen of her led me to believe she was exactly what her shirt said she was, a *bitch*. While I made a mental plan to pull Shawn aside and remind him to ask her on a date, he did just that.

"I think the four of us should go out sometime," Shawn said.

"Like a double date?" Jenny asked.

Shawn shrugged. "Whatever you want to call it."

Jenny looked at Jo. "Sounds good to me."

"I'm fine with it," Jo said with a smile.

Apparently, I was the only one who thought having the crazy cowgirl and my overbearing friend with me on a date would be a burden. A month in the future, just before Jo and I went our separate ways, I might be able to stomach them both for an evening.

As a parting gift for Jo.

"Sounds great." I said. "All we need to do is figure out when we can all get together—"

Shawn scanned the group. "Tonight?"

I glared at him.

"Tonight's good with me," Jenny said.

My attention shot to Jo. Hoping her anxiety would cause her to deny Shawn's double date request, I waited for her to nix the ridiculous plan.

Her eyes glistened with hope. "It'll be fun. Let's do it."

Having Shawn and Jenny accompany us on our date would kill my plan for balls-deep sex. Nonetheless, I didn't want to be perceived as being a prick. Doing so would assure Jo and I got off to a rocky start.

I needed my sexual journey with her to be nothing but smooth sailing. I forced a smile and told her my first of what would likely be many lies.

"I can't wait."

9

JO

SEATED at a booth in one of my favorite Mexican restaurants, I couldn't have been happier. I was another date wit Tyson, and Jenny met a man who just might meet her strange dating criteria.

Shawn's storytelling was second to none. He was cute. He used his hands when he spoke. There were only two questions left.

His loyalty and his dick.

"Guys don't normally go to the bathroom together, do they?" Jenny asked.

I took a quick glance toward the restroom. "I have no idea."

"Shawn's funny," she said.

"Funny ha-ha, or funny weird?"

She reached for a chip. "Ha-ha funny."

"Yeah, he is."

"You know how girls who have a lot in common hang out together?" she asked.

"What do you mean?"

"In school, all the girls who were attention whores hung out together. They were always buying new outfits, comparing purses, wearing the latest styles, and they all got their hair done every four weeks on the dot. And, all the hippies hung out together, wearing their earth-friendly shoes and pull-over hoodies that reeked of weed. It's just, I don't know, people that are alike hang out together, right?"

"Oh. Yeah. *Birds of a feather…*"

She held my gaze. "If Shawn drives a car like Tyson's, they're obviously a lot alike."

"They seem to be pretty close friends," I said in agreement. "I'm guessing they're similar in many ways."

She grinned. "That's what I'm hoping."

"Oh. My God." I giggled. "You're talking about his dick, aren't you?"

"Uh huh."

"What if he's got a Roma?" I whispered.

"Then, this'll be the last time he sees me."

"Seriously?"

She dunked the chip into the salsa and paused. "Seriously."

"What if he's got a great big one?"

"If it's like Tyson's?" She left the chip in the bowl of salsa and leaned against the back of the booth. A glassy-eyed stare followed. "I'll ride him like a dime store pony."

"Would you have sex with him tonight if he wanted?"

"Hell yes." She leaned forward and pulled the chip from the bowl of salsa. "I mean, as long as he's willing to wear a condom. Why wouldn't I?"

"I dunno."

"If Tyson wants to fuck you tonight, would you do it?"

"I'm not sure," I responded, even though I was sure I would if he asked. "Probably."

She laughed. "Probably?"

If Tyson wanted to, I'd fuck him in the women's bathroom, but I wouldn't admit it to Jenny. Being judged for my eagerness to have sex would take an otherwise great night and make it a crappy one.

"Yeah. It just depends," I explained. "I don't want to put out the wrong vibe. I don't want him to think I'm easy."

She rummaged through the chips. After an awkward moment of silence, she forced a sigh and shook her head. "People get too hung up on sex. Fucking is fun. It should be simple and effortless." She looked up. "It only becomes complicated if someone complicates it."

"What complicates it?"

She cackled a laugh. "Falling in love."

I'd never been in love, but I believed in its magic. According to my mother, my grandmother died of a broken heart.

"Falling in love makes matters worse?" I asked, failing to accept it as true.

"It ruins things."

"Really?"

Falling in love never ruined things in the books. There was always some kind of drama, but in the end, everything worked out.

"Believe me," she said. "The woman always falls in love first. When she admits it to the guy, he'll agree that he is, too. He isn't, but he knows if he tells her the truth that things will dissolve. So, he agrees, because he wants to fuck her until something better comes along. Maybe not better, just different. So, the lop-sided couple skates through life with her thinking their love is equal, but it's not. It's not even lop-sided. It's one-sided. The guy's still checking out the asses of every girl in the mall, looking at two-year-old profile pics of some skank he met at the gym, and telling the chick at Starbucks that she's got *amazing eyes*."

I was confused. "If all men are liars and cheats, what does a girl do to keep from being used?"

"Become the user." Her mouth twisted into a smirk. "Ride that dick every chance you get, keeping in mind that its life support system is a pathological liar and an inevitable cheat."

I didn't want to believe her, but she had far more experience with men than I did. I decided to agree with her for the time being and see how things between Tyson and I unfolded.

"Sex should be simple and fun?" I asked in rhetoric.

"Precisely."

Shawn's voice caused my spine to straighten. As if caught with my hand in the cookie jar, I pursed my lips, reached for a chip, and gave Jenny a *not another word* look.

She looked right at the approaching men and cleared her throat. "I didn't realize guys went to the bathroom together. Did you hold each other's junk?"

"He's not strong enough to lift mine," Shawn said as he sat down. "He'll need to hit the gym for a few weeks straight if he wants to give it a try."

Tyson scoffed and took a seat at my side.

Jenny gave Shawn a curious look. "Oh really?"

Shawn nodded. "True story."

As if having little interest in his response, she nonchalantly reached for a chip. "Quite the hunk of flesh, is it?"

"Every time it goes stiff, so much blood rushes to it that it makes me feel faint."

"Sounds like a potential issue." She raised the chip to her mouth and paused. "How long does it take you to recover from this lightheaded state of being?"

"It's pretty instantaneous," he replied.

She chuckled a light laugh. "You feel woozy for an instant, and then it just vanishes?"

"The rush of excitement overpowers the dizzy feeling," he said in a pragmatic tone. "It takes a few seconds."

Jenny's eyes narrowed slightly. "The rush of excitement?"

"If I've gone stiff, you can bet there's someone in front of me that excites the hell out of me."

"Always?" she asked.

"Always."

Jenny gestured toward Tyson with her thumb and then bit off half the chip. "Out of all the times that you've been wingman for your buddy here, you've never *taken one for the team*?"

"Not once."

"You only bone chicks that excite you?"

"That's affirmative, Ghost Rider."

Her brows raised. "Do I excite you?"

"I've been on the verge of collapsing from lightheadedness since we met at the bookstore."

She laughed. "Is that right?"

"It's the damned truth," he said. "I'm feeling dizzy right now."

"What's your position on condoms?" she asked.

He went bug-eyed. "*Excuse* me?"

"Condoms," she said flatly. "What's your position on condoms?"

He coughed out a laugh. "I think they're a great idea for guys with normal sized dicks."

She glanced in his lap and then met his gaze. "You're telling me you can't find a condom that fits?"

"A condom that fits, doesn't *fit*," he explained. He turned sideways in the booth and gave her a serious look. "Do you like ice cream?'

She looked at him like he was a lunatic. "Did you just ask me if I liked ice cream?"

"Yep."

"I love ice cream," Jenny said. "But I wasn't done talking about safe sex."

"Neither was I," Shawn said matter-of-factly.

A puzzled look washed over her. "What's ice cream got to do with condoms?"

Shawn glanced at Tyson and then me. He grinned and shifted his eyes to Jenny. "Favorite flavor?"

"Butter pecan."

"Imagine eating a butter pecan waffle cone. Not at Baskin Robbins or any of the normal three-dollar-a-cone shops. You're at some specialty shop, eating a fifteen-dollar and fifty-cent cone. This is one of those ice cream shops that buys advertisements in the back of those artsy-fartsy architectural magazines that advertise fifty-million-dollar homes that overlook the coast. This place is as gourmet as gourmet gets. You're about, hell, I don't know, six or eight licks in. It's the best goddamned cone you've ever eaten. You've got this shit running out of that little hole in the bottom of the cone, down your forearm, and dripping off your elbow. But, you don't give a fuck. All you can think about is getting another lick in. It's *that* good. Half a dozen more licks in, you're having an ice cream orgasm. All you can think about is that you don't want this buttery cream pecan-filled goodness to end. You look up from your dwindling cone, and some mustachioed maniac grabs you by the neck and starts choking the absolute fuck out of you. He's squeezing your neck so fucking hard that your eyes are bulging out. You're in and out of consciousness, barely clinging on to life. You're not quite dead, but you're not really alive, either. Somehow, you're still clenching that cone."

He paused, looked right at her, and raised both eyebrows. "While you're on the cusp of being choked to death, do you think you can enjoy that blissful cone?"

"Do you seriously want me to answer that?"

He nodded. "I do."

"I don't like being choked," she said. "I wouldn't be able to enjoy *anything*."

"Not even the best butter pecan cone in the world?"

"Nope."

"Well, I love sex. In fact, nothin's better than sex, as far as I'm concerned. Not even a fifteen-dollar and fifty-cent butter pecan cone. And when my cock's being choked to death by some undersized condom, I can't enjoy sex, no differently than you wouldn't be able to enjoy that cone."

Straight-faced, Jenny reached for her purse. After rummaging inside of it for a moment, she tossed a condom on the table, beside the bowl of salsa. "There's a *Trojan*. That fits ninety-five percent of the population."

She threw another one down. "Here's a *Magnum XL*. That fits the four point nine-nine percent of that five percent that can't fit into a *Trojan*."

"And *this*." She tossed a third condom onto the table. "Is a *Beyond Seven, Mega Big Boy XL*. It fits the upper echelon of cocks. The point one percent that are packing some real cock magic."

She slid the three condoms to Shawn's side of the table. "Go see which one fits."

Shawn looked at the condoms, and then at her. "What if the *Beyond Seven* fits? Do I get a prize?"

"That *Beyond Seven* is a glass slipper," she said with a laugh. "If that fucker fits, I've found my Cinderella."

Shawn scooped up the *Beyond Seven* Condom and marched to the bathroom.

I looked at Tyson. "He's insane."

He chuckled. "Tell me about it."

I gestured toward the two remaining condoms. "Do you always carry various condoms in your purse?"

"Yeah," Jenny said. "Don't you?"

I was on birth control, but I really didn't need to be. It wasn't like I ever relied on it, or anything. I damned sure didn't need to carry an assortment of condoms in my purse.

"No," I said. "I'm on birth control."

Jenny looked at Tyson and cocked an eyebrow. "Do you feel like you're being choked out when you wear a condom? Or was he just talking shit?"

"Personally, I hate wearing condoms," Tyson replied. "But, I wear 'em for birth control."

"Does it feel like you're being choked out?"

Tyson shrugged. "Not if they fit."

"I'm not even going to ask," Jenny said.

Shawn strutted down the aisle toward the booth, whistling the entire way. After taking a seat at Jenny's side, he tossed her the condom's empty wrapper. "There you go."

Her brows raised. "Well?"

He grinned. "Got it on now."

"Does it fit?"

"Like a little glove."

She took a precursory look around the restaurant. "Should we have the waitress bring the check?"

"You two can leave if you want." Tyson placed his hand on the inside of my thigh. "But we're going wait to fuck until after we eat. Considering what I've got planned, I'm going to need some nourishment before we get started."

My face flushed. As if aware of my condition, Tyson's hand crept toward my tingling pussy.

I glanced in my lap. I couldn't have placed the spine of Colleen

Hoover's new release between the heel of his palm and my clit. It was the closest I'd been to sex in six years.

I looked up. Completely unaware that my clit might be brushed by the edge of a human hand, Jenny and Shawn were talking quietly.

Tyson's hand inched closer.

I looked down.

There was one sixteenth of an inch of space between his hand and the thin layer of black polyester blend that protected my tingling clit from further stimulation.

Admitting out loud that Tyson's *nourishment* remark pushed me over the edge of the sexual decision-making cliff wasn't going to happen. There were other ways to express my willingness to have my clit massaged while Jenny double-dipped her chips into the community salsa.

With my eyes fixed on Jenny and my waist hidden from view by the table's edge, I gripped Tyson's wrist and pulled his hand firmly against my crotch. If that wasn't enough of a gesture, maybe it just wasn't meant to be. I cinched my thighs together, preventing him from making an easy escape.

If he didn't get the message, we weren't speaking the same language.

Although I'd read that some women's clits were difficult to find, locating mine was a simple task. It was the diameter of my pinky finger, and always peeking out of its hood. Stimulation required nothing more the wind blowing.

I relaxed my thighs and said a quick prayer.

He lifted his hand. The prayer had been answered. My heart sank. He was done.

As the first of what was sure to be many rejection-fueled tears began to well in my eyes, he nonchalantly slid his hand beneath the waist of my slacks.

Guilt shot through me. A tingling sensation followed. My eyes darted back and forth between Shawn and Jenny, wondering who would be the first to figure out that Tyson's hand was touching my cootch. In the amount of time it took my brain's receptors to receive the signal of what was happening, the tip of his finger was parting my pussy lips.

My nipples hardened to a point that I feared they'd rip through the fabric of my silk shirt if I made any sudden movements.

After wetting his finger with my juices, he began massaging my throbbing love button with a precision that I'd spent a lifetime assuming only women could master. The restaurant's dining area started shrinking. Voices became dull and distant. Then, everything went quiet.

Completely consumed by the thought of reaching climax in the booth of a public restaurant while two people sat across from me, my eyes fluttered a few times.

I was seconds away from having an orgasm of epic proportions. I had somehow been cast between the covers of one of the many books that occupied my shelves, and I was loving every excruciating moment of it.

His fingertip circled my clit. Harboring hope for a memorable climax, I channeled my focus on the mountain of pressure that was building between my legs.

Then, it happened.

An orgasm nearly a decade in the making exploded from deep within me, shaking me to my very core. Small electric shock waves followed, rippling throughout each of my Jell-O-like limbs. The euphoric rush paralyzed me completely. When the climactic finale slowed to a dull roar, my eyes opened.

Tyson's lust-filled gaze pinned me in place. I slumped in my seat. A few involuntary sounds sputtered past my lips, escaping in the form of nearly inaudible moans.

Nearly.

"Are you alright?" Jenny asked.

I realized my eyes had gone closed again. After an unsuccessful attempt to straighten my posture, I opened them and nodded eagerly. "I'm uhhm," I muttered. "Yeah."

"Looked to me like she had a fuckin' seizure," Shawn said. "Her eyelids were fluttering and then dribble started oozing down her chin."

I wiped my mouth with the web of my hand, retrieving an ounce of drool in the process.

With his finger resting against my pussy lips, Tyson gave me a mock worried look. "Are you okay? You don't need to go home, do you?"

He was giving me an opportunity to change the evening's course. I weighed my options.

Food.

Or.

A night of sex.

"I hate to ruin our evening." My shoulders slumped. "But maybe you should take me home. I think I might be getting sick."

Shawn chuckled. "What happened? Eat a bad tortilla chip?"

I glanced at Tyson and then at Shawn. "Probably."

I knew Jenny wouldn't care if I left. Nonetheless, I looked at her and mouthed the word *sorry*.

"If you're not feeling good, we should probably go." Tyson slid his hand from beneath my slacks and stood. "I guess it's a good thing Shawn and I both drove."

I edged my way out of the booth. Shawn nodded toward my seat. "You might want to grab your glasses," he said through laughter. "They fell off when you were having that orgasm."

Embarrassed, but not as much as I would have expected, I decided to own the fact that I was fingered into oblivion while Shawn and Jenny watched. After finding my glasses in a blind search of the booth, I draped the temples over my ears and slid from my seat.

"Thanks for pointing that out," I said. "I would have missed them later when I was playing the naughty secretary role."

"Librarian," Shawn responded. "You're the naughty librarian."

10

TYSON

LOCKED IN A PASSIONATE KISS, I pressed Jo's body firmly against the front door. My right hand rummaged for the key while my left massaged her surprisingly ample breasts.

Obviously more interested in kissing her than opening the door, I fumbled aimlessly with the lock. Thirty seconds later, the door was still locked. Jo was dry humping my raging hard on. Ready to abandon my idea to go inside and prepared to fuck her on the front porch, I gave the key one last twist.

The door flew open. Tangled in each other's arms, we stumbled across the floor until coming to a stop against the end of the loveseat.

I broke the embrace and drew a breath. A quick look at her revealed smudged glasses, smeared make up, and disheveled hair. Sexual tension hung in the air like an early morning fog. I reached for my zipper.

She did the same.

In a flurry, shoes flew, and garments followed.

Within seconds we stood before one another stripped of all clothing. Rendered speechless at the sight of her remarkable body, I stood silently and stared while she gave me a quick once-over.

Sexual fervor shot through my veins. If I waited one more second to fuck her, I was going to explode. "We're fucking." I wagged my finger toward the arm of the couch. "Right here. Right now."

She glanced at the loveseat and then at me. "Glasses on, or off?"

I was thrilled that she remembered how much I liked them. I grinned. "On."

Without argument, she complied. My eyes fell to her clean-shaven mound. Her wet folds glistened with desire.

It was all the invitation I needed.

Brimming with the eager excitement of a teen during his first sexual encounter, I guided the tip of my throbbing cock between her legs. As soon as her tight warmth encompassed the swollen head, I knew I was in trouble. After a few failed attempts to penetrate her, I retracted my hips and stared at her pussy as if it were Chinese math.

"No, no, no," she complained, exhaling an uneven breath. "Don't...stop."

Her pussy was so tight I feared I may rip her in two. I gazed down at the milk-colored skin of her lower back and repositioned my hands on her hips. "Is it always this tight?"

"I don't know," she said with a light laugh. "I've never had an arm-sized dick in it. There's nothing wrong with it, if that's what you're asking."

I alternated glances between her pussy and my cock. It seemed like a simple solution. Despite our eagerness to continue, shoving my dick into the mouth of a beer bottle would be easier than trying to penetrate her.

My experience with pussies was limited to fucking them. I wasn't versed in the mechanics of how they worked, and quickly came to regret it.

Confused, I mentally scratched my head. "There's no reason it'd tighten up or anything, is there?"

She glanced over her shoulder. "I'd say this is pretty normal, considering your size. You can make it work, can't you?"

Getting my dick inside of her was going to require hard work and some sexual ingenuity.

"How's your threshold for pain?" I asked.

"I like *this* kind of pain."

"Are you sure?"

"I'm dying here," she complained. "Just fuck me, already."

I had no intention of making her beg me for sex. One way or another, I was going to shove two pounds of dick into her tight passageway.

I drew a long breath. "Ready?"

She gripped the couch cushions firmly. "I've been ready."

I forced the tip into her tightness and closed my eyes. Multiple mini-thrusts followed, each of which allowed me a fraction of an inch of additional entry. The feeling of having even a portion of my dick inside something so tight was glorious.

A few enjoyable minutes later, I looked down. One-third of my length was inside her.

"Everything okay?" I asked.

The response burst from her lungs. "Yeah."

"You sure?"

She gulped a breath. "Uh huh."

I forged on, repeating the same successful mini-thrusts, making minimal progress in the process. I wanted more. I needed to feel myself inside of her. Completely. I took one powerful frustration-fueled thrust.

"God," she gasped. "You feel so good."

"I. Like Your. Little. Pussy," I replied, saying one word with each thrust of my hips.

Progress was slow, yet very satisfying. Then, without warning, she opened like a flower. An extremely small flower, but a flower nonetheless. I sank into her wet confines. Now balls-deep, I gazed blankly at what I'd accomplished.

"Don't move, okay?" she asked in a soft voice.

I hadn't planned on it. I was savoring her warmth. "Is everything okay?"

"It feels." She giggled. "It feels amazing. Just give me a minute."

"Okay."

"Alright." She exhaled a slow breath. "I'm ready."

"Are you sure?"

"Uh huh."

I was sure her pussy was equally amazing, but the bits and pieces of progress I'd made prevented me from knowing what it felt like to actually fuck her. My balls ached, and I yearned to feel my stiff cock take a complete stroke into her impossibly small vagina.

Reluctantly, I withdrew myself. As each inch of my throbbing shaft slid free, I stared in amazement. As the rim crowned, I paused.

I gripped her waist firmly, drew a breath, and said a quick prayer.

Cautiously, I pushed my hips forward. Inch by inch, my entire length disappeared into her wetness. The feeling was unlike anything I'd ever experienced. So much so that I questioned my height of pleasure.

I took another slow stroke, just for the sake of certainty.

Holymotherofallthingssacred.

The breath oozed from my lungs. My head spun. My heart faltered. I was in unfamiliar territory.

I'd been transported into pussy heaven.

Shawn had shared a few tawdry tales of women who possessed magical pussies. After nothing more than partial penetration, these powerful punanis were capable of catapulting a man to the pinnacle of climax. According to him, these temptresses with heavenly honey pots were rarer than hen's teeth.

Privy to their possession of other than worldly vaginas, they traveled the earth tempting men with the lure of their tight twats, rarely allowing mere mortals entry into their legendary lady gardens. The select few who were granted sexual access were treated to a once-in-a-lifetime sixty-second pass into what could only be described as pussy paradise.

I'd always dismissed the steamy stories as being nothing more than fables. Yet. I'd somehow stumbled upon one of the world's secret snatches.

"Are you okay?" she asked.

The answer was *no*. The sheer satisfaction of experiencing her sexual offerings made me an emotional wreck. When the time came, quitting her was going to be difficult.

Impossible. It was going to be impossible.

I looked her over, hoping to find fault. At the beginning of the the evening, her hair was in a bun. Our make out session on the porch caused it to become unkempt, and it now cascaded over her shoulders and onto her back. A back that tapered to a narrow waist and then blossomed into wide hips.

Her ass was a work of art. Athletic legs connected her mouth-watering butt to the cutest feet I'd ever seen. Even her toes defined perfection, each of which had a carefully painted ruby red toenail.

"I think we're good, now," she said, reminding me one more time that she was ready to continue.

I wiped the remnants of a tear from the corner of my eye.

"It doesn't hurt?" I asked.

"Not at all," she responded. "You?"

"It feels good. Great, really."

"It feels *perfect*," she cooed.

I couldn't agree with her more. I took one last look at my accomplishment and grinned at the thought of continuing.

"Here we go," I said.

I began to row my hips fore and aft rhythmically. Her inner walls gripped my swollen shaft like a vise. Each stroke was a reminder that I'd found something special.

Something more than memorable.

Sixty seconds into what I hoped would be an all-night affair, my scrotum tightened. My legs began to shake. The end was near, and the only way to prevent it was to stop fucking her.

But, I couldn't.

I took another stroke. Then, another.

My cock swelled, warning me that I was on the cusp of reaching climax.

Embarrassment encompassed me. Without a doubt, one more stroke would end our night's sexual journey. Disappointed at my performance but incapable of taking pause, I took one last powerful thrust.

When my balls came in contact with her clit, I erupted. In response, she let out a moan of pleasure that echoed off the living room walls. To make sure she realized how much I appreciated her prized possession, I took two powerful full-length thrusts while in mid-climax.

Those two strokes cast me into another universe altogether. When I returned to earth, I collapsed over the arm of the couch at her side.

"Holy. Shit." I drew a choppy breath. "That was amazing."

Her mouth formed a slight smile. Then, her face blushed.

I was embarrassed by my performance and couldn't help but wonder if she was truly satisfied. "What about you? Did you like it?"

She exhaled. "It felt really good."

"Normally, I last longer than that," I admitted. "It's just…your pussy is…it's fucking amazing. I'm sorry."

"It's okay," she murmured. "If we practice at it, maybe we'll get better."

I was all for practicing, as long as she didn't become emotionally attached. I placed the palm of my hand against the curvature of her ass. "They say practice makes perfect."

She raised a shaking hand. "I'll volunteer to find out."

11

JO

THE UNMISTAKABLE SOUND of a clenched fist being thrust against the door three times in rapid succession startled me so much I almost peed. It was type of knock my father always referred to as a "cop knock."

At seven am on a Sunday, my list of potential visitors was short. After regaining my composure, I pressed the heel of my palm against my chest and stood from my seat at the kitchen table.

With hesitation in my steps, I walked toward the door.

BAM!

BAM!

BAM!

I nearly jumped out of my skin. Certain that a SWAT team was clearing the neighborhood so they could conduct an early morning drug raid on my Corvette-driving neighbor, I reached for the door handle.

BAM!

BAM!

BAM!

With my heart thrashing against my ribs, I opened the door just enough to peer onto the porch.

Still wearing the previous night's attire, Jenny stood before me. She looked like warmed over death wearing a smile.

I removed the safety chain from the door and greeted her with a grin. "You look like you had fun last night."

She nudged her way past me and meandered toward the kitchen. Instead of her normal lively gait, she walked as if she'd spent the entire weekend riding an oversized horse.

I locked the door and turned around. "What happened?"

After getting a cup from the cupboard, she removed a pod from the display and dropped it into the Verismo. "I need coffee."

I giggled. "You're walking funny."

"You'd be walking funny, too." She chuckled. "You remember BB Easton's description of Knight's cock, right?"

"I uhhm." I shrugged. "Maybe not."

"BB said. '*All I could see was cock. It looked like there was a log of cookie dough under Knight's clothes.*' I felt like I was in a reenactment of that scene."

"Oh, yeah. I remember."

She let out a sigh and reached for her coffee cup. "Shawn and Knight could have a swordfight with their cocks."

"You guys had sex already?" I acted surprised, even though I wasn't. "You just met him last night."

She sat at the kitchen table. "There's only one reason to be in a guy's presence. One good reason, anyway. To get that dick." Her eyes narrowed. "You're one to talk. FedEx dude finger-banged you last night while a restaurant full of people watched."

I sat down across from her. "He didn't finger-bang me."

"He did *something*."

"He was rubbing my clit," I whispered.

She unraveled her bun and tossed her hair. "Shawn stuck his tongue in my ass."

"What?" I gasped.

"Shoved it right up there." She took a sip of coffee. "It was awesome."

My brows raised in wonder. "He stuck his tongue in your butt?"

"My mouth, my pussy, and my butt." She raised her cup as if toasting the declaration. "In that order."

"So, what did you think?"

"About him? I like him. At least he had the guts to be honest with me before we started. I admired that."

"No. About having him, you know, tongue your butt."

"It was freaking awesome. He's got a talented tongue. It was a great way to end the night."

"What about him 'being honest'?

"Huh?"

"You said he had the guts to be honest before you started."

"Oh Yeah. He said, 'This is going to be sex. That's all.' I respected that. Most guys would lead you on, making you think it was going to be more than that. When a guy says nothing, women believe *less is more*. Me included."

I wondered where Tyson and I stood. I assumed he liked me, but now wondered if I'd fallen trap to the *less is more* trick.

I shrugged. "At least he's honest."

She closed her eyes and forced a dramatic sigh before meeting my gaze. "He's honest and his dick is perfect."

Honesty was a must-have quality for any man that was going to be a permanent fixture in my life. I laughed out loud about the dick comment, though. "A perfect dick? You're walking like you went horseback riding for a week."

"I feel like someone shoved a telephone pole up my ass."

"You didn't let him—"

"I did."

"In the butt?"

She raised her cup. "Oh, yeah."

There was no way his dick was as big as Tyson's. The thought of getting butt-fucked scared me to death. "Compare it to something."

"I told you. Having a telephone pole shoved up my ass."

"No." I chuckled. "His dick. Compare it to something."

She shrugged. "An arm."

"Arms come in all sizes. What kind of an arm?"

She gazed into her cup of coffee for a moment, and then looked up. "You know those steak and cheese things that sit under the heat lamp at Circle-K, beside the hot dogs?"

"Yeah."

"It's thicker than that, but not as thick as a zucchini squash. It's so long that when he was on top of me, it felt like the tip of it was bumping against the bottom of my heart."

"Oh. Wow."

"Yeah. Wow is right."

I sipped my coffee, and then gave her a confused look. "If he's hung like that, how'd that work out? The anal sex?"

"It took a lot of time and a tube of lube. Why do you think I look like haggard shit? I haven't slept yet. We just stopped a few minutes ago."

"When did you start?"

"We dipped out right after you left. I gave him a handy in the car, just to let him know I meant business. We started boning the minute we got to his house."

"At seven o'clock?" I gasped.

"Yeah."

I looked at my watch. It was just past seven. "You guys went at it for twelve hours?"

"We stopped twice," she replied. "Once to eat, and once to mop up the blood."

Blood during sex is never good. My eyes shot wide. "Blood?"

"Yeah. I accidentally punched him in the nose while we were going at it reverse cowgirl style."

It seemed like an impossibility. "How in the heck did that happen?"

She let out a long sigh and rolled her eyes. "You've heard the phrase 'had your brains fucked out', right?"

"Yeah."

"Well, if the guy's hung, reverse cowgirl will turn whatever brain you have to nothing but mush. It's the best sex ever, but it'll make you stupid, that's for sure."

"That's good to know," I said. "But even with cooked squash for brains, you were smart enough to face his feet, right?"

"I was, but it felt like I was being impaled by a freaking lamppost. My arms were flying around like a rodeo cowboy in the PRCA finals. One of my errant fists hit him in the schnoz. We ended the night with cotton balls in his nose and bacon on our breath."

"You stopped to make bacon?"

"Bacon's awesome."

"It's not as good as sex."

"No, but it's a close second." She swirled her coffee and then stood. "We were both starving. He'd already fucked me twice by that time. Bacon sounded good. It was all he had. Bacon, Gatorade, and eggs. After that talk we had the other day, eggs kind of creep me out."

I wasn't a jealous person, but I grew angry that she got an all-night romp with Shawn while I settled for a three-minute stint on the couch with Tyson.

"What?" she asked.

I must have been wearing my disappointment like a crown.

"He poked his dick down your throat again and called it good, didn't he?" she asked.

I shook my head. "No. We had sex."

The words rolled off my tongue dripping with disappointment. I was completely satisfied with what happened until I learned of Jenny getting her anus tongued. I wanted wild, uninhibited, bacon-fueled tongue-in-the-butt reverse cowgirl sex.

Jenny knew I wasn't a promiscuous woman, but she had no idea my dry spell had spanned for nearly a decade. I decided to proceed cautiously.

"We had a few issues with penetration," I admitted. "I guess he's either way too big or I'm way too tight."

"I can shove my fist in my twat," she said with a laugh. "Our biggest problem was trying to get that blood cleaned up."

"Wait? What?" I choked on my coffee. "Your fist?"

"I do it all the time." She giggled. "It feels awesome."

Comparing sex stories with Jenny was going to be amusing, that much was clear. My night with Tyson, regardless of how much I embellished, would pale in comparison to her night with Shawn.

She made another cup of coffee and returned to her seat. "So, you had some entry issues?"

"Yeah. It took a while to get started."

"Once you got going, it all worked out, though. Right?"

"Kind of."

She held my gaze and leaned onto the edge of the table. "What happened?"

I sighed. "He lasted about three minutes."

"Three?"

"He said it felt 'too good'."

"Oh wow," she exclaimed. "That's hot as fuck."

I wallowed in a pool of sorrow. "I didn't even have an orgasm."

"Who cares!" she exclaimed. "You made the sexy as hell Fed Ex dude come in *three minutes*. How many girls do you think can make that claim? That's sexy as hell."

"Do you think so?"

"I *know* so. When a dude is so excited that he can't help but blow his load, that's sexy as fuck. When a guy fucks me and it lasts forever, I wonder if it even feels good to him. I've got some self-esteem issues when it comes to my twat, though." Her gaze fell to her lap. "You could drive a truck in this thing without scraping the mirrors."

I laughed until my ribs hurt. "What?"

"Seriously." She looked up. "It's as big as a barn. If a guy busts a nut a couple minutes after we start going at it, that's hot as fuck. It lets you know he likes fucking you."

I shrugged mentally. "I guess that's one way to look at it."

"It's the *only* way to look at it."

I gazed blankly at my empty coffee cup. "That makes me feel better."

"You should feel like you've got the gold, girl."

I looked up. "What do you mean?"

"Did he say it felt good?'

"Yeah. He did."

"Did he say it was tight?"

"He did," I said. "Several times."

She scoffed. "Guys tell me I'm fun, or that they like my tits. Some of them say I've got a nice tight ass. No one ever tells me my pussy's tight, though."

"I'm sorry."

"Don't be," she said. "It's got its advantages."

I laughed to myself at the thought of her fisting herself. Before I could stifle it, I laughed out loud. "Like putting your fist in it?"

"That's one of the benefits," she said with a laugh. "And, I can take two dicks at once. A DP's nice if it's with the right guys."

"Oh. My. God," I gasped. "You've done that?"

"A couple of times. This big Hawaiian dude and his brother. I was twenty-one, and drunk as fuck on tequila the first time he talked me into it. It was pretty awesome. There were hands everywhere. I mean, think about it. I had hands in my tits, a hand on my ass, and a finger in my butt, all at the same time. And, two dicks in me. It was awesome."

It sounded kind of gross. I grinned nonetheless. "Sounds like it."

"Be thankful your shit's tight, though," she said. "It's an assurance that you'll be the one holding the key in the relationship."

"What do you mean?"

"Girls with tight pussies make the rules," she said flatly.

"I'll keep that in mind."

"I'm serious." She went straight-faced. "Have you ever seen one of those really hot dudes walking through the mall with some ratty-looking chick on his arm? Looks like he's taking his trailer trash cousin shopping?"

"I guess so. Yeah."

"That's what's up. She's got the tightness going on. He screwed her one night when he was drunk, thinking nobody'd find out. Her shit was so tight he couldn't leave her. Now he's stuck with her lame-looking ass, but it's okay because she makes him blow his load every time."

"I'm not lame looking, am I?"

"Not at all." She smiled. "You're beautiful."

Most would find Jenny's willingness to discuss butt sex, fisting, and being penetrated by two dicks at once to be repulsive.

Me?

I found it rewarding.

After all, I learned something valuable. *Girls with tight pussies make the rules.*

12

TYSON

"EXPLAIN to me why you'd say something like that? It didn't even make sense," I complained.

I was surprised that Shawn's comment in the restaurant about Jo being *the librarian* didn't raise eyebrows. He often said things for the sole purpose of getting a reaction out of someone, not taking time to consider the potential repercussions of his actions.

He sipped his beer. "Made sense to me."

"You're lucky she didn't ask you what the fuck you were talking about."

"If she would have, I'd have told her."

"That's the fucking problem. I know you would have. You need to know when to keep your mouth shut."

He gave me a look. "I'm not going to lie to her."

"I'm not asking you to lie to her. I'm asking you to keep your stupid comments to yourself."

"There's nothing stupid about her being a naughty librarian."

"What if she said, 'What do you mean, I'm the naughty librarian?'" I asked. "What would you have said?"

He slid his bottle of beer to the side and met my gaze. "I would have said, 'You look just like the sexy-assed librarian we had in high school'."

"Do you think hearing that comment would have made her happy, or sad?"

His looked as if I'd asked him to explain quantum physics. "How the fuck would I know?" he exclaimed. "I don't know that chick."

"You. Don't. Think. That's the problem. You just yap, yap, yap, like one of those little barking fucking dogs. You need to think about what you say before you say it."

"Okay, *Dad*," he said in a snide tone.

"Fuck you," I said. "Just forget it. I know you're not going to change. I'm just glad she didn't say anything."

He reached for his beer. "I'm guessing you're not going to tell her she looks like Garber."

"Fuck no, I'm not going to tell her."

"Why not?"

"Because no girl wants to think that she reminds a guy of someone else."

"If I told that big-tittied cowgirl that she looked like Britney Spears, she'd probably give me a blowjob. A blowjob and a pat on the back. A fuckin' *attaboy* pat."

"If you told her she looked like Britney Spears, she'd probably slap the shit out of you."

"Why do you say that?"

"Because she would. That Jenny chick is about twenty-five years old, max. Britney Spears is forty, and looks like death."

"She's not forty," he snapped back.

I picked up my phone, typed her name into *Google*, and grinned. "Sorry. She's thirty-seven. Thirty-seven and looks like she's forty."

"Doesn't matter if she's thirty-seven or fifty-seven. In my mind Britney Spears will forever be singing *Baby One More Time* in the hallway in that schoolgirl outfit. Sexy little Catholic schoolgirl lookin' bitch. I'd eat two miles of her shit just to see where it came from."

"You're an idiot. I can't even make a point with you."

"Stop beating around the bush and say what you want to say."

"Okay." I raised my index finger. "If you told Jenny that you wanted her to dress up like a schoolgirl, do you think she'd do it?"

"Chick's a freak, I already told ya. Yeah, she'd do it."

"Alright. If you told her you wanted her to dress up like a schoolgirl and dance in the hallway while singing that song, do you think she'd do it?"

"What part of 'she's a freak' don't you understand? If I told that chick to poke a pickle up her butt while she ate a pineapple pizza and tap danced like Bing fuckin' Crosby in a rainstorm, she'd do it."

Sadly, he was probably right. Making my point wasn't going to come easily if I continued to use analogies.

I forced a sigh and shook my head. "We're friends, right?"

"More like brothers, why?"

"I introduced you to the cowgirl, right?"

He tipped the neck of his beer bottle toward me. "Sure did."

"Do you appreciate it?"

"Sure do."

"In return, grant me this wish. Don't tell Jo that she reminds you, or me for that matter, of Garber? Can you do that for me? You know, because you're so appreciative."

He clanked the neck of his bottle against mine. "All you had to do was ask."

I let out a dramatic sigh. "Glad that's over."

He pushed his chair away from the table, looked me over, and then crossed his arms. "I got a question."

"I'm all ears."

"When you two are going at it, do you have her wear the glasses, or take 'em off?"

"She leaves them on."

"Figures." He scoffed. "Leaves 'em on because she's blind as a fuckin' bat, or leaves 'em on because you tell her to?"

"She leaves them on because I *ask* her to," I replied. "I don't *tell* her to do anything."

"Okay, Mister Congeniality." He leaned forward and arched an eyebrow. "My question is this. She doesn't ask you why you want her to leave the glasses on? Doesn't question your weird hang-ups?"

"It's not a weird hang-up."

"If I asked Jenny – or whatever her name is – to leave her boots on, you'd say I was a weirdo or 'an idiot' or whatever. Leaving the glasses on is a hang-up. Admit it."

"It's a preference."

"What. Fucking. Ever. You like chic geeks and you always have. Flock to 'em like flies to turds." He looked away for an instant, then appeared to have an epiphany. "Okay, when you tell what's-her-name to leave her glasses on while she slobs your knob, she doesn't ask you why you have such *preferences*?"

"She hasn't yet."

"If she does, what are you going to tell her?"

"I'll tell her I'm attracted to girls with big bold glasses."

He dismissed my response with a wave of his hand. "You, my friend, are the idiot."

I wasn't attracted to Jo because she reminded me of anyone. I was attracted to her because she was strikingly beautiful. The similarities between her and Garber were coincidental. The glasses were nothing more than an added bonus.

"Believe what you want to believe," I said. "If Jo wore contact lenses and dressed like a nun, I'd still be attracted to her."

"Tell yourself whatever you want to tell yourself," he responded. "I know you, remember? You're scratching a twenty-year-old itch. Won't matter much in a few weeks anyway, because you'll be dumping her. I just wanted to make *my* point."

"What *was* your point?"

"My point is I tell chicks the truth from the get-go, and you don't."

"I do, too."

"You don't lie to 'em, you just don't tell 'em *nothin'*. I'm a different creature. I told Ol' Cowgirl that I was throwin' her some dick, and that was that. Said, 'This ain't nothing but sex. If you get your freak on and take 'er in the butt like a pro, maybe we can do it more than once. If you're not down to fuck for fuckin's sake, we'll have a beer and call it a night.'"

"And she agreed?"

"Fucked her, didn't I?"

"You question my methods, and I question yours. End result's the same," I said. "Neither of us do relationships."

"But I don't lead 'em to believe there's ever going to be a chance. You do."

I laughed. "Don't think just because you tell them up front that you're just 'throwin' 'em some dick' that they don't secretly hope that it'll turn into more. For a girl to agree to that, she's got to swallow a gut full of self-worth."

"I've never pressured anyone into anything."

"Bottom line is this. You make them feel bad when it starts, and I make them feel bad when it's over. We both make them feel bad."

I wished things were different. That *I* was different. But I wasn't. I never would be. Change would require believing that a relationship could survive.

Flourish.

Go the distance.

I had the luxury of knowing better. Relationships were like turds floating in the toilet of life. Eventually, they all got flushed.

It was just a matter of who did the flushing.

13

JO

MY FATHER WAGGED the tip of his fork toward my plate. "It's not going to eat itself, Jo. Get busy."

"Leave her be," my mother said without looking up. "She might not be hungry."

"She's hungry enough to eat the rice casserole," he replied. "She's done nothing but poke the meat."

"Medley," my mother said. "It's called a rice medley."

The *meat* was gray on the outermost edge and bright red in the center. Regardless of what they'd labeled it, it was fish.

"It's fish," I said. "It's not 'meat'."

"It's a steak," my father argued. "Said so right on the package."

I pushed it across my plate with the backside of my fork. "A *tuna* steak."

He gave me the death stare. "You know the rule."

I glanced across the table. My brother was elbows-deep in his piece of fish, devouring it one over-sized chunk at a time.

I shifted my eyes to my father. "Don't worry, I'll get to it," I assured him. "It'll be last."

"Don't make yourself sick," my mother said.

My father's brows knitted together. He pointed the tines of his fork at her. "Rules are rules," he growled. "She's taking two bites of the steak. End. Of. Story."

He never wavered from enforcing the rules. The *two-bite rule* was my least favorite of them all. We were required to take two big bites of everything we were served. If we didn't like it after two bites, we weren't forced to continue. My father believed two man-sized bites would allow anyone to truly determine if they liked something or detested it.

I didn't have to take a bite of the tuna to know it would be repulsive.

"I met someone," I said.

The statement was more of a diversionary tactic than anything. It was one of the few ways I could draw my brother's attention away from eating. His comments would undoubtedly capture my father's attention. While my father was immersed in my brother's snide remarks, I could cut two bites from my fish and slip them into my purse.

In response to the declaration, my mother and my brother looked up at the same time.

"That's terrific," my mother said. "Tell us about him."

Midway through shoveling a forkful of rice medley into his mouth, my brother paused. "All she knows is what she read about him on his Tinder profile. Let me guess. He's educated, financially secure, drives an Audi, and he enjoys reading books on the couch with his cat after he gets off work. You probably haven't even met him yet, have you?"

"That's enough, Jarod," my mother hissed.

"What the hell's a *Tinder profile*," my father asked.

"It's a dating app," Jarod explained. "From the comfort of your home, you can pick a guy that meets your interests and criteria, just like Jerry Jones selecting a draft pick for the Cowboys. All your prospective *dates* are right there on your phone with their information on display. It's perfect for Jo, she doesn't even have to go out in public and meet anyone. The men all lie, though. Everyone claims to be rich, educated, and single. In reality, they're poor, uneducated, and married. It's a place for guys to get laid."

My father shifted his eyes from Jarod to me. "Is that true?"

"I have no idea," I said. "Sounds like Jarod's pretty knowledgeable about it. Maybe he's been using it."

My father sipped his tea. "Stop trying to piss your sister off."

I cut a one-inch square off the corner of the tuna and raised it within smelling distance of my mouth.

While I struggled not to vomit, Jarod let out a laugh. "The day she meets a normal guy," he said. "Is the day I'll kiss Smokey's hairy ass."

My father gave him a look. "Smokey doesn't want your lips on his pooper."

I snatched the tuna from the tip of my fork and attempted to hide my hand in my lap. The process failed miserably, with the tuna slipping from my grasp at the last minute. A quick scan of the floor revealed the chunk of raw fish had landed at my feet.

Feet that rested on top of a rather elegant Oriental rug my mother purchased while in Barcelona, Spain. With some hesitation, I pressed the toe of my shoe against the wad of fish and smashed it against the irreplaceable rug.

"Stop it, Jarod," my mother said in an assertive tone. She looked at me and smiled. "Tell us about him."

"We met at the store," I said. "He asked me on a date. He drives the FedEx truck. He's really cute, and he's super nice. We went to Lockhart's and ate on Friday night, and then we went out again on Saturday night and had Mexican food."

Jarod chuckled. "FedEx driver? FedEx drivers are old retired child molesters and serial killers. How old is this guy?"

"He's your age. And, he's not a weirdo. He's nice."

"My age? Where'd he go to school?"

"Plano Senior High."

"Does he wear Coke bottle glasses?"

I reached for my glasses. "No, he doesn't wear glasses at all."

"Rules him out as being a pervert," he said with a laugh. "What's his name?"

"Why?"

"Might know him from football, unless he played baseball or

some other stupid sport. Plano hasn't won a championship since 1994. Lost most of their good players in 1999. If he's my age, he would have been a senior before they lost everyone. Did he play football?"

I shrugged. "I pretty sure he didn't play football."

"Is he a pot smoker?" Jarod asked.

"Josephine, I don't want you seeing a pot-head," my mother said.

"He's *not* a pot-head," I insisted. "He's normal."

"If he's normal, he would have played football," Jarod said under his breath. "What's his name?"

I sighed. "Tyson."

Jarod's brows went together. "Not Tyson *Neese?*"

My heart nearly leaped from my chest. Jarod knowing Tyson couldn't be a good thing. A softball sized lump crept into my throat, nearly cutting off my ability to breathe. I swallowed against it and gave Jarod a bug-eyed look.

"I uhhm. You…you know him?" I stammered.

"It's Tyson Neese?" he screeched. "That's who you're seeing?"

"TJ Neese?" my father asked.

"She's seeing T. J. Neese," Jarod blurted. "The kid that threw for six thousand yards his junior year."

"Nineteen ninety and eight," my father said as if reading the facts from mid-air. "Kid nearly set a world record in passing yards. Six thousand and thirteen yards. Beat all my old records to hell. Damned shame about him breaking his ankle. One of the best football players this state has ever seen"

I spent a lifetime detesting football. Oftentimes, it seemed it was all my father and brother cared about. Nonetheless, I swelled with so much pride my posture straightened. "A local celebrity, huh?"

"National," Jarod said. "The summer between his junior and senior year he broke his ankle, or he'd be playing pro right now."

"Sounds familiar," my father said beneath his breath.

According to my mother, my father was a fabulous football player. One would never know it from speaking to him. He would talk about the sport until he was blue in the face but never spoke of his accomplishments.

"Well, we're seeing each other," I gloated. "Oh, and he drives a car like your old car. The red one."

"A Cobra?"

"Yeah. Only it's silver. He rebuilt it. It's got bigger thingamajigs and a closer ratio whatchamacallit, though. He told me, but I don't remember."

He sighed. "I miss that car. Never should have bought that pickup truck."

I cut another section of tuna from the steak and pierced it with the tines of my fork. "Maybe he'll take you for a ride."

Jarod scooped up a forkful of rice. "Bet it's not as nice as mine was."

"I think it's nicer." I lifted the chunk of tuna and waited for the right moment. "He keeps it pretty pristine."

"Have you ridden in it?"

"I have. Twice."

"Is it fast?"

"It's really fast. It makes this horrible whining noise when it takes off."

"Bet it's a *Terminator* Cobra. They've got a supercharger on 'em."

"Yeah," I said. "It's got one of those."

"Bet he put a Kenne Bell on it."

"I don't know what that means. You'll have to ask him."

"When are you going to invite him for dinner?" my mother asked.

I felt that I'd backed myself into a corner. Asking Tyson to come to my parent's home for dinner was a huge step, and one I was certain he wasn't prepared to make. Considering Tyson's near celebrity status with my father and brother, I was going to be pressured until I complied with their wishes.

"I don't know," I replied. "One of these days."

"Sad he's driving a FedEx truck," Jarod said. "He could have been making millions."

My parents had more money than they could ever spend. Oil

SCOTT HILDRETH

leases inherited from generations past provided income in the seven-figure-per-year range. Although I could have relied on my parents for financial assistance, I chose to secure loans for my education, and for my book store.

I didn't derive happiness from wealth, nor did my parents, or my grandparents. Jarod was different. He seemed to view material objects as a means of measuring his successes.

"Maybe he's happy driving the truck," I offered. "He doesn't seem to care."

"He was set to get a twenty-million-dollar-a-year contract. I bet he cares plenty," Jarod argued. "Wouldn't you?"

"I'm happy with what I've got. Maybe he is, too."

"What he chooses to do for a living has no bearing on the man he is, Jarod," my mother said. She looked at me. "I don't care if he's a hobo, I'd like to meet him."

"Are you going to eat that piece of tuna or just let it sit there until it dries out?" my father asked.

"I'm going to eat it, just as soon as I get up a little more courage. It's piece number two," I said with a smile.

My mother winked at me and then cleared her throat. "There's a fly on your rice, John."

His eyes darted to his plate. "Where?"

In one fluid motion, I plucked the tuna from the tip of my fork and tossed it onto the rug beside the first piece. After covering it with my foot, I shoved a forkful of rice into my mouth.

Following his fruitless search for a non-existent fly, my father looked up. "Nasty little bastard got away."

My mother shrugged. "They're sneaky." She looked at me and smiled. "How was the tuna, Josephine?"

"You know how picky I am," I said apologetically. "It was really good, I just don't care much for fish."

"It was your father's idea," she explained. "He's trying to lose weight. We won't have it again. At least not when you're here."

"Thank you."

She gestured beneath the table. "Do you remember when I bought this rug?"

I swallowed heavily. "I do."

She glanced toward my foot and then met my gaze with raised brows. "Remember the problems we had when it came time to import it? After we returned from vacation?"

The process took months after she'd purchased it and was nothing short of an expensive disaster. I attempted to swallow the rising lump in my throat, but only partially succeeded.

"I uhhm." I nodded. "I do."

"I love that rug." She smiled. "You'll bring Tyson for dinner soon, won't you?"

Coercing Tyson to come to dinner was the least I could do to escape the botched fish dinner unscathed.

I pressed my toes against the meat and swallowed heavily. "Yes, Ma'am."

14

TYSON

BOX IN HAND, I walked the length of Miss Everly's driveway. As I bent down to set the object on the porch, the door swung open and two fuzzy gray slippers greeted me.

"Good morning," she said in an exaggerated whisper.

The sound of her voice sent a tingling sensation along my spine. I dragged my eyes up the length of her Barbie-esque frame. She was wearing a pair of wine-colored designer sweatpants and a skin-tight ribbed white tank top, sans bra. Her hardened nipples distorted the thin fabric, commanding the attention of anyone who dared to be in her presence. After a lengthy pause at her oversized assets, I met her downward gaze.

"I've been so anxious for this delivery." She looked me up and down. "Do you have time for a glass of tea?"

I handed her the box. "I should really—"

"I'm going to stop asking if you don't accept." She gave the most provocative of innocent looks. "One glass won't hurt."

I'd screwed so many women during the workday that I'd been reprimanded for it on two separate occasions. My new route was assigned to me as a last-ditch effort to reform me into a less sexually active – and a far more devoted – FedEx employee. So far, the only changes I'd seen was a new selection of available tits and ass.

I had no desire to disrupt my busy schedule for nothing more than a glass of tea. My intentions were sexual, and she needed to know it. "If I come in, we're going to be busy for a lot longer than ten minutes."

"There's something in this box that may excite you." She gestured toward the winding stairway behind her. "Follow me, please."

Curious about the contents of the box, I stepped inside the spacious home and followed her up the ornate staircase.

Tightly wound tendrils of platinum blond hair danced with each step. Her pronounced manner of sashaying caused her ass to shake from side to side in a hypnotic manner. Her intentions were clear. This wasn't her first rodeo. Mouthing the words to Marvin Gaye's *Let's Get It On*, I fixed my eyes on her velour-clad tush and followed her up the stairs.

Upon reaching the upper landing, she turned toward an open bedroom door. She was all business. I liked that quality in a woman.

She promenaded to a dresser at the far end of the room and placed the box on top of it. She turned around and parted her ruby red lips ever so slightly. Marilyn Monroe. She looked like a Marilyn fucking Monroe.

Only better.

She was *sultrier*.

"I want you to treat me like a whore," she breathed in a raspy tone.

I'd spent my entire childhood convinced of two things: dreams didn't come true and prayers were never answered. The curvaceous vixen facing me was clear proof that I was dead wrong.

If she was the filthy slut that I suspected she was, there was no need for small talk.

"Get on your knees," I growled. "I'm going to choke you with a mile of cock."

She fell to her knees. Without an ounce of expressed grace, she ripped off her shirt and tossed it aside. She began massaging her massive boobs. Light moans followed. The kneading of her flesh became more aggressive, as did the sounds that escaped her lips.

Desire shot through my veins like liquid fire.

With my eyes glued to the show, I fumbled to unbuckle my belt. Upon shoving my hand in my boxers, I realized I was as limp as a freshly cooked noodle.

What the fuck?

In my sexual travels I'd been with spontaneous sirens like the one before me. I'd coerced college coeds to copulate. I'd had hanky-panky with horny housewives. I'd tickled the twats of twins. One thing I'd never had to deal with, however, was the dreaded dangly dick.

I looked at it, and then at her.

With her chin up and her eyes fixed on mine, she parted her collagen enhanced lips. "I'm such a dirty whore," she murmured. "Use me up. Cover me in your come. I want to bathe in it."

At that moment, the only thing I could have used her for was getting me a tissue to wipe my tears. Since meeting Jo, I'd suffered a three-minute lackluster performance and one inability to perform entirely.

Something was wrong.

Terribly wrong.

I gripped my limp dick in my fist and attempted to stroke it. I would have been more successful at stroking a handful of mashed potatoes into an erection.

There are very few things in life that we know for absolute certain. However, I knew beyond a shadow of doubt that I wasn't going to get hard. If anything, my cock was shrinking in size.

It was running away from her.

No matter what Miss Everly did, or how badly I thought I wanted to fuck her, it wasn't happening.

I shoved my limp dick into my boxers, pulled up my shorts, and buckled my belt. If I played my cards right, I just might be able to escape with a speck of self-esteem.

I shot Everly an exaggerated glare. "You're a dirty fucking whore. You don't deserve this dick."

The nearly inaudible moans that had crept from her lungs for the last few minutes increased in volume.

Tenfold.

"Oh my God," she moaned. "Please. Give it to me. I need it. Slap me with it."

"You're nothing but a slut." I shook my head in mock disgust. "A dirty, filthy slut."

"You're right," she murmured. "I'm nothing but a dirty whore. Fuck my dirty pussy and come all over my face."

I'd have loved to use her. Sadly, short of getting her to scramble me some eggs, I had no other use for her.

I turned toward the dresser and grabbed the box. After tearing it open, I retrieved a curved dildo fashioned from golden chrome. Heavy in my hand, and futuristic in appearance, it was a work of art. A quick search of the box revealed a tiny wireless remote control. I pressed the button on the remote. The cock-shaped device shook violently. I pressed the button again. The vibrating lessened to more of a *thump, thump, thump*. A third press caused it to jolt back and forth methodically.

I turned it off and handed her the golden schlong.

"Stick that in your twat, whore."

She wrestled her sweats to her thighs, taking her panties with them in the process. After arching her back and leaning against the end of the bed, she inserted the tip of the battery-powered penis past her beef curtains.

I crossed my arms and cleared my throat. "All of it."

Her eyes fell closed as she began to fuck herself senseless with it. After a few lengthy strokes, all ten inches of it vanished.

I pressed the remote's button twice.

The sound of her moaning permeated through the room.

I turned toward the door. "Don't you dare move," I commanded. "Stay right fucking there until you've had six orgasms." I faced her. "Do you understand me?"

"Yes," she muttered.

Refraining from bursting into laughter, I shot her a sharp glare. "I am a *Sir*. You'll address me as such."

A breath of satisfaction shot from her lungs. "Yes, Sir."

"Six!" I barked. "Nothing less than six. I *may* give you some cock if you learn to follow my commands, whore."

Enveloped by the sound of her moans, I gingerly walked down the steps and toward the front door. After setting the remote control on the sideboard, I opened the door and sauntered to my truck.

There was one place I could go to determine if my cock was truly broken.

Admitting there was only one didn't come easily.

15

JO

"THE FED SEX delivery man is here," Jenny exclaimed. "Ho-Lee-Shit, look at this. He's freaking nuts!"

Immersed in a book order, I looked up. Tyson's FedEx truck was cutting across four lanes of traffic in the middle of the busy street. After screeching to a stop directly in front of the store, he leaped out of the truck's open passenger door.

Upon seeing him, I stood and turned toward the door. Wearing a straight-faced expression, he rushed past Jenny, offering her nothing more than a wave of his right arm. Before I cleared the edge of the desk, he was standing in front of me.

Without so much as a greeting, he gripped my biceps and leaned into me. As his face came to rest against my neck he drew a slow breath.

Goosebumps rose along my upper arms. I pressed my jaw against his cheek. "What are you doing?"

He pulled away and looked me over. "It's a good thing you're wearing a dress."

I was lost. The look of confusion plastered across my face was proof. "Huh?"

"Grab my cock," he said flatly.

My face flushed. "Tyson!" I whispered. "Not here."

"Grab it," he demanded. "Squeeze it."

"Jenny's right behind you," I said in protest.

"I don't give a fuck." He gestured toward my hand with his eyes. "Grab it."

"Are you serious?"

"I need you to do this for me," he pleaded.

His back was facing the door. For the time being, no one could see his front side but me. I glanced toward the entrance. Unaware of her surroundings, Jenny was busy practicing the steps to a line dance.

I pressed my palm against his crotch and gripped his girth in my hand. Instantaneously, it began to grow. Within seconds, his FedEx shorts were stretched to their limits.

I raised my brows. "Now what?"

"Tell what's-her-name to watch the store."

"Why?"

"I wanna fuck."

"Seriously?"

"Seriously."

My eyes darted around the store. "Where would we go?"

"I don't care." He coughed out a laugh. "I'll bend your sexy ass over that fucking desk and shove you full of dick right here."

My entire body began to tingle at the mention of it. After a few seconds of erotic thoughts, I came to my senses.

"Right here in front of her?" I argued. "What if someone comes in? That's crazy."

"You got me hard, now it's your responsibility to take care of it," he said as if it were a known fact.

"Says who?"

He glanced at his cock. "That's the rule."

I had no idea if it was a rule or not. I'd never heard it, but then again, I possessed nothing more than a thimble full of sexual wherewithal.

I scrunched my nose. "Really?"

He nodded. "It's common knowledge. If you make it hard, you've got to get me off."

I considered complying with his wish and wondered if there was a place where we could pull it off. A small storage room or the mop closet were the only two viable options that came to mind.

My dripping wet pussy believed that getting fucked in either location would be the epitome of hotness. I glanced at his crotch. His rock-hard dick was parallel with the floor, holding the material of his navy-colored shorts outstretched like a sideways tent.

I scanned the length of his muscular frame. A light scruff of whiskers peppered his strong jaw. His hair appeared that he'd combed it with a brush of his hand. His eyes gleamed with sincerity.

The corners of his mouth, however, were curled up slightly and struggling not to spring upward any further.

"You're full of shit," I insisted. "There's no rule."

He popped his neck and then grinned. "Maybe there isn't."

It didn't matter. I wanted him to fuck me. It could last three minutes, or thirty, I didn't care. Opportunities like this weren't presented to girls like me with any regularity.

"Rule or no rule, I'll do it."

His eyes lit up. "Where?"

The storage room was at the rear of the store, behind the last bookcase and off to the side. Although the entrance was visible to anyone who might meander past, the room itself – as long as the door was closed – was hidden.

"Storage room." I turned toward the back of the store and glanced over my shoulder, at Jenny. "We'll be back in a few minutes!"

Still dancing to a song that only she could hear, she didn't even bother turning around. "Don't do anything I wouldn't do."

Giddy about mid-day sex – even if it was going to take place in an eight-foot square room – I led Tyson to the back of the store. Upon opening the door, my heart sank.

The small space was filled from floor to ceiling with donated books, swag, and other miscellaneous items, leaving very little room to do anything but stand face to face between the stacks of boxes.

"It's a little more…it's…there's not much room," I stammered.

He rested his chin on my shoulder, peered inside, and then sighed. At the instant I expected him to declare screwing in the overstuffed room wasn't a possibility, he turned me to face him.

His hungry eyes scanned me from my head to my feet and then back. Upon meeting my gaze, he grinned.

I glanced at Jenny and then at him. "What?"

"You make my cock hard."

"I'm glad I can—"

He kissed me deeply, sucking the remaining words from my lungs before I could speak them. Caught completely off guard by the kiss, I stumbled backward until I came crashing to a stop against the corridor wall.

I no more than realized his hand was sliding up my thigh, and he'd already slid his finger beneath my panties and penetrated me. My heart palpitated. He fingered me into a frenzy, then began to rub my clit feverishly.

My legs wobbled. The kiss continued, as did the teasing of my clit. After swirling his finger around my swollen nub long enough to produce a few micro-orgasms, he tugged against my panties. Although I probably should have, I offered no opposition whatsoever.

His body pressed against mine, pinning me to the wall. One of his hands tweaked my right nipple. The other lifted the hem of my dress.

Receiving no objection on my part, he grabbed my ass and hoisted me from my feet. His stiff dick pressed against my wetness. I wanted to feel him inside if me.

Every inch of him.

I ground my pussy against his swollen shaft. Desire ran through me so deeply I shook. I sank my teeth into his lower lip. The sound of a horn honking brought me to my senses.

I pulled my mouth away from his and sucked a choppy breath.

Mentally prepared to tell him that I wasn't about to fuck him in the open hallway, I parted my lips. No one word escaped me.

Instead, I simply looked him in the eyes and waited for him to do it.

The pressure increased. My jaw tensed. My eyes widened as he pushed the length of his massive girth into me, inch by inch. Unlike the first time we had sex, the pain was very pleasurable.

The impromptu visit. Grabbing his cock while we stood at my desk. The smell of his cologne. The kiss. Being pressed against the wall. Forcing himself into me. Everything rushed together, consuming me completely. In response, I gripped his face in my hands and kissed him as if it was the last time we'd ever have an opportunity to do it.

With our lips pressed against one another's and our tongues tangled in a feverish kiss, he began fucking me like he was mad at me.

Every inch of angry dick he shoved into me was welcomed by my warmth. With each powerful thrust, my back slammed against the wall. The impact was marked by carnal grunts that shot from my lungs.

I eagerly accepted each stroke without opposition or complaint. My vaginal canal had somehow conformed to his massive size, leaving the sex nothing short of the most pleasurable event I'd ever had the opportunity to experience.

While I became lost in what was surely the most passionate kiss to ever exist, he fucked me like a man possessed.

It felt so much different than the first time. I'd never imagined sex could feel like heaven, but it was just that, and nothing less. Hovering above the ground in a blissful state of being, I continued to accept all he had to offer until we were both breathless.

He pulled his mouth from mine.

His eyes were filled with energy. I gazed into his magnificent orbs, not knowing what to say, but feeling that I should say something.

"I love fucking you," he said beneath his breath.

"Thank you," I said, and then felt like an inexperienced fool for saying it.

With our eyes locked, he pressed me to the wall using nothing more than his hips. Holding me in place with his stiff cock, he slipped his hands under my dress. His fingers quickly found my aching nipples. While he rolled them between his thumb and forefinger, he began to fuck me slowly.

The rhythmic nature of his thrusts combined with the twisting of my nipples brought me to the brink of climax. I tightened around his shaft. He withdrew half his length and paused.

"I want to watch you come," he breathed.

His expressed desire to watch me reach climax was all it took to push me over the edge. Tension mounted, and there was nothing I could do to prevent it. In one more stroke, I was going to explode.

Before I could respond, he pushed what remained of his cock into me, slowly.

That was it. I was officially done.

"Ohmygod," I stammered. "It's happening."

Upon hearing my declaration, his pace increased. Feeling strangely guilty, I looked him in the eyes. On the heel of one of his thrusts, a tingling sensation ran through me, taking with it my ability to resist any further.

My inner walls contracted around his shaft.

His cock swelled.

In unison, while gazing into each other's eyes, we reached climax. There was no sound. There were no surroundings. There was Tyson, and there was me. For that period of time, nothing else existed.

I came so hard my entire body shook from the inside out. When the orgasm ended, I was in his arms, still suspended above the floor. After regaining my wits, I glanced toward the front of the store.

Jenny was nowhere in sight

"That was amazing," I breathed.

He kissed me softly. "We're not stopping."

"Stopping what?"

He looked me up and down. "This." He grinned and lowered me to my feet. "Just wanted to let you know."

I had my first quasi-assurance of recurring sex. I did a mental fist pump and smiled in return. "I was getting ready to tell you the exact same thing."

16

TYSON

I OFTEN WONDERED if I worked on my car to relax, or as a means of escape. For all practical purposes, the vehicle was perfect. Even so, I found myself doing *something* to it two or three nights a week.

Shawn handed me the ratchet. "What do you mean, 'my shit was like a piece of spaghetti?'"

"Imagine holding a piece of cooked spaghetti and trying to poke it through a keyhole," I explained. "That was my cock."

He looked at me as if I'd taken a shit on his dining room table. "You were completely limp?"

I leaned under the hood. "As limp as a noodle."

"Jesus, dude. So, you just left?"

"Not exactly. I had her poke a dildo in her twat. Told her to have six or eight orgasms, I don't remember. I said when she was done, she could get up. Then, I just walked out. She didn't know I couldn't get hard. I acted like the dildo was her punishment for being a dirty whore."

"Go back to the *I had her poke a dildo in her twat* part of that story," he said. "How'd you wrangle that?"

"Acted like a Dom. I think she liked it."

"What do you know about Doms?"

I tightened the supercharger pulley bolts. "Not much. More than you, I imagine."

"Doubt it. Been reading that chick's books. It's pretty interesting shit."

I paused and glanced over my shoudler. "What chick?"

"CD Reiss. I'm on one now called *Marriage Games*. They've got a place like a bar, and you go in there and hang out. All the chicks are submissive, and the dudes are Doms. If the chick's hang-ups are in tune with the dude's desires, they work out the details, go to a room upstairs, and sign a contract. Then, it's 'go time'. Shit's crazy."

"Doubt places like that exist in the real world."

He shrugged. "Shows what you know."

"What do you mean?"

"Already checked. There's places like that in Dallas. Shit they're everywhere. And, there's munches that people go to. If they're *in the scene*, that is."

"Munches? They have muff-diving contests?"

He laughed. "A munch is when people that are into that type of shit all get together. Might be couples, might be single people. It's a way to meet other people in the scene. That's what they call their lifestyle. *The scene*. It's like a party or a mixer. Might be dinner, or whatever. But it's a way to meet one another. New people that are just as fucked up as you are."

I handed him the wrench. "You think people with those desires are 'fucked up'?"

"I think it's cool, but they're not normal, no."

I took exception to his position. "What the fuck is *normal*? Poking shit up chicks' butts isn't normal. You like to poke shit up girl's asses. So, I guess you're fucked up."

"Never said I wasn't."

I took off my rubber gloves and set them on top of the radiator support. "I think different people get off on different shit. When someone's fantasy isn't in line with yours, that doesn't make them abnormal."

He picked up the gloves and turned away. "Good point." He

tossed the gloves in the trash can and faced me. "Back to mister noodle dick. What are you going to do about that? That's serious shit."

"It's subconscious. There's nothing I can do about it. Live with it, I guess."

His eyes narrowed. "Be limited to one chick?"

"For now, I guess."

"What's the world become?" He crossed his arms and looked me over. "T. J. Neese is spoken for."

"I'm not spoken for."

"Sounds like you are."

"I'm choosing to slow down a little. Until my cock recovers."

"You can't perform with anyone else. You're impotent." His brows shot up. "Might be the onset of love."

The words *impotent* and *love* caused me to cringe. "Fuck you," I spat. "I'm not impotent, and it's not love. For right now, I'm enjoying fucking Jo. It's that simple."

"It's much more complicated than that."

"No, it isn't."

"That chick with the tits. The one you told to stick the dildo in her twat." He folded his arms over his chest. "How hot was she?"

Before I could respond, he shook his head. "Strike that, counselor. If you hadn't met Jo, how hot would you say she was? If you met the platinum-haired seductress three months ago, what would you be telling me about her?"

"She's okay."

"Okay?" He laughed. "Just okay, huh?"

"Yeah. She's alright."

"Compare her to someone. Alright like Katy Perry, or alright like Emily Ratajkowski?"

"I think Katy Perry looks like a weasel. Who the fuck's Emily Ratajkowski?"

"Baddest bitch on the planet. Did that video with Robin Thicke."

"Who the fuck's Robin Thicke?"

He pulled his phone from his pocket, tapped his finger against the screen, and then shoved the phone in my face.

"*Blurred Lines*," he said. "I know you've danced to this motherfucker in private."

The song was familiar. The woman dancing naked in the video reminded me more of Jo than anyone else. "That's the Ratajkowski chick?"

He nodded. "Yep."

"Reminds me of Jo."

"Dude, you need medical attention. Your problems aren't limited to your cock, Jo's got your eyesight fucked up, too. You're a goddamned mess."

In my eyes, the resemblance was uncanny. "If her hair was darker and she was wearing glasses, she'd look just like her."

He rewound the video, played a few seconds of it repeatedly, and then turned it off. "I can see that. So, which one is it? Katy Perry, or Em-Rat?"

"She's built like that Sofia Vergara chick, and looks like Christina Aguilera, if Aguilera is having a good day and her hair isn't one of those shades of weird orange."

He went bug-eyed. "And you couldn't get it up?"

It seemed strange the more I thought about it. "Maybe I was dehydrated, or something."

"You didn't just get done fucking Jo, did you?"

"Now?"

"No, dumbass. When you were at Christina Aguilera's place."

"No, I fucked her afterward."

"Who? Jo?"

"Yep."

"You fucked her after you couldn't get it up for the Aguilera chick?"

"Right after. Yeah. I was worried my shit was broken, so I hot-footed it over there and fucked her in the hallway."

"Which hallway?"

"Back of the bookstore."

"Remote hallway, or visible?"

"Visible."

"You been reading those books? From her store?"

"Nope."

"Just felt like fuckin' in the hallway while the dirty cowgirl watched?"

"She wasn't watching."

"I bet she was."

"She wasn't."

He sighed. "Got bad news, Kemosabe. If you couldn't get it up for Aguilera, and you got it up for Jo, it wasn't dehydration. It's much deeper than that. I think you're falling in love."

I knew better than to allow myself to fall into the false belief that love existed. Love was a farce, and I knew that from first-hand information.

"There's two things you need to understand," I said adamantly. "It isn't love, and the cowgirl wasn't watching."

17

JO

FACING one another with our ears pressed against the wall, Jenny and I listened as the city manager tried to negotiate with the masseuse.

"Forty dollah hand job. Happy ending," she explained. "Feel good. You like for sure."

"What about a blowjob?" he asked.

"Blowjob?" she screeched. "You find skanky girl for blowjob. No blowjob here. This respectable place. Massage parlor, not whorehouse."

"I want a blowjob."

"You police? Mistah blowjob police man?"

He chuckled. "I'm not the police."

"I see you on TV. You mistah big time. You police, mistah big time?"

"I'm not the police."

"Blowjob one hundred dollah, mistah big time."

"Can I come in your mouth?"

"For one hundred dollah? What, you think I'm a whore, muthahfuck? You come on washcloth. Feel good for you. Wipe you clean when we done. Nice and warm."

"I want to come in your mouth."

Jenny leaned away from the wall. "This is freaking hilarious," she whispered. "Think she'll let him come in her mouth?"

I shrugged.

She leaned against the wall and grinned.

"Come in mouth, two hundred dollah. No swallow."

"Two hundred dollars?" he bellowed. "That's crazy."

"Not crazy. You like. Come in mouth. Two hundred dollah."

"Two hundred dollars, and you swallow."

"No swallow for two hundred dollah. Swallow two-fifty."

"Two."

"Two-fifty, mistah big time. You like for sure. Come back next week, two hundred. You ask for Linda."

"It's the one that drives the BMW," Jenny whispered. "Linda, the thick one. She's funny."

I pressed my finger against my lips. "Shhh."

"Okay," he agreed. "Two-fifty. But, you've got to call me Spanky, and I'll need you to tell me I've got a huge cock while you're sucking it."

"You fuckin' crazy, mistah big time. Role play fifty dollah. Three hundred dollah, I tell you anything you like."

"Three hundred?" he wailed. "That's crazy."

"Crazy good. Linda suck you long time."

"Fine. Three hundred. But you're going to call me Spanky, and you're going to tell me my cock is huge."

"Three hundred dollah for massage. Put money under lamp. No check. No credit card. You like for sure."

"But you're going to—"

"Three hundred dollah. For massage. You like."

"Ohhh. For *the massage*. I gotcha."

The room fell silent for a moment, and then he began to moan.

"Oh, Sparky, you so big," she cooed. "Hard for little girl to fit in mouth."

The moaning sounds became more visceral. A light thumping sound followed, and then the paper-thin wall began to shake.

"Sparky, your cock so big. You come in little girl mouth, Sparky? Me want you come in mouth."

"Spanky," he groaned. "Spanky!"

"Spanky extra fifty dollah," she demanded. "I use special paddle. You like."

Jenny covered her mouth with her clenched fist. While mistah big time re-reminded Linda of his preferred nickname, Jenny sprinted toward the bookshelf and then let out a laugh.

"You couldn't make this shit up." She giggled. "We ought to write a book."

"Shhh."

"I can't listen to any more of it," she whispered. "I'm going to pee my pants. It's almost as entertaining as you and FedSex going at by the storage room yesterday."

I pushed myself away from the wall and tip-toed to where she stood. "Oh my God. You heard us?"

Her face washed with guilt. "I watched you."

"You watched?"

"Fuck yeah. It was hot as fuck."

"You watched? Like, you *watched* us?"

"From right here."

"For how long?"

"All of it. He's hung like a freaking donkey. That shit's crazy."

My face went flush. I covered my cheeks with my open palms. "Oh. My. God."

"What did you expect? He lifted your dress up, slammed you against the wall, and shoved you full of dick. There wasn't much else going on here, so I watched."

I found it strangely sexy that she watched us have sex without my knowledge. It was almost like I was the star in one of the porn videos I'd spent so many evenings masturbating to.

I lowered my hands. "I didn't look stupid, did I?"

"You looked sexy as fuck."

"Really?" I asked.

"Really."

"Have you ever watched porn?" I asked sheepishly.

She spit out a laugh. "Are you being serious?"

My shoulders slumped. "Sorry."

"Fuck yes, I watch porn." She laughed. "Who doesn't?"

"Oh." I let out a sigh. "I thought you were thinking I was, I don't know, a weirdo."

"I'd think you were a weirdo if you didn't watch it."

"Did we look, I don't know. Did we look as good as the people in the porn videos?"

"Pfft." She waved her hand in my direction. "Better. You two looked sexy as fuck."

"Really?"

"Some people have chemistry, and some people don't. In those videos, the people look like they're just getting paid to fuck. You two? You were fucking because you had to."

"What do you mean?"

"If you wouldn't have fucked right then and there, both of you two would have spontaneously combusted into flames." She threw her hands in the air. "Poof. Up in flames."

I grinned at the thought of looking like I had such chemistry with Tyson. "Why do you say that?"

She gave me a worried look. "Don't get mad, okay?'

"Mad?"

"Yeah. Don't get mad."

"I'm not going to get mad," I said. "Why would I get mad?"

She reached in her pocket and pulled out her phone. After unlocking it, she extended her hand, with the screen facing her. "Don't get mad."

"Okay."

She turned the screen to face me.

The picture was of me with my back against the wall. My legs were spread, and my feet were even with Tysons midriff. My dress was crumpled around my waist, and my ass was bare. The fingers of Tyson's left hand gripped my butt cheek firmly.

He was looking to the left slightly, and his jaw was tense.

My eyes were fixed on him. The look on my face told a story that words were incapable of.

I was in sexual heaven.

The mood captured in the picture was amazing. I studied it for some time, and then handed Jenny the phone.

"I'm not mad," I said. "You're right. That's sexy. Will you send it to me?"

"Sure."

"I can't believe you caught that moment so perfectly."

"I took about fifty pics." She laughed. "A little video, too."

"You took a video?"

"Just a little one."

"Can I see it?"

"Sure."

She fidgeted with the phone, and then handed it to me. "Don't go scrolling around after you watch it. There's shit on there you don't need to see," she warned.

"Of me?"

"No," she said. "Of me."

"Oh." I giggled. "Okay."

I pressed *play*.

Tyson's shorts were around his ankles, and he was fucking me slowly. My dress was up to my shoulders, and my boobs were bare. Tyson's right hand was on my left boob, squeezing it firmly. His left hand rested under my butt cheek.

With each stroke, my back was pressed against the wall.

My arms were draped over his shoulders, and my hands were clenching his shirt in balled fists.

After half a dozen thrusts, I arched my back. "I'm going to come. Right now."

The muscles in Tyson's legs flared as he began to fuck me ferociously. Each savage thrust slammed my back against the wall. Both of his hands squeezed my boobs as if doing so brought him great pleasure.

After a several second-long pounding, my back arched. My eyes widened.

No one in porn could duplicate the look on my face, that much I was sure of. It was one of sheer and utter satisfaction.

The video ended, mid-orgasm.

I found it odd that my recollection of the event, and the event itself, were different. Watching the video was strangely satisfying.

I handed her the phone. "Send me that, too."

She smiled. "Sexy, huh?"

A long breath escaped me. "Yeah."

"Chemistry," she said as she fiddled with her phone. "You two have it. There, I sent you both."

"Will you delete that stuff?"

She looked at the phone, and then at me. "Do I have to?"

"I don't want anyone to see it. It makes me nervous."

"Not to sound weird, or anything, but I like watching you two fuck. It's sexy as hell."

"I guess you can keep it, as long as you don't show it to anyone." I chuckled. "I'll just tell myself you deleted it."

"Cool. Thanks."

I took a step toward my desk, and then paused. "I wasn't going to say anything, but the thought of you watching us have sex is kind of sexy."

"The *thought* of me watching might be kind of sexy, but actually watching you have sex is sexy as hell. Best shit I've seen in a while."

"You didn't show it to Shawn, did you?"

She seemed offended. "No," she snapped.

"Okay. Don't, please."

"Don't worry. It's for my eyes only."

"Thank you."

"So, you two are like, what, an item, or whatever?" she asked.

"What do you mean?"

"Well, there at the end, he said he never wanted to stop fucking you. You agreed. I just thought that meant you two were, I don't know, *together*."

I'd given the comment Tyson made in the throes of passion little, if any, consideration. The thought of being in a relationship was impossible for me to fathom. I was the permanently single nerd who was lucky enough to get fucked once upon a time by someone who happened to smell the desire leaching from my pores.

"I don't know," I responded. "We haven't talked about it since."

"Well, you should. I like the thought of you two being together. It's a cute story." She slid her phone into her pocket and shrugged playfully. "And, I like watching you fuck."

I wasn't sure if Tyson and I would ever be in a relationship, but from the little bit of video I'd seen, I liked watching us fuck, too.

18

TYSON

I DESPERATELY NEEDED to resolve my issue with impotence. Convincing myself that Jo was more than an object of sexual desire was crucial. If I could find a way to once again see *all* women as being attractive, and not just Jo, I could get back to normal. The first step was to be in her presence, and *not* fuck her.

I had no idea if I possessed the ability to spend time with a woman if we *weren't* engaged in a sexual act, but I intended to find out. Seated at a quaint little Italian joint across from Jo, I asked the first question that came to mind.

"Of all things, what made you choose an erotic book store?"

Her eyes thinned a little, and her gaze fell to the table. After some thought, she looked up. She brushed her hair behind her ear. "A love of reading, I guess."

"Have you always loved reading?"

"I have. I started before I was four, from what my mom says."

"You were a natural." I admired her hair, which was down and curly, and then met her gaze. "Why an erotic book store? Why not a run of the mill, one store covers all type affair?"

She chuckled. "I get asked that, a lot. Well, my senior year in college, the Indie book world was just starting to gain momentum. It had been around for a few years, but it wasn't perceived as producing worthwhile literature. I read a few Indie published books and liked them. I always known I wanted to do something with books but didn't know what. Maybe be a freelance editor, or work for a firm as a literary agent, or something. When I realized the books written by the Independent authors were as good, or oftentimes, better than the books that were published by the big publishing houses, I decided to do what I could to assist those authors in getting their names out there."

"I want to ask something, but don't think I'm a complete idiot, okay?'

She smiled. "Okay."

"What, exactly, is an independently published book? What's the difference?"

Her eyes lit up. "Good question." She rubbed her palms together and leaned forward. "Traditionally published books go through *this* process: The author writes the book, or a portion of the book, and pitches his or her book to an agent, usually through an email. An agent is the only way to get the book in front of a publisher. Without an agent representing them, an author has no hope of a publisher ever seeing their work. So, the author submits his or her query to hundreds of agents. Maybe one in ten thousand, if that, turn into a published book. Over the years, there's been all these books, authors, and ideas that have just evaporated because an agent either didn't take time to read the query or didn't like the book. Amazon came along and gave authors a platform to publish their books independently. It allowed the author to upload their book, develop a cover, and publish it into an ebook that could be read on Kindle, which was Amazon's e-reader. Amazon took thirty percent of the revenue, and the author got seventy percent. The authors who had a room full of unsellable manuscripts were now able to publish them and see if anyone liked them. Some of the authors learned that their ability to write was as good as anyone out there."

Her level of excitement showed just how much she enjoyed doing what she did. "I had no idea how that worked," I admitted.

"Hell, it sounds like the process was pretty shitty before Amazon came along."

"It was."

"So, I could, theoretically, write a book, and publish it?"

"Sure."

"Has anyone really succeeded?"

"Have you seen the movie, *The Martian?*"

"Yeah. Matt Damon? Gets stuck on Mars?"

"That's the one."

"Yeah. It was great, why?"

"Independently published book. The author's name is Andy Weir. You've heard of *Fifty Shades of Grey*, right?"

"Yeah, who hasn't?"

"Independently published," she said. "E.L. James."

"Damn. Okay. Well, that's awesome that you've devoted your bookstore to those types of books."

She beamed with pride. "Thank you. Do you like to read?"

"I will if I have to. Honestly, I think my escape is my car. I work on it even if it doesn't have anything wrong with it."

"There could be worse hobbies."

"I suppose."

"Did you do well in school?"

I picked up my fork. "I did okay."

"Did you play any sports?"

It was a question I hated to answer, because it often opened a floodgate of memories I hated to recall or admit. I opted to answer truthfully, but without giving her reason to press the issue any further.

"A little football," I responded.

"Anything else?"

"No, just football."

"Were you good at it?"

I wasn't willing to travel down that particular path of memory lane with her, or anyone for that matter. Football was off-limits with me and had been for eighteen years.

I cut the corner off my lasagna and raised it to my mouth. "Not bad."

"Not good enough to make it a career?" she asked. "Or to be a coach, or something?"

I poked the food into my mouth, and then shrugged. "Hurt my ankle."

I chewed my food, realizing I'd opened the gate. I lowered my left hand beneath the surface of the table and crossed my fingers in hope that she'd change the subject.

"How'd you hurt it?"

There I was. Between a rock and a hard place. I realized I'd placed myself there and wondered if my subconscious mind wanted to talk to someone about it. Consciously, I had no desire to reveal that part of my life to her, or to anyone for that matter.

I tried to swallow but struggled to do so. After taking several drinks of water, I realized I was sweating profusely.

"Are you okay?" she asked.

I wiped my brow with my forearm.

I was far from okay. I pressed my fork through the edge of my lasagna and paused. After a moment, I began to shake.

I set my fork aside and wrung my hands together. I'd lived my adult life telling myself everything happened for a reason. That theory left me wondering if Jo's presence in my life was for more than simply having sex with her.

My subconscious mind decided she was in my life for other reasons. Before I could stop my lips from moving, they were telling her what I'd shared with no one.

"I was," I stammered. "I was in a car wreck."

It was over. I said it. There was no reason for me to elaborate, or to explain the horrible sequence of events that transpired that night.

She would say she was sorry, and I'd shrug it off.

"Oh my gosh," she gasped. "I'm so sorry."

I gazed blankly at my food. "It's okay."

I desperately wanted to change the subject but couldn't seem to get my mind pried away from thoughts of the horrific event that changed my life forever.

"Was anyone else hurt?" she asked.

No one else was "hurt" that night. It was much more complicated than that.

My chest felt heavy. I pressed the heel of my palm against my ribs. Much to my disappointment, the pain sharpened, as if someone had poked an ice pick into my heart. Reserving hope that telling her would provide relief, I did just that.

I didn't need to tell her everything. Just enough to ease my pain.

"My father," I muttered. "He was killed."

Surprisingly, the words came past my lips with ease. As I extracted them from the compartment where they'd been hidden, however, they cut through my soul like razors.

She stood, walked around the edge of the booth, and sat down beside me. After draping her arm over my shoulder, she nestled at my side. Overcome with sorrow, I laid my head against her chest. Memories of my childhood, and of my mother, came to mind. As a young boy, resting my head against her chest brought comfort.

I mentally hummed the words to Third Eye Blind's *How's It Going To Be*. Halfway through the song, I cleared my throat.

"The car I drive now...it was...it was my father's first new car. We picked it out together. It was only a few months old when he died."

"You remind me a lot of my dad," she said with a smile. "Your father would be proud of what you've done with it. I'm sure of it."

I hoped she was right. I desperately yearned for his approval and felt keeping his car in tip-top condition would pay homage to what was once his pride and joy.

I drew a long breath. "I hope so."

"Your mother? She wasn't in the car?"

I should have expected Jo would ask, but the question hit me like a sucker punch, nevertheless.

I lifted my head from her chest and gazed blankly at the adjoining booth, which was empty. "When I was in sixth grade, my father found out my mother was having an affair. He confronted her about it and gave her a chance to work on repairing their marriage. Instead, she left. They got a divorce a few months later. She moved away with someone completely different as soon as the divorce paperwork was signed. I haven't seen her since."

"Tyson, I'm—" She covered her mouth with her hand. "I'm sorry."

A tear trickled along her cheek. I wiped it with the edge of my finger. "What about your parents?" I asked. "Are they still together?"

She nodded. "They got married the instant they graduated high school and were married for almost twelve years before they had kids. My brother is your age. They've been married forty-seven years."

"That's cool."

"They're great people." She wiped the corner of her eye with the heel of her palm. "I'd like for you to meet them sometime."

Someone staying married for forty-seven years was commendable. Unbelievable, in my eyes. "Forty-seven years, huh?"

"Forty-eight here in five weeks."

"That's admirable," I said. "Quite an accomplishment."

"I go over there every Sunday and eat dinner with them and my brother. He had a car just like yours, by the way. It was a Cobra."

I nodded in acknowledgement. Her brother sounded like my kind of guy. I folded my arms over my chest. "No shit? A Cobra?"

"It was red. Other than that, yours and his are pretty much the same. His didn't have a supercharger, though. At least that's what I remember him saying about it. You two would get along great. He takes care of cars just like you do."

I grinned. "I'm sure we'd have a lot to talk about."

She removed her glasses and brushed her hair behind her ear with the tip of her finger. "You're welcome to come meet him and my parents, anytime. You could come to dinner if you like."

"Does your mom like to cook?"

"She loves it. She's an amazing cook."

The only home-cooked meals I'd eaten since my father passed were tossed together by Shawn's mother. She was single, worked two jobs, and couldn't cook a decent meal to save her ass.

My mind drifted to the dinner table, talking to my father about the modifications he'd one day make to the Cobra. With my mouth salivating, I gazed blankly at my lasagna and recalled my father's go-to Sunday dinner.

"My father was an amazing cook, too. Chicken-fried steak, mashed potatoes with cream gravy, and green beans with sautéed onions and chunks of bacon was my favorite meal."

I stole a quick look at Jo. Despite the sorrowful look that she wore, her brown eyes glistened with innocence. As I admired them, I realized until that moment, I had no idea what color her eyes were.

I hated to bring her the grief that came with my childhood. I hadn't spoken to anyone about losing my father since it happened and speaking to her came easy. I wondered what was different about her. Maybe I needed to speak to someone more than I realized. Maybe I trusted her. Maybe we were just in the right place at the right time. Whatever the reason, I continued to explain the most trying time in my life.

"After he died, I went to live with Shawn," I explained. "His mother didn't have the time to cook. Shawn's dad dipped out before he was born, and she worked at least two jobs the entire time we were in school. Frozen pizzas were her specialty. I miss siting down to eat a meal."

She grinned. "You're welcome to join us, anytime."

One half of me wanted nothing to do with meeting a girl's parents, ever. It was the first step in relationship development, and I didn't do relationships. The other half of me wanted to believe it was possible for a relationship to last a lifetime.

Forty-eight years, if nothing else.

The latter half of me spoke. "I'd kill for a home-cooked meal."

Her eyes gleamed with hope. "Are you busy Sunday?"

"Not yet."

"Well," she said with a smile. "You are now."

19

JO

WHEN I SHUT the front door, my father woke from his nap. After wiping his eyes, he glared at me from across the room. "What on God's little green earth is going on, Jo?"

"I wanted to talk to everyone at the same time."

"This couldn't wait for four more days?" He collapsed the footrest of his recliner and stood. "You know I don't do well with surprises."

"Is that Josephine?" my mother asked from the kitchen.

"In all her glory," my father said in snide tone.

I huffed out a sigh. "Where's Jarod?"

"Ask your mother," he said. "I've been busy tending my weak heart since I heard you were rushing over here to make an announcement."

"It's not that big of a deal," I said. "I just wanted to make everyone aware of something."

"That T.J. fella didn't knock you up, did he?" he whispered.

"Daddy!"

He stretched his arms high over his head and yawned. "Well, it's a question worth asking."

My mother wandered into the living room. "What's the occasion, dear?"

"I had something I wanted to tell everyone," I explained. "When Jarod gets here, I'll tell you."

"Is it about that boy?"

"No. Yes. Kind of," I babbled.

She let out a sigh. "Now, I'm worried."

I gave her a look. "Why?"

She wiped her hands against her apron. "Just tell your father and me, and you can tell Jarod when he gets here. He's never on time, you know that."

"It can wait."

She crumpled the edges of her apron, and then released them. "Give me a hint."

"It's not a big deal, how's that for a hint?"

"If you called an impromptu meeting, it's a big deal," my father complained.

"It's not a big deal," I insisted.

"A big deal to your generation and a big deal to my generation are two completely different things," he said. "Kids nowadays will kill someone who calls 'em a name. Back when I was a kid, all we had to worry about was getting hit in the mouth if we said something offensive. And, let me tell you, every kid in high school had a pickup truck with a gun rack, and those racks were filled with guns. Damned parking lot was like an armory, and nary a one of those guns was ever carried into school. Say what you've got to say, Jo."

"It's not a big deal."

The front door swung open. Jarod looked at my parents and then at me. "What's going on?"

"She won't say," my father responded. "But, it's about that football player."

"Jo called this meeting?" he asked with a laugh. "Should have known."

I glared. "Shut it, Jarod."

Jarod looked at my father. "I was afraid something happened to your heart."

"Something happened with my heart in nineteen and sixty-nine, when I met your mother. It was my junior year, right after History class." He kissed her on the cheek. "That was the day I fell in love."

My mother and father's relationship was something to envy. They'd fallen in love as high schoolers. My mother was like me, reserved and quiet. My father was loud, boisterous, and the quarterback of the football team. According to my mother, he brought out all the good in her.

Over the years, their love never faded. Seeing them interact with each other was rewarding.

"Let's sit down," I said.

"If that'll let us get to the crux of this situation, I'm all for it," my father said.

We each took a seat, with me letting out a long breath as I sat down. I looked at each of them and let out another. "Tyson is coming for dinner on Sunday."

"That's exciting news," my mother said with a smile.

"That's not exciting enough to have me so worried I feel like I'm gonna shit my pants," my father said. "I've been half sick since your mother told me you called. Now, I've got bubble guts for no reason."

"You were asleep when I opened the door," I argued.

"Exhaustion from pacing the floor for the last two hours," he replied.

"Well, he's coming for dinner, and I need to set some ground rules before he gets here."

My father's eyes narrowed. "Like what?"

"No razzing him about his ankle," Jarod quipped. "Right?"

I drew a slow breath, and then glanced at each of them. "There's more to it than that. I've struggled all day with what to tell everyone, and then I decided just to tell you the truth."

"Well, thank God for that," my father declared. "I must have done something right."

"Daddy..."

"I'll listen."

I looked at my mother.

She folded her hands and rested them in her lap. "I'm ready when you are, Josephine."

"His ankle was broken in a car wreck," I explained. "In that same wreck, his father was killed."

My mothers face washed with grief. "Oh heavens," she gasped. "I'm so sorry, Josephine."

I swallowed against my dry throat and continued. "Someone crashed into the driver's side of the car, killing his father on impact. The car he drives today is the same car his father was driving when they were hit. I just want to make sure no one mentions football, his ankle, his parents, the wreck, or asks how or why he rebuilt the car. I want him to be comfortable."

"That's just awful," my mother murmured. "Was his mother hurt?"

I sighed. "She left when he was little. His father raised him. He hasn't seen or heard from his mother in over twenty years."

My father stood and began pacing the floor. "I know a little something about being attached to a car."

I rolled my eyes.

I looked at Jarod. "Nothing about the ankle. Okay?"

"I won't say a word."

"No football questions," I said.

"I won't." He stood. "I always wondered what happened. I heard he was in a car wreck, but I didn't know if that was what broke his ankle. I'm sorry, Jo."

I forced a smile. "Thanks."

"What kind of a mother could leave their kid?" my father bellowed. "Was she wacked-out on dope?"

"I don't know, Daddy."

"I bet she was wacked out on that meth-a-phetamines."

"Meth-AM-phetamines," Jarod said.

"That's what I said. That shit's gonna be the downfall of this nation. People lose their minds on that crap."

My mother reached for my knee and rested her hand there. "I'm sorry, Josephine. I really am. Anything we can do to make him comfortable, you just tell me."

152

"That's another thing," I said, looking toward my father as I spoke. "Can you give up your diet for a day?"

"Suppose I can." He put his hands on his hips. "Why?"

I looked at my mother. "His dad used to cook this: chicken-fried steak, mashed potatoes and gravy, and green beans with bacon and onions. I'd like for you to make that when we come."

"Sounds like my kind of fella," my father said.

"He said he hasn't had a good home-cooked meal in years," I whispered. "After his father died, he moved in with his best friend. I guess this guy's mom didn't cook very well, if at all."

She patted my knee. "I'll cook the best I'm able, Josephine. If he doesn't like it, he's not a Texan."

"He was born and raised here," I said. "He's a Texan."

"I imagine he'll leave full, and happy," she said with a smile. "I'll use my mother's recipes. They're southern through and through. The secret is to let the steaks marinade in the buttermilk overnight."

My father clapped his hands together. "Is this the recipe with the cayenne?"

"It sure is."

"Whoo-eeee. This fried steak will make a puppy pull a freight train," my father bragged. "Fry up some green tomatoes with it."

My mother lowered her chin and gave a playful glare.

"If we're frying dinner," my father said. "We just as well *fry dinner.*"

She grinned. "I might fry a few tomatoes."

"What if he brings up football?" He glanced at me. "What do we do?"

"I guess tread softly. Be sensitive of his loss, now that you know about it."

My mother wagged her index finger at my father. "If you say one word, John, mark my words…"

"I'm not saying a damned thing," my father assured her. "But, if he brings it up, I'm not going to be rude."

"If he brings it up, you better just change the subject to the Texas weather." She looked at Jarod. "And, you, mister come-late-or-not-at-all, can talk about cars."

"Yes, Ma'am," Jarod replied.

My mother dusted off her apron. "I'm going to need to pick up this pig sty."

"It looks, fine, Mother."

She glanced around the room. "I'd be ashamed to have him here with the way it looks."

"I'm nervous," I whispered.

She looked up from her survey of the room. "Why?"

My shoulders slumped. "I just want him to like me."

"Don't be nervous." She put her hand on my cheek. "If you act like yourself, he can't help but like you. The good Lord put him in your life for a reason. If it's not for him to like you, I sure don't know what else it would be for."

Sex was the other viable option, but I didn't mention it. While my stomach churned at the thought of having Tyson over for Sunday dinner, I simply offered my mother a smile. "I hope you're right."

20

TYSON

WELL-MANICURED LAWNS, neatly trimmed shrubbery, and driveways occupied with the occasional children's play toys lined the streets.

I pulled into the steep drive and admired the two-story cottage. Each of the mullion-fitted windows were free of any draperies, allowing a full view into the home. Situated on an oversized corner lot and constructed of weathered white-washed brick and white lap siding, the home could have easily been placed along the coast of Chesapeake Bay.

An inviting brick sidewalk led from the edge of the driveway to the uncluttered front porch. I came to a stop alongside the walk and took one last look at the home before getting out of the car.

I meandered to the porch and brushed the wrinkles from my shirt. Before I had a chance to knock, the door opened.

Her hair was up, in a tightly-braided bun. Wearing a coral-colored sleeveless summer dress and flats, she looked remarkable. Breathtakingly beautiful was more like it.

She gave me the once-over and then smiled. "You look nice."

I was lost in admiration. Her dress came to mid-thigh. Long enough to cover her assets, and short enough to garner my interest.

I gave her a nod of approval. "So do you. That dress is…wow. It's perfect."

"Thank you." She pulled the door closed behind her. "I like that shirt. It looks nice on you."

I'd worn my favorite pearl snap shirt, jeans, and a pair of well-worn – but polished to perfection – black leather boots. I reserved the shirt for special occasions, wearing it infrequently, at best.

Beaming with pride that she'd mentioned it, I turned toward the driveway. "Thanks. It's a favorite. I rarely wear it."

"Why? It looks good on you."

"I hate the thought of something happening to it," I explained. "It's got sentimental value."

"Well, it looks nice."

I walked to the passenger door and opened it for her. "Thank you."

She turned her backside toward the open door and paused. I noticed she wasn't wearing her glasses. Her eyes twinkled with content. I raised my finger to her chin, lifted it slightly, and kissed her.

Before I met Jo, kissing was something I never really cared for. With her, I found it satisfying, but wasn't quite sure why.

When our lips parted, she looked at me with wonder in her eyes. Her lips parted.

I kissed her again, before she had the chance to speak.

With reluctance, I leaned away. The surprised look on her face vanished, only to be replaced with one of content.

"Sorry." I shrugged and gave her one last kiss, a quick one. "I couldn't help myself."

"That was uhhm." She wiped her lips on the back of her hand. "That was nice."

With our eyes locked, she smiled and lowered herself into her seat. I sauntered around the car, wishing we were going somewhere else. I was anxious about having dinner with her parents, and it was worsening the closer we came to our dinner date.

I sat down in my seat and buckled my seatbelt. "This was my

father's shirt. He hated spending money on clothes for himself, but never hesitated to buy me things. I bought this for him as a Christmas gift. He wore it all the time."

"If he looked as nice wearing it as you do, I bet he wore it with pride."

"He did. He loved this shirt."

"What about your boots?" she asked.

I glanced at my feet and chuckled, surprised she'd asked. "They were his, too."

"He had good taste. Was he built like you?"

I started the car. "He was. The older I get, the more I realize I'm going to look just like him in a few years. He was thirty-nine when he died. If you saw a picture of him, you'd think we were twins."

"Do you have one?"

I searched through my phone, retrieving one of the many pictures I'd converted from photographs to .jpeg files.

"Look at this one." I handed her the phone. "It's when we got the car."

The photo was of my father and I standing beside his car, right after we bought it. She studied it for some time, alternating glances between the phone and me.

The corners of her mouth curled up as she handed me the phone. "You were a really cute kid. He was a very handsome man. He looks just like you. Or, you look just like him. Whichever way you want to look at it."

I looked at the picture, and then at my reflection in the rearview mirror. I hadn't made the comparison in some time, but she was right. I looked just like my father.

I set the phone aside and backed out of the driveway. "It's crazy how much we look alike."

"You're his doppelganger."

Her saying the word caused me to recall her likeness to Miss Garber. Although those similarities were what originally drew me to her, I now saw them as nothing but coincidental.

Jo was attractive in many ways other than her looks. She was kind, caring, and had a softness that surrounded her. I found an odd sense of comfort being in her presence, especially after we spoke of losing my father. The accident had been an off-limits subject since my father's funeral, even to Shawn. My admitting to Jo about losing my father opened a door of recovery for me that had been shut since the day he was buried.

In short, I'd become grateful to have someone like Jo in my life.

"Doppelganger." I chuckled. "I told you. We look like twins."

"Do you have any of his mannerisms or characteristics?"

I smiled a prideful grin. "He picked up things with his toes. Socks, little toys I'd leave on the floor, that kind of stuff. I do the same thing. He had a little Nerf ball he'd throw at the TV, when someone did or said something he thought was dumb. I do that, too. I find myself saying, 'What in the everlasting fuck' more often than I probably should. That was his go-to phrase. I shave like him too. Sideburns first, every time."

She seemed to savor what little I'd revealed, choosing to simply smile slightly in lieu of speaking.

I fixed my eyes on the road ahead and began reciting my father's words of wisdom. "An unmade bed is the sign of a cluttered mind. When you're wrong, admit it loud enough that everyone can hear. When you're right, brag silently. Nobody likes a tattletale. Be conscious of the weight of your tongue, use it sparingly and wisely. Don't ask questions if the answer is obvious, it'll only make you appear foolish. Never leave a tip that's less than five dollars; if you can't afford to, you should be eating at home. Routines are recipe for good health; make them and stick to them. Treat your car the same way you treat your woman; with respect and kindness."

I barely choked out the words of the last phrase. He'd reminded me of it on many occasions, as we were cleaning his cars or changing the oil.

I was a walking contradiction. It hit me like a speeding freight train. I lived my life in my father's footsteps, making every effort to be the man he was. To make him proud.

Yet.

I'd spent my adult life treating women like sexual objects, not people. I gave the cashier at HEB more respect than the women I'd allowed into my life. I swallowed a mouthful of shame, and then looked at Jo.

"What...what do we have?" I asked. "What is *this*?"

Her face contorted. "I don't understand what you're asking."

"I'm going to your parent's house to have Sunday dinner. We obviously like each other enough to orchestrate something like this. Are we *dating*?"

Her face lit up like a Christmas tree. "Well, we haven't discussed it. Do you want to? Be exclusive, or whatever?"

My father's policy was to love one woman and love her with all your heart. My mother's inability to adhere to the same rule was what caused the collapse of their relationship, and of my subsequent life. If I was going to mirror one of my parents, my mother certainly wouldn't be that person.

Yet.

I had become the woman I'd spent a lifetime resenting.

"I've got no plans to be with any other woman," I assured her. "If that's what you're asking."

"I'm satisfied completely..." She wagged the tip of her index finger between us. "With you. With *this*."

"Okay," I said as I took the off-ramp. "Let's be official. If that's okay with you."

"As long as." Her smile faded. A look of apprehension replaced it. "Be truthful with me, please. Always?"

My future would embrace a truthfulness and transparency matched by no man.

I nodded. "I will."

She nodded eagerly. "As long as we can be truthful with one another, I think I'm okay with that." She smiled and then covered her mouth with her hand. "I know I am."

I was okay with it, too.

Very much so, to be honest.

I rolled to a stop at the traffic light and tilted my head back.

After momentarily closing my eyes, I spoke silently to the man I'd undoubtedly disappointed.

Sorry, Pop.

Without you here to remind me, some things are easy to forget.

I'm back on track, though.

And, my bed's made, just the way you taught me.

21

JO

I REACHED for the door knob and paused. I was so excited about my new relationship status that I feared I'd make a complete fool of myself in front of my parents. Batting my eyes at Tyson, hanging on his every word, and saying things that made no sense whatsoever while my parents looked at me like I was a lunatic was not the way I wanted to spend the evening. Knowing me, it was more than likely the way it would go.

After inhaling an inaudible breath of courage, I looked at Tyson. "Ready?"

"Almost." He kissed me gently, leaned away, and brushed the wrinkles from his shirt. "I am now."

I pushed against the handle and peered inside. "We're here."

My father stood just inside the door. He was obviously either prepared to open it, or he was spying on us.

Spying was my guess.

"John Watson." He extended his hand toward Tyson. "Pleasure to meet you."

"Tyson. I'm uhhm, Tyson." Tyson babbled. "Tyson Neese." He shook my father's hand. "Are you *the* John Watson, by chance?"

"Depends." My father chuckled. "You're not the tax collector, are you?"

"John Watson who threw for fourteen thousand and thirty-three career yards?" Tyson asked. "John Watson who was named Scholastic Coach's All-American in 1970? John Watson who gave up a career of football to work on his father's farm? John Watson who inspired me to…"

Tyson wiped his brow, and then looked my father over as if sizing him up. "You are, aren't you? You're John Watson."

Apparently, Tyson knew more of my father's football accolades than I did. Filled with a smug pride, my heart swelled at the thought of Tyson knowing my father.

Knowing *and* admiring him.

My father's eyes darted to my mother, and then to me. Fearing admitting who he was would lead to contradicting my request of *no football talk*, his eyes locked on mine and paused.

I nodded in approval, hoping the discussion that followed didn't lead to something that upset Tyson.

I'd never seen my father blush, but his face was as red as a ruby. He gave Tyson a fake look of confusion and raised his index finger to his lip as if pondering his response. "Fourteen thousand and thirty-three yards rings a distant bell. If memory serves me correctly, I took my parent's farm over when I graduated high school. Hell, you might be standin' on that sacred ground as we speak." He put his hands on his hips and smiled. "I suppose I'm *the* John Watson, yes."

"Pleasure to meet you, Sir," Tyson said. "You were an inspiration to my father, and to me."

My father patted him on the shoulder. "Pleasure to meet you, Tyson. Did you bring your appetite?"

Tyson nodded. "Yes, Sir."

"Good," my father said, winking at me as he spoke. "Because we're having my favorite meal."

"I can't wait." Tyson gleamed. "I still can't believe it's you. You inspired my father to be a quarterback, and he inspired me with tales of your high school days. My father loved the sport, but never made it past second string. I made a pretty good showing in passing yards when I was in school. Game's much different today than it was when you played, though. Back then, it was a rushing man's game. Today, it's all about winning."

"Couldn't agree with you more." My father looked at my mother. "How close are we to eatin'?"

"It's ready now."

My father patted Tyson's shoulder. "We've only got two dinner table rules. No feedin' the dog table scraps, and no discussing sports."

Feeding the dog was a rule I was aware of. Abolishing discussions of sports was something I wished would have happened long before Tyson came for dinner. I gave my father a lingering look. "I keep forgetting that second rule. You know how I love talking about football."

With his arm draped over Tyson's shoulder, he turned toward my mother. "This is my wife, Jackie."

Tyson extended his hand. "Pleasure to meet you, Ma'am."

"The pleasure's all mine, Tyson."

"So, it's ready?" my father asked.

"It's ready if we're ready," my mother responded.

My brother cleared his throat. "I'm Jarod, the often-forgotten brother."

My father turned around, bringing Tyson with him. "This is my son, Jarod. Hard to remember if he's here or not. He's never on time."

Tyson shook his hand. "Get yourself another Cobra, and you'll never be late."

Jarod grinned. "Isn't that the truth."

"I'll show you mine when we're done eating."

"Jo says it's got a supercharger."

"She's right," Tyson said. "I put a Kenne Bell two-point-eight Mammoth on it. Liquid cooled."

Jarod's eyes widened. "How many ponies is she pushing?"

"A thousand fifty on e85," Tyson said, beaming with pride as he spoke. "About nine hundred on 93 octane."

"Jesus jumped up Christ," my father coughed. "That thing's got a thousand horsepower?"

Tyson nodded. "It sure does."

While the men walked to the dining room together, I stepped to my mother's side. "Tyson and I are officially exclusive," I whispered.

"What does that mean?" my mother whispered in return. "Official?"

I searched my mind for a term she'd understand. She was two generations behind me, at least. Only recently did she give way to the cell phone *craze.*

"We're going steady," I said.

She gasped a breath. "I'm so happy for you. He seems like such a nice man."

"He's slow to come out of his shell, but he is really nice."

She let the men make it all the way to the dining room, and then stepped in front of me. "You'd be slow to come out of your shell, too, if you'd been through what he's been through. You give him all the room he needs, Josephine. Men need time and space to figure things out. Don't crowd him. Now, or ever, for that matter. All of what's good comes from waiting."

I was giddy with excitement about Tyson and I being official. If my mother recommended it, I was all for doing it. If anyone knew how to make a marriage last, it was her.

I nodded. "Yes, Ma'am."

She dusted her hands against her dress and gestured toward the kitchen. "You can help me with the food, Josephine. Let's make Tyson feel like this home is just as much his as it is ours, shall we?"

I was so happy I could have screamed, but I smiled instead. "Tell me if I'm doing anything dumb, will you?"

"Just smile and nod at everything he says," my mother offered. "I've been doing it with your father for almost fifty years, and it works wonders."

If that's all I had to do to keep Tyson happy, I'd look like one of those bobblehead dolls with a painted-on grin.

22

TYSON

DURING THE TIME I'd lived with Shawn, I felt like an outsider, a nuisance, and a burden. Although I was sure the feelings I harbored were at least partially due to my delicate state of mind, I experienced them as if they were accurate and true.

At the end of my senior year, I legally inherited my father's home and his belongings. I then began spending time in my childhood home, but soon found out I was uncomfortable living there. For the following year I continued to stay with Shawn, feeling awkward in my home without my father being present.

Strangely, I felt welcomed in Jo's parents' home the instant I walked inside.

I glanced around the dinner table, making note of each person in attendance. I pierced the last morsel of steak, dragged it through the remaining potatoes, and lifted the fork to my mouth.

"Ma'am, the food was second to none," I said.

"Thank you," Jackie said. "I'm glad you enjoyed it."

She was roughly sixty-five years old by my calculations, but she looked – and acted – many years younger. She was tall and thin, like Jo, and had shoulder-length snow-colored hair that she wore straight. I imagined the frosty-white strands were darker in her youth, like her daughter's.

Her floral pattern dress with embroidered pockets sewn onto the front indicated an age that her appearance otherwise kept hidden.

"Best damned steak in Texas," John said. "No one fries a steak that can compare."

"My father cooked a darned good chicken-fried steak. His wasn't better than this. It was just different. I'd call them equal."

He mopped his plate clean with half a dinner roll and raised it to his mouth. "Sounds like he was a fine cook."

I chewed the last bite, and then responded. "He was."

"Well, Jackie can rustle up a thing or two that are worth eatin'." He poked the gravy-soaked roll into his mouth. "Make Sundays a regular engagement, and you can judge for yourself."

"Don't talk with your mouth full, dear," Jackie said.

He swallowed. "It wasn't full."

"It was close enough."

He shifted his eyes from her to me. "Could have fit two of those rolls in there, but she'd have complained that I was eatin' too much bread. She's got me on a diet."

"*I* don't have you on anything," she snapped. "*You*, my dear, said you wanted to lose ten pounds."

John gestured toward the kitchen with his eyes. "Might be lookin' to lose more than that after we eat that peach cobbler she baked."

"You made cobbler?" Jo asked, her tone filled with excitement.

"I sure did. I'll whip some fresh cream to serve with it." Jackie looked at me with apologetic eyes. "We'll have to use store-bought ice cream. The handle's been broken on the ice cream maker for years. John refuses to replace it."

I wiped my hands on my napkin. "I like to think I can fix anything. I can have a look at it if you'd like. Homemade ice cream sounds pretty good."

"That thing's is a hundred years old. It belonged to John's parents," Jackie explained. "We need to get a new one."

"We're not getting a new one," John bellowed. "I'll take that

SOB to the city and get someone to fix it."

I wondered, in considering the tale of John's past, if he had the same sentimental attachments to the ice cream maker that I had to my car.

John's story was unique. In his day, he was as good of a quarterback as had ever existed. At the end of his senior year, his father fell ill, suffering from occasional high spikes in his blood pressure.

Although every college in the nation wanted him to play football for them, he opted to forfeit his college education – and a possible career in professional sports – to tend to his family's farm while his father recovered. He vowed to return to the sport as soon as his father was in better health.

His father died soon thereafter. John never returned to the sport. According to Texas football folklore, his mother lived for another decade, dying on the tenth anniversary of her late husband's death.

If one chose to believe Texas legend, she died of a broken heart.

I looked at Jarod, and then at John. "If you'd like, we can look at it. Maybe see if we can fix it."

John smiled and gave a sharp nod. "Alrighty."

I pushed myself away from the table and glanced at Jackie. "Ma'am, if you'll excuse me--"

"Absolutely," she said. "But, don't waste any time on that old thing. You'll want the cobbler while it's still warm."

"Yes, Ma'am."

I offered Jo a smile and followed John and Jarod to the overstuffed – but very tidy – garage.

Jarod was a typical Texan. Wearing boots, tight-fitting Wrangler jeans, and a button-down long-sleeved shirt, his belt was fitted with a buckle large enough to catch the attention of passersby at one hundred yards.

He was lean and lanky with closely-cropped hair that he wore just long enough to comb. Like his mother, he appeared much younger than his thirty-five years.

John may have been striving to lose ten pounds, but he didn't look overweight in appearance. Still a barrel-chested man with massive biceps, he lacked the beer belly that most men his age had obtained much earlier in life.

He wore his gray hair in a crew cut. The photos I'd seen of him in his athletic years bore such a resemblance that recognizing him came easily.

He removed a dusty the tarp from the ice cream maker and set it aside. "Here she is. Made many a bowl of ice cream with this thing. Hell, my parents made me ice cream with this SOB when I was a kid." He looked at Jarod. "Remember your thirteenth birthday? You demanded we make blueberry ice cream. Worst tastin' shit I've ever eaten. Looked like hell, too."

Jarod laughed. "It did taste pretty bad."

"Don't think there's much you'll be able to do to fix it," John said, pushing the wooden bucketed contraption aside. "Worm gears are messed up."

I bent down and looked the churn over. After just a moment of trying to get it to work, I realized the threads on the handle's shaft were worn to a point that repair – short of re-threading the shaft – would be impossible.

"It's not the gears. The shaft's worn smooth," I said. "I can probably re-thread it if it's not stainless steel."

John laughed. "It might look shiny, but my guess is that shaft's carbon steel. They didn't use much stainless back then. Hell, that thing's a hundred years old. That thing's so worn out that someone's gotta sit on top of it to hold down the churn while someone else cranks their arm off. Tastes like heaven when you're done, though."

I stood and turned toward the open garage door. "If it's cold-rolled carbon steel, we might be in luck."

"Be in luck if someone had a tap and die set," John mumbled.

"I've got one in my car."

"Who in the hell keeps a tap and die set in their car?"

"A thousand horsepower tends to break bolts off from time to time." I glanced over my shoulder. "I keep one for such occasions."

"Well, hot damn!" He rubbed his palms together briskly. "Run out there and get that SOB."

After retrieving the tap and die set, I re-threaded the entire shaft one size smaller. After removing the die, I wiped the newly cut threads clean. "All we need is a nut and washer, and we should be good for another hundred years."

"I'll believe it when I see it," John said flippantly. "What size nut? I've got a bolt bin full of options."

"Three-quarter inch. Sixteen threads per inch," I said.

He turned toward the far wall and returned in an instant. He extended his arm in my direction, holding his clenched fist even with my chest. It was the same way my father used to give me special coins, and small trinkets.

I placed my open hand beneath his. He dropped a nut and washer into my palm.

"See if that works," he said.

A few seconds later, the nut was in place and tightened. I stood, placed my hands on my hips, and admired my work. "Give it a try."

John bent down and cranked the handle. As the paddles began to spin, he clapped his hands together. "Hot damn. We're back in business." He alternated glances between Jarod and me. "Jackie's gonna have a conniption fit."

"Why's that?" I asked.

"Hell, we used this contraption to make ice cream after we got married, right on this very farm." He picked up the churn and admired it. After a moment, his eyes went into a glassy-eyed stare. "That was a mighty long time ago," he murmured.

I gestured toward the door. "Let's take it inside and see what she has to say."

Clutching the wooden bucket, John looked up and met my gaze. His eyes were welled with tears. He swallowed heavily, and then cleared his throat. "Thank you, Son."

A lump rose in my throat, all but blocking my ability to breathe. I hadn't heard those words in eighteen years. After a lengthy struggle, I stepped to John's side and patted him on the back. "Let's see if we can get some made before the cobbler gets cold."

Still holding the bucket in his arms, he looked at me and grinned. "You crank, I'll sit."

I smiled in return. "Wouldn't have it any other way."

23

JO

WEARING nothing more than my panties and bra, I was on my back in bed, staring blankly at the ceiling. Tyson was lying beside me, in his boxer shorts. We weren't engaged in sex, nor had we been. At any other time in my life, I would have viewed the chaste situation as a complete and utter failure.

On that night, however, I saw the celibate moments we shared as progress.

"You have no idea of how much that meant to my father to get the ice cream maker going again," I said.

"I imagine it's the same feeling I had when I got the Cobra running. When I drive it, I feel close to my father. Your dad will probably have the same feelings when he makes ice cream."

I tilted my head to the side. "You're probably right. His mom and dad made him ice cream with that rickety thing. They were pretty frugal. My father is, too. It's probably at least part of the reason he hasn't replaced it."

I never had a chance to meet my grandparents, but I'd heard plenty of stories about them and their meager way of living life. They farmed the land they owned, making use of everything the land produced.

The farmland had three oil wells on it. My great-grandparents had farmed the land for their entire lives, never relying on the earnings from the oil as a means of income. They believed a hard day's work was a necessary element of living a fruitful and rich life.

My grandparents believed the same thing.

My father had no knowledge of the amount of money produced by the oil wells. It was his belief that the farm provided the income required to keep his parent's heads above water.

He'd no more than graduated high school when his father was hospitalized due to problems with his heart. Within weeks, my grandfather was paralyzed and blinded by the spikes in his blood pressure. A short period of time later, he died.

My father worked on the farm for over a decade, keeping the bills paid, the family fed, and the cupboards filled with canned vegetables that the farm produced.

Upon my grandmother's passing, my father learned of the wealth the family earned from the oil wells. He never mentioned any resentments for having forfeited his career in football, or his college education. Instead, he claimed a feeling of pride for having done what needed done in a time of need.

"I think everyone from your parent's generation is frugal." He rolled onto his side. Our eyes met. He held my gaze. One corner of his mouth curled up slightly. "You went on and on about my father looking like me, but you didn't bother telling me you and your mother look so much alike. She's beautiful."

I blushed at the remark. "Thank you."

He kissed me.

I liked it when he kissed me.

It wasn't like that was in the books. Actually, nothing was like what was in the books. The sex we had was earth-shattering. A chapter had yet to be written that could accurately describe the feelings I felt when Tyson was inside me.

Every time he kissed me lightly my mind went blank. My body tingled. My heart raced.

When the kisses were more aggressive, my legs shook. My pussy tingled. I became soaked.

The reality of Tyson was so much more pleasing than the fictional equivalent.

"I like it when you kiss me," I said.

"I like kissing you," he replied. "It's weird. I've always hated kissing."

I felt blessed. And curious. I was always curious. It was hard not to be. "What makes it different with me?"

"I'm not sure."

"Well, whatever it is, I'm glad you're feeling it."

His eyes smiled. "Me, too."

He remained motionless for quite some time. During that time of silence, his eyes scanned every visible inch of me, up and down, up and down. As I prepared to ask him what it was that he was looking for, he kissed me again.

While embraced in that kiss, he slipped his hands beneath the cups of my bra and began kneading my breasts to a rhythm I matched with my gyrating hips. In a moment, he was on top of me, grinding himself against my leg.

The kiss became more aggressive. Juices flowed. My face flushed. His erection grew against my thigh, making clear that he was as pleased with the kiss as I was.

I'd never been in such an intimate embrace. Having his firm cock between us while we kissed drove me wild with desire.

Our mouths parted.

I couldn't wait another second to feel him inside me. Pressed between him and the bed, I slid along the length of his body until my wet panties were all that prevented him from entering me. I kissed his chest while I writhed against his cock, further fueling my passion with each thrust of my hips.

I wanted him so badly I ached.

He forced his arm between us and clenched his stiff dick in his fist. After pulling my panties to the side, he guided himself into my throbbing mound.

His girth entered me, inch by inch, until I was filled with his stiffness. Our bodies merged. His naked chest melted into mine.

With our desire-filled eyes locked, we thrust our hips against one another in perfect timing. With each rhythmic stroke, the freshly-shaved flesh above his cock bumped against my clit, sending an electric jolt throughout my entire body.

Our bodies were making music. Somehow, we both knew the tempo, and were dancing to it as if we'd done so many times in the past. It was passion, defined. He was giving me all he had to offer, and I was eagerly accepting it into my warmth.

He pushed himself into me fully and paused. A hint of his cologne-laced sweat found its way into my nose. At that same instant, he pressed his mouth to mine.

Our tongues touched. My body tensed.

My pussy clenched his cock like a vise. The tips of his fingers dug into the flesh of my back, pulling me hard against him.

Without sharing so much as a word during our love-making session, we reached climactic bliss together, as one.

Tremors shot through me with each wave of pleasure the orgasm brought with it. His breathing became choppy. At the height of my breathless climax, he erupted deep inside of me.

I was so filled with euphoria, I felt like crying. When the sensation eventually subsided, he collapsed against me. I listened to his breathing until it became less labored and rhythmic. I wondered if he listened to mine.

I wrapped my arms around him. Hoping to make the moment we were sharing last forever, I held him against me. We fell asleep in each other's arms, each satisfied so deeply that speaking of our accomplishment bore no measurable value.

I opened my eyes, not knowing how much time had passed. He lifted his head. The corners of his mouth curled up slightly.

He kissed me softly.

When our mouths parted, I gave fair warning. "Be careful," I breathed. "It was a kiss that started this."

He looked me over with admiring eyes as he traced the tip of his finger along the edge of my clavicle. "I think we should start and stop with a kiss. Every time."

Upon hearing those words, my heart melted.

I agreed wholeheartedly. Starting and stopping with a kiss was perfect. Conveying my thoughts verbally, however, was going to be impossible. A big wad of emotion was trapped in my throat and it wasn't leaving anytime soon.

Trying to speak through it would undoubtedly bring tears, and I wasn't interested in being *that* girl.

Incapable of replying, but feeling the need to do or say *something*, I lifted my head and pressed my lips against his.

I once read that a kiss can say what words cannot.

I prayed it was one of those times.

24

TYSON

SHAWN LEANED over the jewelry case and peered inside. After surveying the contents, he shook his head lightly and coughed out a laugh. "I'm confused."

"About what?"

"About what's going on."

"With what?"

He waved his hand over the top of the display. "About *this*. Are you trying to piss her off, or make her happy?"

"That's a stupid question."

"If you're trying to make her happy, buying her a bracelet isn't a step in the right direction. In fact, it's a nail in your relationship's coffin. A big one."

It had been a month since Jo and I started seeing one another. I needed to do something to mark the achievement. Something noteworthy.

I shot him a glare. "Since when are you versed on relationships?"

"Since forever."

I couldn't help but laugh. "You've never been in one."

He folded his arms over his chest and huffed a breath of

discontent. "Whenever I get in one, you can bet I won't buy the girl a fucking *bracelet*. That's a relationship no-no. At least not at the beginning. Maybe for a birthday or some shit, after you've been together five or six years. Not *now*."

I crossed my arms and looked him over. "Where do you come up with this shit?"

"I watch a lot of reality TV."

"Reality TV?"

"Yeah. You know. The real-life shit."

I shook my head in disbelief. "According to reality TV, bracelets are a no-no?"

"Haven't you seen *Southern Charm*?"

"Afraid not."

"T-Rav bought Ashley a bracelet for her first gift. You should have seen the look on her face. Dude picked out a nice fuckin' bracelet from a swanky custom shop. When she opened the box and looked inside, you would have thought he handed her steamin' cat turd."

"Who the fuck's T-Rav?"

"He's a reality TV star, and he was almost a senator. He would have been elected, but he got busted for trafficking dope."

A drug dealing almost senator with his own television show. It was part of what was wrong with the nation. I chuckled. "And you think I should take relationship advice from this guy?"

"No. His relationship advice sucks. You should take *my* relationship advice."

I looked down my nose at him. "Based on your vast relationship experience?"

"No, motherfucker," he huffed. "Based on the look on Ashley's face when T-Rav handed her the goddamn bracelet."

"You're out of your mind."

"Is there something I can help you with?" a female voice asked from behind me.

I turned around. A buxom blond in her early thirties stood on the other side of the display case. Her skin was the burnt orange color reserved for those who opted to spend their idle time in a tanning booth. Dressed in a black dress with a plunging neckline, her over-baked boobs bulged from the cups of the bra that pushed them skyward.

"Sorry," I said. "We were just arguing about a TV show."

"As a matter of fact——" Shawn leaned against the display case. "I have a question."

She grinned her pre-programmed department store sales clerk smile. "I'll do my best to answer it."

Shawn looked her up and down and then held her curious gaze. "I'm asking for a friend."

Her smile turned genuine. "Okay."

"You meet this guy, and instantly you feel like your personalities are magnetic. On the first date, you say 'what the hell', and you decide to, well, give him a blowjob…"

He leaned closer. Naturally, she did the same. With their noses mere inches apart, he continued.

"So, he undoes his belt, reaches into his boxers, and pulls out his penis. It's huge. As big around as your wrist and ten inches long," he whispered. "On that night, all you do is suck him off. On the next night, he bends you over the arm of his couch. When you're together, all you want to do is screw. You screw in the bookstore, in her car, in his FedEx delivery truck, in the shower. Each time you fuck, you have so many orgasms you damned near go blind. Then, things get romantic between the two of you. You decide it's much more than sex. It's nothing short of heaven. Hell, you're happier than Daryl Dixon at a crossbow convention."

Shawn leaned away from the display case.

She remained bent over, revealing enough overly-tanned cleavage to wage a war.

"So, one night, you two go out for dinner," Shawn continued. "After they serve the wine, but before they bring your first course, he reaches under the table and pulls out a box. He hands it to you. What do you hope it is?"

Enthralled by his story of the big-dicked FedEx man, she made a 'V' with her hands and placed her chin against her open palms. "Is it a small box?"

Shawn glanced at her tits. "You pick the size."

Leaving her boobs on display for Shawn to ogle, she looked away for a moment while contemplating her answer. When her focus returned, she stood. "Is it the first gift he's given me? Or is this one of many?"

"The first."

She grinned. "Flowers. I want it to be a big box of flowers."

Shawn gave me a dismissive wave of his hand. "Told you."

She shifted her eyes from him to me, and then looked me over. "You're the friend?"

"Excuse me?"

She twirled her hair with her index finger while continuing her inspection of me. "You're the FedEx driver?"

At any other point in time in my life, I would have seen her expressed interest as an invitation. At that moment, I saw it as irritating and inappropriate.

"Yeah, I'm the guy that's *in a relationship*." I pointed at Shawn. "He's single."

She gave me the once-over before looking at Shawn. "So, what's with the question?"

"He wanted to buy her a bracelet," Shawn said. "I told him it'd send the wrong message."

"Bracelets are nice," she said, twisting her mouth to the side as she spoke. "But, she'd probably like flowers more. A bracelet is a strange gift. It's what you give someone you *haven't* had sex with. It's a pre-sex gift. One that leads to sex. You know, it lets her know you're interested. After sex, bracelets are weird."

I couldn't believe my ears. I may have been wrong but being chastised by Shawn and the tanning booth queen wasn't easy to accept.

I gave her a look. "Bracelets are weird?"

She nodded like a child who'd been offered a second serving of ice cream. "Uh huh."

"Let me get this straight," Shawn said. "Bracelets are a pre-sex gift? A gesture to let the woman know you *want* to fuck?"

She looked at him and scrunched her nose. "Kind of. Yeah."

Shawn pointed to the collection of bracelets that were on display in front of her. "Pick one out."

Her face washed with confusion. "Huh?"

"I'm going to buy you a bracelet."

Her eyes thinned. "Why?"

Shawn raked his eyes up and down her five-two frame and waited.

Enough time passed for me to make a sandwich, eat it, and clean up the mess. When I was mentally wiping the countertop free of crumbs, her eyes widened.

"Oh. My God." She giggled. "You're funny."

I closed my eyes for a moment and then opened them, hoping I could make her go away, but it didn't work. I'd seen enough over-baked flesh to last me a lifetime. I flicked the back of my hand against Shawn's bicep and pushed him toward the door. "Come on, Casanova. We're going to the flower shop."

"I work until ten," she said as we turned away.

Following me to the door with reluctance in his steps, Shawn glanced over his shoulder. "I'll be back."

"Dude." I huffed a sigh. "She's orange."

"Orange, and sexy as fuck," he insisted. "Did you see those titties?"

There was nothing sexy about her. She, her titties, and her discolored skin were disgusting. "The ones she flopped onto the glass case?" I chuckled. "Yeah, I saw them."

"She needs to be titty-fucked." He glanced in her direction and then looked at me. "I'd come all over that cute little face of hers."

I paused. "Cute? You think that chick was cute?"

"She looked like Alicia Silverstone with big fuckin' titties."

The movie was popular when we were thirteen. He never ceased to amaze me with his references to celebrities, and I gave him a look to make my position clear. "The chick from *Clueless?*"

"Yep."

I pushed the door open and gestured toward the parking lot. "You need to grow the fuck up."

"Fuck you, T.J."

I walked to the car without further discussing flowers, Alicia Silverstone, bracelets, discolored titty flesh, or coming on the face of shopping mall sales associates.

Although I couldn't blame Shawn for the sexual antics of my past, being friends with him had certainly contributed to my desire to bang as many women as possible. Sharing tales of lewd behavior and the inflated qualities of the women we had sex with was commonplace between us.

I was afraid those days were over.

He reached for the door handle and paused. "On to the flower shop?" he asked over the top of the car. "Get a big arrangement of cool shit?"

"Nope. I'm going to the bookstore."

"Without a gift?"

"I've got a gift."

"What?" he asked.

I grinned, knowing my response would fall on argumentative ears. Nonetheless, I said what I felt was appropriate.

"Loyalty."

25

JO

I EAGERLY ANSWERED MY PHONE, excited to see that he'd taken time to return my call. "Good morning, this is Jo Watson."

"You left a message for me to return your call," he said. "What can I do for you?"

"As I said in the message, my name's Jo Watson. I have a small bookstore in Texas that's devoted to independently published romance novels. Every month, we hold a contest. We choose ten winners from a long list of entrants. Each winner is provided a paperback from the pre-selected author of the respective month. That author is what we call the 'author of the month'. We spend the entire month decorating the store with the author's photos, flyers depicting his or her books, posters of the newest release—"

"Stop!" he insisted.

"Excuse me?"

"I'm sorry," he said. "I don't get wrapped up in the distribution of propaganda."

"Propaganda?" I asked. "Maybe you misunderstood…"

The phone clicked.

"Hello? Hello?"

I lowered the phone and looked at the screen. Somehow, we'd

become disconnected. I called the number again. After two rings, he answered.

"Hell-low," he said, his tone making his level of frustration clear.

"Mister Hildreth, I'm sorry. I was in the middle of explaining our procedure for the monthly contest, and we were disconnected."

"No, we weren't."

"Actually, we were."

"Actually, we *weren't*," he said in a snide tone. "I hung up."

"You hung up?"

"Sure did."

I was appalled. Appalled, but not surprised. "May I ask why?"

"Because," he said. "I was done talking to you. I don't fuck with propaganda. Don't believe in it. It's not how I do things."

"What portion of our earlier conversation led you to believe—"

"Posters, flyers, photos." He sighed into the phone. "Propaganda, propaganda, propaganda. I write a book, I publish the book, and I write another book. I don't do photos, flyers, or posters. Sorry."

"We wouldn't require anything from you. We'd do that for you, Mister Hildreth. It's part of what we—"

"Stop!" he barked. "You won't do it for *me*, because *I don't fuck with propaganda*. Is there anything else I can help you with?"

"I guess not."

"Have a nice day, Miss Watson."

I sighed. "You, too."

I hung up the phone and slid it across my desk.

"SD Hildreth?" Jenny asked.

I nodded.

"Didn't go well, did it?"

I looked up. "No, it sure didn't."

"When you said you were going to pick him for next month, I thought it was a bad idea."

"Why? He's got, like, fifty books out there."

"He's a dick, that's why."

"I've read some of the Facebook posts from his signings," I said. "People say he's nice in person."

"You weren't 'in person'," she explained. "You were talking to him on the phone. I don't think he's a very trusting person. Personally, I thought he was a girl for the first couple of years. He was writing under 'SD' Hildreth, not Scott."

"Yeah, I thought he was a girl, too," I admitted.

"I friended him on Facebook, thinking he was a she," Jenny said. "Then, I found out he was a guy. I sent him a message and was trying to explain how much I enjoyed his books, and that I thought he was a girl, but that I was glad to find out he was a dude. About two PMs into it, he got mad, blocked me, and unfriended me. Like I said, he's a dick. All guys are dicks. If you remember that, you'll be safe."

"Well, crap. I wanted to market a guy next month."

"Do that photographer-author guy," she said excitedly. "Golden Czermak. He writes hot male-male stuff and shifter romance."

"Ooh. Shifter romance is hot stuff right now. Wait? Is *he* a dick?"

She shook her head. "Not at all."

"But he's a guy. You said all guys are dicks."

"He's gay, so he doesn't count," she explained. "Gay guys are cool. Straight guys are dicks. Gay guys can be trusted. Straight guys can't."

"At all?"

"Not at all," she said, wagging her raised index finger from side to side as she spoke.

"Can you see if you can get that Golden guy's contact info?"

"Sure." She turned toward the door, and then quickly spun around. "Oh, I almost forgot. The reason I came over here in the first place was to say that FedSex is out at the curb. He's been there for, I don't know, maybe thirty minutes."

"Thirty minutes?" I glanced toward the front of the store. His car was parked right beside the entrance. "What's he doing?"

"Not sure. Looks like he's on the phone."

Despite our commitment to one another, I was far from comfortable with all matters when it came my and Tyson's relationship.

Jenny's constant talk of men being assholes, acting in unpredictable manners, and cheating left me fearful of one day doing or saying something that would be perceived as being pushy or overbearing. I didn't want to give Tyson any reason to be anyone other than the man I knew him to be.

"Thanks for telling me," I said. "I'm sure he'll come in when he's done."

A few minutes later, while I was researching male romance authors, Tyson stepped in front of my desk and cleared his throat.

"How's your day going?" he asked.

"Pretty basic Saturday afternoon," I responded with a smile. "Kind of slow. What are you out doing?"

He set his phone down and lowered himself into the seat on the opposite side of the desk. "Just wanted to stop by and let you know that I'm devoted to you."

I thought we'd already discussed the matter but acted as if the subject was new to me. "Well, that's nice, Tyson. I'm devoted to you, too."

He extended his clenched hand over the desk. "Here."

"What is it?" I gave him a cross look. "It better not be a spider."

"It's not."

I held out my hand, but quickly retracted it. "What is it?"

"It's for you," he said with a nod. "Trust me."

According to Jenny, men couldn't be trusted. I placed my upturned palm under his hand and prayed she was wrong. He opened his fist. A key fell into my hand.

"What's this?" I asked.

He nodded toward my hand. "A key to my house."

I was flattered. Flattered and somewhat confused. More confused than anything, really. As I gazed at the key, not quite understanding what was going on, he handed me a small sheet of folded paper.

"That's my address, and the code to my alarm system," he said. "There's a pad on the edge of the left garage door frame. Just like it says on the paper, press the number, then the pound symbol. The alarm will disarm. The asterisk symbol will open the garage door, and the key will open any door that goes into the house. They're all keyed the same."

"Uhhm. Okay." I looked at the items, and then at him. "Are you planning on going somewhere?"

"No, I just wanted to, I don't know." He shrugged. "I wanted to be as transparent as possible. You can come over any time. I've got nothing to hide."

I had no idea why he was doing what he was doing, but I liked it. I struggled not to giggle. "Okay. Thank you."

He slid his phone across the desk. "Look at that."

"I've seen it. It's the new Samsung. It's pretty."

He pointed to the phone. "Look at it. Swipe the screen and have a look."

"At what?"

"My contacts," he blurted. "Or, my lack of contacts. I took all the women out of my phone that I've...that I..." He gestured toward the phone. "Let's just say that there's no women's numbers in my phone except for my insurance agent, my doctor, and maybe a few other that are clearly professional."

"I believe you." I pushed the phone toward his hand. "I don't need to look at it."

Using the tip of his finger, he flicked it to the center of my desk. "I *want* you to look at it. I deleted pictures, too. About three thousand of them."

I choked out a laugh. "Of what?"

"I don't know. Stuff. Girls tits and shit like that."

"You had pictures of three thousand women's boobs?"

He raised his brows and shrugged. "Some were duplicates."

"Still, that's a lot of boobs."

"Well, they're gone. I just wanted to stop by and let you know that I'm truly devoted to this. I want everything to work out between us. I'm not trying to be sappy or a pussy or anything, but I want to be honest. It's important that you know I'm being straightforward. I want you to trust me."

"I do," I said. "I want you to trust me, too. I don't have any dick pictures or guy's numbers, though. I do have a lot of porn sites saved to my favorites on my laptop, but I don't communicate with those guys, I just look at their dicks."

He crossed his arms over his chest and lifted his chin a little. "You watch porn?"

If he was going to be transparent, so was I. Honesty was the key to our relationship surviving long-term.

"Yeah. Pretty much nightly," I admitted. "I think I might have a problem with it, but we can discuss that some other time."

"That's cool," he said. "I'm okay with you watching it. I think."

"Your dick is prettier than those guy's dicks, just for what it's worth," I whispered.

His eyes narrowed. "Pretty?"

"Yeah. It's pretty."

He cocked his head to the side and gave me a look. "My dick and my phone are pretty?"

"Personally, I prefer the iPhone, but as far as Androids go, the Samsung's pretty nifty. I like the suede cover. Your dick, on the other hand, is the prettiest dick I've ever seen."

He leaned his jaw against his clenched fist and looked right at me. "How many have you seen, if you don't mind me asking?"

I knew one day the question was going to come up. I hoped he'd let me combine all the dicks I'd seen into one big pile and make reference to that number. It would be staggering, but far less embarrassing.

"In real life, or on the internet?" I asked.

"Give me two separate numbers. Real life, and then the internet."

I gazed up at the ceiling and let out a long breath before looking at him again. "Four, in real life. On the internet, probably…" I multiplied the number of days in a year times twenty, and then multiplied that number times the thirteen years I'd been watching porn. I gave him a look of innocence, just to soften the blow. "Ninety-four thousand, nine hundred, if my math's correct. There's a possibility I've seen some twice, but that's impossible for me to know for sure."

His eyes bulged.

"A hundred thousand cocks?" he half-whispered. "Jesus."

I raised my brows. "I know, right?"

He glanced over each shoulder, and then leaned forward. "You've only had sex with four guys?"

That question was the one I feared the most. Admitting my lack of experience would either be a blessing or a curse, and I knew not which. I drew a breath and then let it out.

"Actually, I've only had sex with one," I admitted. "I sucked two guys cocks, which would count for dicks number two and three. Then, when I was ten, I went into he bathroom while Jarod was messing with his, and I saw it, by accident. Just part of it, though. That's number four, for a total of four real-life dicks."

He looked like he'd seen a ghost. "You've had sex with one guy, besides me?"

"Uh huh. Just so you know, it wasn't a big deal. He came to my second-cousin's wedding, on my mom's side. He was from Seattle and was a friend of the groom. I don't even think he gave me his real name, and I didn't get his number or anything. It was a pretty strange deal. I was so drunk I couldn't walk, and we did it in his rental car in the parking lot." I shrugged. "Sorry."

"No," he said. "I'm not uhhm. I'm not concerned."

"What about you?" I asked before I could stop myself. "How many have you seen?"

"Mine and Shawn's, up close. All the guys in gym class, but not like a dick inspection, or anything. Just as they walked past. And the football team, of course. We showered together."

I laughed. "No," I whispered. "How many pussies?"

"A lot more than four." He chuckled. "Let's leave it at that."

"Okay."

I was satisfied with his response, kind of. After chewing on it for a moment, I decided I wanted more.

"I know they all *look* different," I said. "But, what do they *feel* like? Can you describe the differences?"

After raking his fingers through his already mussed hair, he arched one eyebrow just a little. "They're all different. Some are tight, some are loose, and some are just fucking weird. Yours, for what it's worth, is perfect."

I started to say thank you, but before I did, he continued.

"It's better than perfect," he said. "It's pussy heaven."

"It feels *that* good?" I asked, trying to hide my excitement. "Heavenly?"

"Heavenly is pretty accurate. Maybe better than heavenly, I just don't know what else to compare it to."

I had the pussy of an angel. I beamed with pride. "Heavenly is good," I said with a smile. "Let's stick with that."

"Okay." He nodded toward my hand. "Put that key in your key ring and keep that piece of paper in a safe place, you're making me nervous."

Still floating on my pussy compliment cloud, I'd forgotten I was holding it. "I will," I assured him. "Sorry."

He gestured toward his phone. "You're not going to look at my phone, are you?"

I wanted to, but not while he was watching. I wanted to spend an afternoon going through it while he was working on his car or taking a nap. I wondered if he ever took naps and decided probably not.

"No," I said. "I trust you."

He picked up the phone and shook his head.

"What?" I asked.

"That was a pretty big deal to me, and you act like it's nothing."

"I'm sorry," I said. "It's a big deal to me, too. I'm glad you're being transparent, but I trust you."

"Thank you."

He fidgeted in his seat for a moment, and then glanced over each shoulder before looking at me again. "Show me your tits."

His request took me by complete surprise. I wrinkled my nose and glared through thinning eyes. "What?"

He cleared his throat. "Your tits. Get 'em out."

"I looked to my left, down the aisles of books, just to make sure Jenny wasn't videoing our conversation. After satisfying myself that we were alone, I gave one of the reasons I was opposed to doing so.

"I'm wearing a tee shirt," I said. "It's not that easy."

"Get. Them. Out."

The tone of his voice was different. Stern. Demanding. I reached for the hem of my shirt.

He cocked his head, as if frustrated with my lack of compliance.

In one motion, I raised it, catching the underwire of my bra with my fingertips as I pulled the shirt past. My boobs rose slightly and then fell into place. His eyes followed them, paused for an instant, and then met mine.

Having my tits out in the open office was more liberating than I expected it to be. Holding my shirt against my shoulders, I raised both brows. "Good enough?"

He reached across the desk and pinched my left nipple so hard I had to clench my jaw to refrain from making any discernable noise. When his hand returned to his lap, I still felt the pressure of his fingers on my hardened nipple.

My pussy was soaked.

"Holy crap," I said through my teeth. "Was there a reason for that?"

He smiled. "I didn't want you to think because I've been being sweet that I'm getting soft, because I'm not. I'm committed to you, but that doesn't mean I'm going to go easy on you."

I swallowed heavily. "I don't want you to."

"Good. Because I know what I want." He gestured behind me with his eyes. "Doing things like fucking you against that wall back there is part of it. So is this."

"Okay."

He gestured toward my swollen nipple with his eyes. "You can put your shirt down now."

"Thank you."

He stood and leaned over my desk. "Kiss me."

Deciding *how* to kiss Tyson was like choosing which pair of shoes I should purchase off the sale rack – regardless of the decision I made, I'd second-guess myself later. Hard, soft, aggressive, tongue, no tongue, nibble or not to nibble.

I never knew which one was fitting. Nevertheless, I complied with his wish, giving him a lot of lip and a little tongue. One thing was immediately clear. It was the right moment, he was the right man, and I'd chosen the right kiss.

When our mouths parted, I met his gaze. His smiling eyes confirmed we shared the same belief.

Best. Kiss. Ever.

He wiped his bottom lip with the edge of his index finger. "That was nice."

"I've got more where that came from."

"I can't wait." He picked up his phone and put it in his pocket. "Come by when you get off work?"

"Be in bed naked," I said, trying to remain straight-faced. "I'll just let myself in with my new key."

He winked. "Atta girl."

"Is that a yes?"

He turned away. "I guess you'll find out when you get off work."

As he walked away, I raised my right hand and gave the same wave a child gives at a parade as the floats roll past. His arrival, the visit, and his departure had me in a complete daze. I stared blankly at the door, uncertain if I could work another five hours without making a trip to the bathroom with my trusty vibrator.

Jenny's voice reminded me of the risks associated with demonstrating affection in the workplace. "You've got really nice tits, by the way."

My eyes bulged. "You saw that?"

"Afraid so."

I stood. "Pictures?"

"A few."

"Will you send them to me?"

She smiled. "Already did."

26

TYSON

SHE WAS DRESSED in a flowing white tank and dark jeans that were skin-tight from her waist to her ankles. Dark hair draped along either side of her chest, coming to a rest just above her elbows. Her glasses had worked their way down her nose and were positioned half the distance between the bridge and her little button tip.

She studied the shrine devoted to displaying my accomplishments. Framed newspaper clippings, a Sports Illustrated cover, numerous magazine articles, action photos and an array of medals filled the lighted case. It was difficult to claim modesty in the presence of such a display, but I was just that.

Modest.

"You looked so young," she said.

"I looked like I was fourteen until I was twenty."

She looked at everything on display at least twice, and then glanced over her shoulder. "This is really impressive."

"He collected everything when it came to me and the sport of football," I said. "I just left it the way it was when he passed."

She admired a framed photo of me releasing the ball just before being tackled. "Do you miss the sport? Being competitive?"

I was surprised she asked the question. It was an easy one to answer but answering wasn't easy.

"Parts of it," I responded. "The bond. The friendships."

"You don't miss playing?"

The truth was that I didn't miss it at all. Football was my father's passion, and I played it to please him, not myself. Admitting the complete truth, even in his absence, seemed like an impossible task.

"Not really," I said. "Not the playing, anyway."

"Oh." She pushed her glasses up the bridge of her nose. "I wonder if the tinkering with the car filled that gap in your life."

The 'gap in my life' was filed with me sticking my dick in women at an unprecedented rate, but I found no value in admitting it to her. I'd changed my ways, and that was all that mattered.

"Probably." I glanced around the poorly lit den. It felt creepy to be in there without my father. "Have you seen enough?"

She took one last look at the collection of memorabilia. "I suppose so."

I flipped out the light and turned toward the hallway. "It's about time to eat."

Although she'd been inside my home before, I hadn't bothered showing her any of my personal effects. Now that I was being truthful, I felt compelled to do so. It didn't make the process any easier.

She followed me into the living room and circled the furniture like a cat trying to decide where to sit.

An island surrounded by barstools separated the kitchen from the living room. I sat down there and admired her as she perused the living room. Still undecided on where to land, she turned to face me.

Her face wore a look of concern.

"Is everything okay?" I asked.

"It's fine," she said. "I was just, I don't know. Looking at all those pictures of you got me thinking."

"About?"

"I want to uhhm." She scrunched her nose. "Try something."

In a display of my childhood antics, I swiveled the barstool from side-to-side. "Care to elaborate?"

Her lips parted slightly, revealing her desire to speak. For a lingering moment, she remained silent, gazing at me with her mouth open just enough for me to get a glimpse of her snow-white teeth.

In an expression of her innocence, she pushed her hands into her pockets and rocked back and forth on the balls of her bare feet. "The *reverse cowgirl*," she whispered. "Can we try it after we eat?"

Desire rushed through me like a fever. I tried to act indifferent.

The lasagna was on the counter behind me, waiting to be served. There was no doubt watching her ride my cock would be far more satisfying than eating. I picked my jaw up off the floor and gave a deadpan response.

"Rumor has it that lasagna's better cold than it is hot."

Her perfectly-sculpted eyebrows raised. "Oh really?"

"Want to give it a try now?"

"Which one?" she asked. "The lasagna? Or the sex?"

"The cowgirl, Cowgirl."

"I've got a lot of eating experience." She reached for her belt. "And, a lot of catching up to do on sex."

The mere mention of sex had my cock standing at full attention. I slid off the edge of the barstool and pointed at my distorted shorts. "There's only one way to change that."

I'd spent seventeen years screwing every woman that would give me an opportunity. Jo, by her own admission, had done just the opposite. Despite my desire to fuck her every waking moment that she was in my presence, I hoped to spend at least a portion of our idle time growing closer to her on a more intellectual level.

She, on the other hand, yearned to experiment with sex.

I decided to combine the two efforts. I could explore her intellectual side while we explored her sexual desires. Considering the books that she'd read, she undoubtedly had a mountain of ideas stored away. By the time we'd satisfied all her wishes, we'd be closer than a married couple.

Satisfied I'd thwarted one of our relationship's potential

problems, I rid myself of my shorts and boxers in one shove. After tossing my shirt to the side, I glanced in her direction. Topless and bent at the waist, she was struggling to remove her fitted jeans, pushing them along her silky-smooth thighs one frustrating inch at a time.

"I. Am. Never. Wearing. These. Things. Again." She shoved against the spandex-infused denim with each abruptly spoken word. "This. Is. Ridiculous."

The jeans seemed to be stuck, just above her knees. Bare-assed with her legs bound together by the skin-tight material, she looked up and met my gaze. "Can I get some help?"

In a hilarious effort to maintain her balance, she hopped across the floor with her pants tangled around her knees, bumping into nearly every object in her wake.

"Please?" she pleaded, bouncing off the arm of the loveseat as she spoke.

Before I could provide her with any assistance, she came crashing against the edge of the coffee table. The impact caused her to go reeling in the opposite direction, head over respective ass.

When she came to a stop, she was midway between the fireplace and the couch, face down and resting against one shoulder, with her bare ass high in the air.

I glanced at her glistening twat and grinned. "Nice pussy, my dear. Didn't wear panties today, huh?"

She flopped onto her side. "Will you help me? Please?"

With my eyes fixed on her cute little ass, I ambled to her side, struggling all the while not to laugh out loud. "Lift your feet, *Grace*."

She extended her legs. I gripped the hem of her jeans and pulled, fully expecting them to simply slide off her legs. They stretched a foot in length and popped right back into place. Frustrated, I pulled against them so hard I lifted her from the floor. After several all-out tugs, she collapsed onto the floor and I held the jeans.

"Jesus." I looked the jeans over. "These things are ridiculous."

"I'm never buying another pair of jeggings," she exclaimed. "Ever!"

I tossed the jeans aside. "What did you call them?"

"Jeggings."

"What the fuck's a *jegging?*"

"Jeans and leggings," she said. "Combined."

"Jeggings." I laughed. "That's the most absurd amalgamation I've ever heard."

"I'm not even wearing those stupid things home. You can give me a pair of shorts or something. I'm done with them. Throw 'em in the trash."

I was wearing my birthday suit, and she was equally as naked. The mood to have sex, however, seemed to be lost during the commotion.

"Are you out of the mood?" I asked.

"No," she huffed. "This little scrape isn't going to stop me."

"You look cute down there," I said.

She adjusted her glasses. "Put your dick in my mouth."

If I let her suck my cock, it'd be over before it got started. She was far too good at it. I put my hands against my hips and let out a sigh. "The last time we tried that, you sucked me stupid. I'm not falling for that trick again."

She rose to her feet and squatted in front of me, taking my flaccid cock in her hand as she did so. She licked her lips. Paralyzed by anticipation, I watched as she guided it into her mouth. Two strokes of her mouth later, I was as hard as a rock.

"That's enough of *that.*" I retracted my hips and extended my hand. "Come on, Cowgirl. I'll carry you."

I carried her to the bedroom and carefully lowered her to the edge of the bed. Still sporting a rather hard dick, I laid beside her and laced my fingers behind my head. With my erection pointed at the ceiling, I gave the first of what was sure to be many instructions.

"Alright," I said. "Here's how this is done. The girl straddles the guy, and she faces——"

Mid-sentence, she straddled me. Her fabulous ass inched toward my cock. Despite her lack of experience, she obviously had enough of idea of how to position herself to get started.

I began to give my first verbal instruction, but she was one step ahead of me, guiding the head of my swollen cock between her legs before I could speak.

Her dark hair dangled along the center of her narrow back. In complete contrast to her porcelain-colored skin, the long curly locks danced back and forth as she tried to get comfortable. Considering her innocence, seeing her in that position was erotic as hell.

Mesmerized by her body's beauty, I watched as she forced herself against my swollen shaft. As it disappeared, so did my desire to do anything but make love to her. After taking one-third of it into her warmth, she paused.

"Holy crap," she breathed. "This feels *good*."

My eyes were fixed on the gap between her ass cheeks. Seeing my length disappear a little more with each gyration of her hips was hypnotic. Speechless, I gawked at the sight until my entire cock had vanished.

"Ohhh-kay." She glanced over her shoulder. "Are you ready?"

She may have lacked physical experience, but of the ninety-thousand cocks she'd seen on porn sites, it was obvious at least some of them had been in the reverse cowgirl position. I fixed my eyes on her bold black glasses and gave the same nod of approval a professional bull rider gives the gate attendant.

Slowly and methodically, her pussy devoured my entire length. Awestruck, I watched as I disappeared into her wet confines, repeatedly. With each well-timed stroke, my scrotum tightened a little more.

"I..." She lowered herself until her clit was against my balls.

"Love..." Her hips pivoted upward, slowly revealing the length of my stiff girth.

"Your..." She forced herself along the shaft, until the tip bottomed out.

"Dick..." She gave three quick successive strokes.

The last three strokes elevated me to the point of no return. If I didn't make a change quickly, it was going to be over.

I drew a shaky breath and tried to clear my mind. During that lull, she began to ride me like a rented mule.

"What's your...dream vacation...spot," I asked in a broken sentence.

Bouncing on my cock like a kid on a Christmas gift pogo-stick, she glanced over her shoulder.

"What?" she spat.

"Favorite. Vacation. Spot." The words escaped in three distinctly different breaths.

She stopped moving her hips.

Her eyes grew angrily narrow. "Whatinthefuckiswrongwithyou?"

"I'm trying to bond with you," I explained. "On an intellectual level."

She removed her glasses and tossed them at her side. "You're going to come, aren't you?"

"Not if you slow down a little bit and talk to me."

She glared for an instant and then turned around. The charade was over. My weakness had been exposed.

Her hands slid to just below my knees and gripped the flesh firmly. Her hips began the same predictable rhythm of gyrating fore and aft, milking my swollen length of its ability to resist her.

She arched her back as her sexual tirade gained momentum.

I gazed blankly at the outline of her body against the sun-lit drapery in the distance. A tingling sense of satisfaction ran along my spine. She'd made me weak for her, and I was enjoying every minute of it.

Absorbing her beauty was easy. Like a rose transforming from a bud to a fully blossomed flower, she opened a little more each day. I eagerly took in all she offered, yearning for any glimpse into what made her so uniquely attractive to me.

My scrotum tightened. My cock swelled. My breathing became choppy and unpredictable. It was coming to an end.

Intellectual banter couldn't save me. I was past the turning point. Resistance was impossible, so I embraced the inevitable.

The time had come to fuck.

My hand came down against the side of her cute little ass with a *thwack*!

"Fuck me, you sexy little bitch," I said though my teeth. "Fuck me!"

I sat up and gripped her waist with both hands. Although she needed no assistance, I offered enough to remind her that sex was a two-way street.

"Fuck me!" I forced her downward and my hips skyward, taking the breath from her lungs with the force of my thrust. "Fuck me!"

"Holy crap," she moaned.

I gripped her waist firmly. With my eyes fixed on her sweet little pussy, I fucked her feverishly. "Sexy. Little. Fucking. Bitch."

She glanced over her shoulder. "Yes! Yes! Yes! Keep going!"

It was clear that I'd met my match.

I slid my hands to her boobs. While cupping them in my hands, I pinched her nipples between my thumbs and forefingers. It was a weakness of her, and I knew it.

With the same rhythmic passion that we'd shared in the past, we fucked one another fervently. Animalistic grunts and words of encouragement echoed throughout the bedroom as our lovemaking session reached its peak.

Pressure built within me until I could resist no longer.

Her body tensed.

Mine followed.

"Fuck yes," I bellowed. "I'm going to come."

"Do it," she groaned.

I sank my teeth into her shoulder, pulling her against me in the process. Together, as a sexual unit, we reached climax.

Sparks flew.

My head spun. The ensuing orgasm was mind-blowing.

I looked around the room and blinked a few times, not quite certain of what had happened. Upon regaining my wits, I collapsed onto my back.

She came to rest beside me. After catching her breath, she rolled to her side.

Her eyes thinned a little. "What was that intellectual vacation spot crap about?"

"I don't know." I sighed. "An idea I had. Getting to know each other while we fucked."

"Can we keep the intellectual stuff confined to the dinner table?" she asked. "If we're going to talk in the bedroom. I prefer the dirty stuff."

Calling her a sexy *bitch* was a risk. I was pleased she enjoyed it. "Intellectual talk in the kitchen, dirty talk in the bedroom. Got it."

"Good." She gestured toward the door with her eyes. "Cold lasagna? I'm starving."

"Cold lasagna and a little intellectual conversation." I sat up. "Sounds good."

"Save the intellect for tomorrow." She twisted her hair into a messy bun and reached for her glasses. "I'm kind of vacant upstairs right now."

"What's wrong?"

"I think you might have fucked my brains out."

"I'm kind of vacant up there too," I admitted. "You did a number on me."

Her mouth twisted into a smirk. "By the time this night's over, you're not even going to remember how to tie your shoes."

27

JO

LOST IN A DAYDREAM, I answered the phone without so much as looking at the screen. "This is Jo."

"Good morning, Miss Watson. I'm Jessica, SD Hildreth's wife. How are you?"

"I'm doing well, thank you," I responded. "How are you?"

"I'd be a lot better if my husband wasn't such an ass. He told me about the conversation he had with you, and I've called to apologize for his narrow-mindedness."

"Oh, that's okay," I said. "I started reading his memoir, and I kind of understand now that he's a little different than most. It's part of what makes him unique, I guess."

"Different?" She laughed. "You should try living with him. It's *interesting.*"

I reached for Hildreth's memoir, which was sitting at the corner of my desk. "From what I've read, you two get along really well though, don't you? I mean, I'm not done with the book, but it sure looks like that's where everything's headed."

"Oh, we get along great. He's a wonderful man, if he knows you *and* likes you. His problem is that he doesn't trust people. *Anyone.* So, he goes through life with this crappy look on his face, convinced he's not going to let anyone get close enough to him to hurt him."

I hated to say anything, but after reading the part in his book about what the government did to him, I can't say that I blamed him. "That's understandable though, considering what happened to him."

"I suppose," she said. "Again, I'm sorry."

"It's no big deal, really."

"If you're still open to it, he'd love to participate in your promotion," she said. "We'll donate whatever you need. As long as it's successful for you, that's what matters."

I sat up in my seat. "He agreed to that?"

"He didn't have a choice." She laughed. "Yes, he agreed."

"Oh. Wow. Uhhm. Well, ten paperbacks is what we like to give away each month. Can you do that?"

"Sure. What about swag?" she asked.

"If you've got extra, I'd love to have some. Bookmarks. Pencils. Whatever. We use it to promote his work, and, of course, the store."

"Are you sure ten books is enough?"

"If you want to send a few more, that'd be great. We can do a bigger giveaway."

"This helps your bookstore, too. Is that right?" she asked.

"It brings us a lot of traffic, yes. You know how romance readers love signed paperbacks."

"I'll send fifty," she said.

"Holy crap," I gasped. "Seriously?"

"If you can make use of them, I'll send them."

Having fifty books would be a game changer for me. I could do all kinds of contests and drive tremendous traffic to the store, and to Mister Hildreth's work.

"That would be awesome," I said.

"I'll put together a nice box of swag, too."

"That's just. That's fantastic. I can't wait."

"I sent you a friend request on Facebook," she said. "I'll forward the tracking numbers. You can get with me anytime by PM."

"Okay. Thank you, again."

"It's the least we can do," she said. "I feel awful about what he said."

"It was harmless," I said.

She sighed. "It's not always harmless. A few months ago, a publisher sent him an email about a manuscript. He was waiting for her to contact him, but when she did, she didn't identify herself, so he didn't realize it was her. She just said, *send me the manuscript to your most recent piece of work* or something like that. He responded, saying *send me the passwords and log-in information to your fucking bank accounts.* She sent an email back and said, *excuse me?* He responded, and said, *go fuck yourself, lady. I don't send manuscripts to anyone.* She responded by saying, *I'm the representative from XYZ Publishing, and you're the rudest individual I've ever had the opportunity to speak to.* He didn't apologize. He sent her another email, explaining that if she'd have identified herself, everything would have been fine. He went on to say that her lack of doing so proved that she was either ridiculously pretentious, or ridiculously unprofessional. Either way, he told her, he wasn't willing to do business with someone like her. Needless to say, that relationship ended long before it even started."

"That actually happened?"

"It sure did. About six weeks ago. He lost a pretty big contract because of it."

After hearing her stories, I thanked God Tyson wasn't like Mister Hildreth. "That's crazy," I said with a laugh. "But, like you said, at least he's a good cook."

"He sure is." She chuckled. "I'll ship your things by end of day tomorrow, and like I said, I'll forward tracking numbers to you on Facebook."

"Thank you."

"Thank you, Miss Watson."

"Tell Scott thanks, too."

"I will."

"Bye.

"Bye."

I hung up the phone and bounced from my seat. "Jenny! Guess what?"

In the middle of two-stepping alone, she paused, and turned around. "The FedSex man poked his tongue in your butt?"

"No, not yet. This might even be better news."

"Better than a tongue in your ass?

"Maybe."

"What's better than that?" she asked.

"SD Hildreth's wife called. She's sending *fifty* books!"

Her eyes shot wide. "Fifty?"

"Fifty."

"We can make a huge banner and hang it on the canopy," she said. "This place will be crawling with horny housewives."

"I know, right?"

"Was she nice?" she asked.

"She was really nice."

Still facing me, she began to two-step again. "Makes sense, then."

"What makes sense?"

"That she's nice." She shuffled to the left, spun in a circle, and then shuffled to the right. "For a relationship to work, there's got to be darkness *and* light. Without experiencing the stench of a pile of horseshit, you'll never truly appreciate the aroma of the honeysuckle along the fence line."

I laughed. "You're funny."

She tipped her imaginary hat. "Funny and *right*."

If she was right, I couldn't help but wonder why Tyson and I got along so well. It was quite possible that I was the light to his darkness, but I wasn't sure that I was aware of what his darkness was.

While Jenny continued to shuffle across the floor, I wondered if I'd ever find out.

28

TYSON

WE'D REACHED YET another Saturday and were out on what had become our ritual *date night*. Headed to a steakhouse we'd both agreed on, I recalled the night of our first date, and chuckled at the thought of Jo barfing on my car.

"I was just thinking of the first night we went out," I said.

"It seems like so long ago," she replied.

I chuckled. "The look on your face when I stomped the gas pedal was priceless. I thought you were going to shit your pants."

"I'm not saying this because I'm trying to impress you or something. Believe me, I'm saying it because I mean it," she assured me. "I *really* mean it."

In the midst of changing lanes, I glanced over my right shoulder. "Shit. I'm scared to ask what you're talking about."

"This car," she said. "I love it. It's, I don't know. It's exciting not knowing what's going to happen next. When you get frustrated and stomp the gas, it's like riding a roller coaster. I love it."

I grinned. "It can be exciting, that's for sure."

"When you mash it, it just goes. It scares the crap out of me," she explained. "But at the same time, I find it exhilarating. Exciting."

"For me, it's therapeutic," I said. "When I get depressed, or when I've been having a bad day, I'll drive this thing for half an hour. After that, all is well."

"I can't imagine having a car like this. I'd either be in a ton of trouble, or…" She looked at me as if apologizing for something she intended to say. She swallowed heavily. "I'd get a lot of tickets, for sure."

"I haven't received a single ticket in it."

Her eyes went wide. "How can that be?"

I pointed at the row of LED lights in the dash. "It's got a built-in radar detector. And, I use *Waze* on my phone when I'm driving on the highway."

"Waze? What's that?"

"It's a GPS app that allows drivers to load information showing where the police are running speed traps."

She shook her head. "I don't even speed that much, and it seems I've always got two speeding tickets on my record."

I laughed. "You'd lose your driver's license if you owned this car."

She adjusted her seat belt's tension, and then relaxed in her seat. She looked at me and grinned. "I'd have no driver's license and a wet pussy."

I gave her a look. "A wet pussy?"

She nodded. "When you go fast, it makes my pussy wet."

"Really?"

Her eyelids fluttered. "Uh-huh."

I glanced in the rearview mirror and then checked both side view mirrors. After making sure there was no traffic, I downshifted two gears and pressed the gas pedal to the floor. The shrill whistle from the supercharger was drowned out by the sound of the exhaust as the engine climbed to 7,000 RPM.

I shifted gears and glanced at the speedometer.

125 miles an hour and climbing fast. I shifted again.

145 miles an hour. As the needle reached 155, we approached a slow-moving truck. I shifted the car into neutral and changed lanes.

With both hands on the steering wheel and my eyes fixed on the road ahead, I asked the only question that mattered.

"Is your pussy wet?"

"Soaked."

"I guess I'll always know how to get you wet," I said.

She laughed. "You get me wet when you look at me."

"What?" I looked her up and down. "When I look at you?"

"Look at me. Kiss me. Touch my shoulder. Kiss my neck. Rake your fingers through your hair. Wet, Wet, Wet, Wet, and wet."

"Really?"

She raised her right hand. "I swear. Scout's Honor, or whatever."

I'd felt like a weak-minded idiot since Jo and I met, because merely looking at her caused my dick to go stiff. Consequently, I only looked at her for short periods of time, and never took time to truly appreciate her beauty.

At least not in public.

If she suffered the same level of arousal I did, it was no wonder we ended up fucking every time we saw one other.

"I get stiff by just looking at you," I admitted.

"I know."

"What do you mean, you *know*?"

"I can see it," she said. "You're hard all the time. I can see the outline of it in the leg of your shorts. Even when you wear jeans."

"I've always wondered if people notice."

"Oh. They notice." She laughed. "Believe me."

A state trooper parked at the side of the road caught my attention.

"Cop!" Jo shouted. "Cop! Cop! Cop!"

"Thanks. I saw him." I glanced at the speedometer. Our speed was 72 miles an hour, only two miles an hour above the speed limit. "We're fine."

"How fast are you going?" she asked.

"Seventy-two."

"Thank God," she said.

As we rolled past the trooper, he pulled out into traffic. Ten seconds later, his lights were flashing, and his sirens were wailing.

I changed lanes.

He changed lanes.

I pulled onto the shoulder on the right side of the highway.

He did the same.

"I won't say a word," Jo said. "Don't worry."

I watched in the rearview mirror as the officer spoke in the hand-held receiver of his radio. My muscles tensed. He had no reason to pull me over, other than his desire to be a prick. As the twenty-something trooper sauntered toward my car, my blood began to boil.

He stepped alongside my door.

I rolled my window down approximately one inch.

"Roll the window down, Sir," he barked.

With my hands positioned on the steering wheel and my eyes fixed on the windshield, I responded. "I can hear you just fine."

"License and registration," he said.

"What's the reason for pulling me over?"

"Speeding."

I looked at him. "I find that hard to believe," I said. "I was in neutral and preparing to take the off-ramp. Do you have my speed recorded on radar? May I verify it?"

"License and registration, please."

I cleared my throat. "I have a legally owned, properly registered, and loaded weapon between my right thigh and the console of the car, Sir. Would you instruct me as to how you'd prefer I obtain my license? It's in my right rear pocket."

The officer pulled his gun from his holster and trained it on me. "Keep your hands where I can see them."

My mind flashed to the night my father died. The blood. My crying. I desperately wanted to wipe my brow but didn't dare move my hands.

"I'm not moving, Sir," I said, my voice cracking from emotion. "Neither is my passenger."

"Keep your fucking hands where I can see them," he shouted.

"I'll advise you that this is being recorded, officer," I lied.

If his ridiculous overreaction was being recorded, I felt that he might refrain from shooting until he felt he absolutely had to, and I had no intention of giving him *any* reason to do so.

"Driver," he shouted. "Keep your hands on the steering wheel."

"Understood," I said.

"Passenger," he barked. "Using the index finger and thumb of your left hand only, lift the weapon and place it in the vehicle's rear seat. Slowly."

Visions of the day my father died came to mind. I hated that Jo was being brought into the equation, but there was nothing I could do to prevent it.

"Take your time, Jo," I said. "Just like he said. Left hand. Thumb and forefinger."

Jo complied by lifting the gun's holster from its resting place. After placing it in the rear seat, she returned her hand to her lap.

Clenching the steering wheel as if my life depended on it, I cleared my throat. "What now, officer?"

"Roll down your fucking window!" the officer demanded.

I shook my head. "I can hear you just fine."

"Tyson," Jo pleaded.

My jaw tightened.

"Keep your right hand on the wheel," the officer said. "Use your left hand to retrieve your license. Hand me the license through the window."

I did as the officer asked, performing the awkward task without giving him reason to be alarmed. After handing him the license, he asked that we both get out of the car.

"For what reason?" I asked.

With his weapon still pointed at me, he explained his reasoning. "My safety."

He was young and inexperienced, that much was certain. There were over a million civilians in the state of Texas that were legally licensed to carry handguns. One would think he'd be more versed on how to handle such matters professionally.

The last thing I wanted was for Jo to live her life after having witnessed an unarmed citizen being shot by an overzealous, inexperienced cop.

"Instruct me on the procedure you'd like me to use to get out of the car, officer," I said, my tone rich with frustration. "Step. By. Step."

"Driver, use your right hand to disengage your seatbelt. Slowly," he barked. "Use that same hand to open the door. Passenger, use your left hand. One at a time. Driver first."

I complied. Once I was safely out of the car, Jo followed.

While the officer ran my license check, we stood facing one another with our hands flat on the top of the car.

Jo's frustration was clearly etched on her face. "You should have rolled your window down," she whispered. "That made him mad. He scared the crap out of me with that thumb and forefinger thing."

"He wasn't mad about the window. The fact I had a handgun in the car was what ticked him off," I argued. "I'm sorry you've been put through all of this. It's completely unnecessary."

"Why do you insist on carrying that thing?"

"What thing?"

"The gun."

"For my safety, and for the safety of those I love," I responded adamantly. "There's far too many criminals in this state carrying guns *illegally* for me not to carry a gun. I'm not planning on becoming a statistic."

She forced an exhaustive breath and then looked at me. "I'm guessing the odds of ever actually using it are pretty low."

"You're right. They are." I held her gaze with angry eyes. "But, I've lost the two people I loved the most, already. I'm not willing to lose a third."

"I'm glad you're willing to protect those you love, but carrying that thing causes a lot of problems."

"The problem is that a police officer pulled me over without cause," I seethed. "He's got a job to do. Fucking with me because he's got a hard-on for guys who drive fast cars isn't it."

"Why are you so mad?" she asked. "Because we're out here with our hands on the car like criminals|?"

I thought I was doing a good job of hiding it. Obviously, I was wrong.

"Personally, I'm not pissed off about *this*." I drummed my fingertips against the top of my car. "I'm pissed off because he pulled me over. He didn't have any right to do so."

"You were speeding. Earlier."

"His car was pointed away from me. He has no proof. I guarantee you that he pulled me over because my car has a loud exhaust and *looks* fast. He's hoping I have an outstanding warrant, so he can arrest me and look like a fucking hero."

"You don't think he's going to write you a ticket?"

"If he does," I warned. "He'll probably end up arresting me. I'm not signing a fucking speeding ticket. I can guaran-goddamn-tee you that."

"Why do you hate cops so much?" she whispered.

My gaze fell to my feet. After an unsuccessful attempt to calm my nerves, I looked up. It was time to tell her the rest of the story.

"Because," I seethed. "They killed my father."

29

JO

I WANTED ANSWERS, but I had no idea what to say or how to say it. Driven by nothing but instinct, I proceeded with caution and the utmost respect.

"I thought your father died in a car wreck?"

"I alluded to that, but I didn't specifically say it," he explained. "I wasn't at a point that I was ready to talk about it yet. I guess I am, now."

My topsy-turvy stomach gave warning. I didn't want to know what happened. If Tyson was ready to talk about it, however, I needed to be ready to listen.

"Whenever you're ready to talk," I assured him. "I'll listen."

He looked past me, beyond the edge of the highway's overpass. "His car was a six-speed, and I had no idea how to drive it. He was persistent, always demanding that I learn. 'A man needs to be able to drive a stick shift' he'd say. We'd gone out every night that week, practicing stopping, shifting, and taking off from a dead stop."

He gestured toward the roadway below with a nod of his head. "We were down there somewhere, driving in a residential neighborhood, because there wasn't much traffic. It was getting dark and we were ready to call it a night. A kid came out of nowhere on a bike. I went to push in the clutch and hit the brake instead. The car stalled, and I stomped the gas by accident. We shot right toward the kid. I yanked the wheel. The car spun out and slid sideways. I lost control and slammed right into a telephone pole. It tore the left side of his new car open like someone had done it with a can opener. Headlight. Fender. Door. Hood."

He looked away and shook his head.

"I was pretty shaken up. My father wasn't even mad. He took the driver's seat, and we headed home. Just after we exited the off-ramp, there was a police roadblock set up. When we came to a stop, he looked at me, said 'shh', and set the brake."

Gazing blankly at the front of the car, he blinked a few times, and then continued. "They were looking for an escaped prisoner who'd stolen a car and eluded the cops. There was a helicopter, dogs, the whole bit. One of the cops saw the damage on the car and asked where we'd been. He told the cop he didn't think it was any of his business where we'd been. To be honest, it wasn't. We weren't escaped convicts, we were just a father and a son, going home on a Sunday night. The cop took offense and got an attitude. He asked for my father's driver's license."

With my hands pressed against the top of the car, I stood on shaking legs, waiting for the conclusion to a story that I already knew the ending to. An ending I feared I didn't want to hear a detailed description of.

He shifted his eyes to meet mine. "He didn't have his wallet, and I knew it. I wanted a Gatorade when we started, and he realized he'd left it at home. He did it all the time. He hated carrying that thing. My father told him he didn't have any reason or right to see his license. He explained we'd done nothing to warrant being detained or being searched. He said we were just trying to get home, which was only a few blocks away. The cop called the canine officer over. When the dog got to the car, it uhhm. It started barking. That's when things went to hell."

The primary color of his eyes had changed from green to brown, making them seem much darker and far less inviting. He didn't need to continue. I felt sick. In fact, I was mortified, and he hadn't even finished the story.

"Everything happened...it all happened at the same time. The helicopter shined its light in the windshield. Shadows flickered. Someone screamed 'don't move'. Someone else screamed 'show me your license'. And then, someone screamed...he uhhm...someone yelled, 'gun!'. The uhhm. The first shot was deafening, but not so much that I didn't hear the other two cops empty their service weapons into the car." He looked up. Tears were streaming down his cheeks. "I watched him die, Jo. For nothing. For absolutely fucking nothing."

It was worse than I imagined. Much worse. I couldn't get my words past the lump in my throat, so I joined him in mourning his father's loss by crying.

The officer stepped to Tyson's side. "It's your lucky day, Mister Neese."

Tyson's gaze fell to his hands. The muscles in his jaw flexed. "Is that right?"

Studying the paperwork clipped to his metal clipboard, the officer didn't bother looking up. "I'm going to let you off with a warning."

Tears rolled down Tyson's cheeks. He glanced at the officer. "For *what*?"

The officer, still studying the paperwork, hadn't noticed Tyson's state of being.

"Speeding," the officer said.

A vein along the side of Tyson's neck expanded. He was clearly on the verge of snapping. If he did, there was no way it would end well.

I needed him to remain calm. I cleared my throat. "Ty-son."

His eyes met mine. I raised my index finger and mouthed the word *please*.

He exhaled a breath through his nose and looked at the officer. "I appreciate that, officer," he said through clenched teeth.

The officer tore the warning ticket from the clipboard and

handed a copy to Tyson, along with his license. "Again, it's not a citation, and there's no notice to appear."

Tyson glared.

"Have a nice afternoon," the officer said.

Tyson didn't respond. He merely rested his forearms against the top of the car and clenched the wadded warning ticket in his hand. After having just recalled the loss of his father, I could only imagine where his mind was.

As the officer drove past, my muscles relaxed. It was over. We were free to go on about our business, but I felt I couldn't move. With tear-filled eyes, I studied Tyson. What I saw was an angry little boy who'd been stripped of his youth. Of his innocence. Of his father.

Through the course of the tension-filled event that we'd narrowly escaped, I realized something. I didn't want to lose Tyson.

I couldn't lose Tyson.

"Tyson," I said.

Still leaning against the car, he was staring at the ticket he held. His eyes were narrow, and his jaw was tight. He shifted his gaze to meet mine.

His fierce brown eyes were filled with anger. "Yeah?"

I wanted to protect him, but a gun wasn't my weapon of choice. I needed to provide him the warmth of reassurance that I wasn't going anywhere. That through the thick and the thin, I'd be there at his side, no matter what.

That he could trust me.

Saying it was a huge risk, but one I was willing to take. I swallowed heavily, and then offered him a smile.

"I love you," I said.

The angry look he was wearing faded. Sheer content replaced it. Green eyes with amber specks glistened as they held my gaze.

He exhaled a soft breath. The corners of his mouth curled up. "I love you, too."

30

TYSON

WHILE JO and her mother prepared what would be my third home-cooked Sunday meal in as many weeks, I followed John toward a metal building that was positioned behind their home.

He seemed preoccupied, kicking a small piece of a fallen tree branch as we walked. A lawn tractor sat in front of the remote building's open doors. The smell of freshly-cut grass lingered in the air. Upon scanning the adjoining field, I realized the acre or so of grass that surrounded the home had just been cut.

"I love the smell of fresh grass," I said.

He lifted his head. "Used to hate it when I was a kid. Grown to like it, though. It smells like progress."

Although the city had grown around them, the land his family had spent two generations harvesting vegetables on remained unchanged. I wondered how long John would be able to continue to look after the acreage, and just what would happen to it when he was too old to continue.

"Is Jarod coming today?" I asked.

"He always comes," he replied. "Anybody's guess when he'll be here, though. World's biggest procrastinator, that boy."

I chuckled. "Jo says the same thing about him."

He looked up from the stick that he'd nearly kicked all the bark from and smiled. "Jo's the opposite. Always on time, no matter what. Hard to believe they're brother and sister."

He paused at the back corner of the building and put his hands on his hips. A lone oak tree fifty yards in the distance had a large tractor tire hanging from one of its larger branches. The tire was far too big to be a swing.

I studied it, puzzled by what purpose it served. "What in the heck's that for?"

"Peace of mind," he responded. "This is where I do my thinkin'."

A large steel horse trough placed thirty feet or so from the tree puzzled me. I studied it for a moment, and then looked at John. "Do you have horses?"

"Never cared much for 'em," he responded. "One of the SOBs stepped on my foot when I was a kid. Mashed it all to hell. They're too big and too unpredictable for my likes."

He sent the stick sailing with a swift kick of his right foot and stepped to the edge of the watering trough. Much to my surprise, it was filled with sun-faded footballs. He picked one up and looked at it.

"That store that sells everything for a dollar right off Stacy Road sells these things, cheap. They're not a buck, but they're damned affordable. I buy fifty of 'em every three years or so. Sun makes 'em all wappy-jawed after a few years. SOB's don't fly straight after that. Not bad for four bucks a piece, I suppose."

He raised his arm, hesitated, and then threw the football toward the tire that hung from the tree's branch.

Like a guided arrow, the ball flew through the tire's opening without so much as touching the surrounding rubber. When it rolled to a stop in the distance, I looked at John.

"Still have quite an arm on you, Sir."

"Come out here every chance I get. Keeps my head straight." He reached for another ball and then looked at me. "Ever miss the sport?"

I'd spent eighteen years trying to forget entirely that football existed. Sharing my story with Jo was allowing me to heal, but I still grew extremely frustrated when thinking about the sport.

"Not so much. No."

His gaze fell to his feet. After a moment, he looked up. "I'm not asking you to talk about it, but I feel like I need to say something. Hard for me not to, knowin' what I know now."

I had no idea what he was talking about. I shrugged. "Okay."

"Jo told us about what happened to your father. Goes without saying, but I'll say it anyway. I'm sorry, Son. I truly am."

I sighed. "It's been eighteen years. I'll never forget it, but it doesn't eat on me like it used to."

He raised the ball over his right shoulder. "My father wasn't murdered, but I lost him when I was a youngster. I still feel like I was robbed of what I was entitled to." He threw a perfect spiral toward the tire. Like the first, it flew right through the center. "Ain't a day go by that I don't miss spendin' time with that man."

He picked up a ball and handed it to me. Before I could resist, I was holding it.

I hadn't held a football since the day of my father's death. Although I would have expected it to feel awkward, it didn't. I hoisted its weight, squeezed it, and grinned. "Feels pretty good for four bucks."

He nodded toward my hand. "You gonna squeeze that thing like a titty, or are you gonna throw it?"

I doubted I could match John's accuracy and stammered to make an excuse not to throw the ball. "I haven't had a football in my hand since the day my father died."

He picked up another ball. "You said the day I met you that your father loved the sport."

"He did."

"Did you make him proud? When you played, that is."

My father told me every day how proud he was of me and my abilities. "Very much so," I replied.

"Do you believe in God?" he asked.

"It's hard to explain," I said. "So, I'll just say *yes*."

"Suppose your father's up there somewhere looking down on you right now?"

I didn't have to think about it. "I do."

"Suppose he'd be proud of you if a sixty-six-year-old man showed you up out here? Out-threw you?"

I hoisted the ball, took aim, and threw it. No differently than John's, it flew right through the center of the tire. Although accomplishing the task would have been meaningless to most, I swelled with pride at what I'd done.

John looked at me and grinned. "Feels good, don't it?"

I nodded. "It does."

He picked up a ball, squeezed it, and then took aim. With the ball hoisted behind his right shoulder, he paused. "Jo told her mother that you two have messed around and fallen in love."

I coughed out a lungful of surprise. "We uhhm. Yes, Sir. We admitted that to each other a few weeks ago. Thirteen days, to be exact."

He threw the ball. As expected, it went through the center of the tire. As it rolled to a stop, he folded his forearms across his chest. "She's always been different, that girl. Scared of her own shadow. I never understood why, but she was. Her mother thought we did something wrong. Held her too much, didn't hold her enough, kept her on the bottle too long, too much time in the crib, *something*. Personally, I always wondered if it was a fear of rejection, or something like that. Suppose I'll never know. I do know this."

He reached into the trough. With is arm hanging at his side and the ball gripped firmly in his hand, he continued. "Men and women these days are different than they were when I was young. They're too quick to get pregnant, get married and get divorced. Being in a relationship's no different than being married. Succeeding requires one to be understanding, forgiving, and, above all, open-minded. Saying 'I love you' is easy, but there's a big responsibility that comes with those three words, and it's damned tough to live up to."

I swallowed heavily. "I don't think I'll have any problems, Sir. Living up to her expectations, that is."

He faced me. "Mind if I ask you why you think that?"

"Can I be honest?" I asked.

He laughed. "Wouldn't expect you to be otherwise."

"After losing my father, I walked away from football. I didn't break my ankle. I wrapped it, made my own plaster cast, and told everyone I'd broken it in the wreck. I couldn't think about playing the game without my father in the stands watching me. He was in the stands during practice, and he was in the stands during every game. I didn't have to look, I *knew* he was there."

Thinking of my father spending so much time sitting on the hard bleachers brought a smile to my face. "It was *our* sport. After my mother left, it brought us together. Without him sitting up there watching me from the stands, I had no desire to continue. I gave up on something I truly loved, and I've spent every day since regretting it. I've spent eighteen years running from the truth and wondering what could have been. I'm not going to make the same mistake again."

I met his gaze. "Walking away from something I love, that is."

He threw the football toward nothing in particular. It tumbled to a stop in the distance. "What could have been?" He shook his head and looked away. "You remind me of myself, Son. All of this." He waved his hand toward the trough and then the tree. "This is me wondering what could have been. There's nothing wrong with wondering. But, when I walk away from this little spot, I forget about what could have been. During the walk back to the house, I always thank the good Lord for what I have."

The sound of a distant bell ringing captured my attention. John glanced toward the house. "Sounds like Jackie's ready for dinner."

The sound resembled what I'd heard from many of the churches I'd driven past during my Sunday drives throughout the state. It was a sound that was impossible to escape.

"That's an impressive bell," I said.

He waved his hand toward the western sky. "I could hear that SOB from the far end of the fields when I was a kid. There's no better reminder of having been graced with another week's blessings than the sound of the Sunday evening dinner bell ringing."

He draped his arm over my shoulder. We faced the house. As we walked, I gave thanks for Jo, her parents, and for my willingness to change. When we reached the driveway, I felt a strange sense of guilt.

I hesitated and gestured toward my car.

"I'll be right in," I said. "I need to grab something."

He turned toward the door. "Don't be long. If she rang that bell, you can bet it's ready to eat."

"I'll be right in."

After he disappeared into the house, I lifted my chin and gazed toward the cloudless sky.

I'm sorry I gave up on football, I just…I couldn't imagine playing without you. I hope you understand.

I lowered my head, took a few steps toward the door, and paused.

I promise you I'll never give up on something I love again.

31

JO

WHILE WAITING for Tyson to get ready, I enjoyed looking at the pictures of him that were on the display in the den. Imagining his father's pride was easy. All one had to do was take a quick look around the room.

I glanced at the many bronze medals that were in the lighted glass case and wondered what they were for. Some had footballs on them, while others did not. In studying them, I realized a portion of them were sitting on top of one of his yearbooks.

I wanted to look in it but didn't dare open the case without his permission.

I paced the room for a few minutes. Curiosity got the best of me. I went the bathroom door and knocked.

"Come on in."

I opened the door a few inches. Tyson stood in front of the mirror, shaving.

"Can I look at what's inside the glass case? I'll put it right back where it goes."

He smiled. "Sure."

"Are you sure?"

"Absolutely." He shaved a swath along the side of his face. "I'll be ready in ten more minutes."

"I'll be in the den, drooling over your pictures."

He blew me a kiss. "Okay."

I closed the door and walked into the den. After carefully opening the door to the case, I picked up the yearbook from his junior year, the last year he played football.

PLANO SENIOR HIGH 1998-1999

I opened the cover and flipped through the pages. After finding the index, I was pleased to see that Tyson was pictured on sixteen pages.

I went from picture to picture, feeling as if I'd been given an opportunity to take a glimpse into Tyson's life long before I knew him. His hair was longer, he looked younger, and he was much smaller. Even so, he was undeniably Tyson.

I wondered if he knew me during high school if we would have fallen in love. After remembering that we were six years apart in age, I decided it must have been fate that kept us apart until the time was right.

After looking at all sixteen pictures more than once, I flipped through the pages, searching for Shawn. After finding his class photo and learning his name, I looked through his photos as well.

I laughed knowing he now wore the exact same haircut he wore in school. As I went to close the book, it fell open to a page that was filled with personal notes that had been written to Tyson. Despite my desire to read them, I closed the book.

I carried it back to the case and leaned down to put it on the shelf. Curiosity tickled at my ability to resist. Eventually, I decided to read one page of notes, just to learn a little more about the man I loved.

I read the first passage that caught my attention.

TJ,

Congrats on the yardage, bro. Go Wildcats! Seniors next year, and I can't friggin' wait. Maybe you can get Garber to wrap those DSLs around your Johnson this summer. If you do, I want to hear all about it.

Class of '00 Rocks!

Binter

I knew what DSLs were, but I had no idea who *Garber* was. In wondering what Tyson's junior year sweetheart looked like, I went to the index and looked up the name 'Garber'.

Suzette Garber 21, 34, 47, 68, 101, 119, 121, 145, 161, 190, 211, 217, 232, 255

She was nearly as popular as Tyson. I eagerly flipped to page twenty-one, just to see what she looked like.

Upon opening the book to that page, my mouth fell open.

My twin sister was looking back at me.

Dressed in dark slacks, a white button-down blouse, and what looked like a two-inch pair of heels, she was wearing glasses that could have very well been a pair of my own. Her hair was even cut like mine.

Shocked, I flipped to the next page, and then the next. Upon getting to page two hundred and fifty-five, I learned that she wasn't a student, she was the librarian.

Then, like a punch to the stomach, Shawn's words from the night in the Mexican restaurant came back to me.

"Librarian. You're the naughty librarian."

I felt dirty. Used. Cheap. I tossed the yearbook on the couch, stood, and stomped to the bathroom.

Without knocking, I pushed the door open. Wrapped in a towel, and in the middle of rubbing lotion on his arms, Tyson looked up.

I cocked my hip and glared. "Do you want to tell me who Garber is?"

His Adam's apple rose, and then fell. "Huh?"

"Garber," I snarled. "The librarian. Binter wanted you to let him know if she sucked your dick with her 'DSLs' during summer break. Remember?"

"Jo, it's coincidental," he stammered. "She was just the librarian. I didn't—"

"Save it," I snapped back. "It's far from coincidental.

Remember when Shawn said, 'you're the naughty librarian'? Well, I do. That was right before I wrapped my DSLs around your cock the first time. Why don't you call Binter and tell him about that?"

I slammed the door.

With tear-filled eyes, I stomped to my car. While Tyson stood at the front door wrapped in a towel, my DSLs and I backed out of his driveway for what I was sure would be the last time.

32

TYSON

SHAWN TOSSED the yearbook onto the loveseat. "I hate to say, 'I told you so', but *I told you so*."

I was hurting from areas I had no idea possessed pain receptors. Even my *soul* ached. "I'm not looking to get a fucking lecture," I complained. "I'm here for advice."

"I already told you. The cowgirl said she's madder'n fuck and doesn't want to ever see you again."

I pressed the heels of my palms against my temples. "She won't answer my calls, or texts. I've been by her house twice. I just need to explain everything to her."

"What the fuck are you going to tell her?" he asked. "That you picked her out of the crowd, so you could fantasize about drilling your high school spank bank queen?"

I stood up and shot him a glare. "Fuck you."

"It's true."

I turned toward the kitchen. "You're an asshole."

"Truth's a bitch, ain't it?"

I spun around. "Who the fuck are you to tell me how to fix a broken relationship, anyway? You bang chicks like you're turning yourself in on Monday to start a life-long prison sentence."

"But I tell 'em the truth," he said. "How many times do I have to remind you of that?"

I crossed my arms over my chest and flexed my biceps in anger. "What the fuck are you saying? That I should have told her she reminded me of Garber on the day I met her?"

"If you didn't want this to happen, yeah." He looked me up and down, and then shook his head. "Either that, or you never should have told her you loved her."

"But I do love her."

He twisted his mouth to the side and stood. "I'd say you fucked up, then. Big time."

That was my fear. That I'd fucked up big time. Her likeness to Garber seemed so insignificant when the relationship started. Now? It seemed like I'd been a liar and a creep.

I gave him a look. "If you wouldn't have said anything that night about the naughty fucking librarian, I could have talked my way out of this."

"You fuckin' prick!" He puffed his chest. "Don't you try to spin this and make it my fault. If you had told her the truth from jump street, we wouldn't be having this conversation. You made the decision to do what you did. Be a fuckin' man and own it."

As much as I hated to admit it, he was right.

At the time I met Jo, I had no intention of ever falling in love. My plan was to have sex with her and walk away. How was I to know walking away wouldn't be an option?

I sat down. "My whole body aches."

"From what? Flexin' your fuckin' muscles at me? You're lucky I like you, asshole. I ought to whip your ass."

"Shut the fuck up," I complained. "I need to fix this."

He exhaled a breath through his teeth and shook his head. "Just find another chick to screw, you'll be fine in no time."

"You don't get it, do you? There are no other chicks to screw. I'm done. It's Jo, or it's no one."

He shrugged. "Looks like you're going to be single, bro."

"I can't live without her," I stated. "I've got to fix this."

Since my father's death, there'd been very little I cared about.

My car, my memories of him, and his home. Since meeting Jo, she was *all* I cared about. In her absence, there was nothing else in my life that mattered.

I'd shared things with her that I hadn't shared with anyone. I'd confided things in her I'd spend a lifetime concealing. Having her in my life caused me to admit that I was living life on a collision course with no one other than myself.

Before meeting her, I was my own worst enemy. Through her actions and innocence, she proved to me that I could trust a woman. In trusting her, I realized what a crucial part a woman plays in a man living a rich and rewarding life.

With her came a comfort that I never knew existed. In her presence, I could be me without fear of repercussion. She was kind, caring, and considerate of all those she encountered. She gave while taking nothing. I loved her easily and unconditionally. In return, she loved me equally.

Until I betrayed her trust.

I tilted my head toward the ceiling and covered my face with my hands. "Fuuuuuck!"

33

JO

MY BROKEN soul lay at my feet. Shattered into a thousand pieces, my heart was littered along the sidewalk that led from the driveway to my parent's front door. My trust in mankind had been cast into the Texas wind, leaving me incapable of placing so much as an ounce of faith in anyone I encountered in the future.

The little of me that remained intact came to rest at my mother's side on the front room couch. She raked her fingertips through my hair. "Whenever you feel like talking, Josephine."

I felt so foolish for believing that Tyson was interested in *me*. To think, for one moment, that it was possible showed my vulnerability when it came to mankind in general.

I exhaled an unsteady breath. "I. Hurt. So. Bad."

"Sweetheart, I'm sorry," she said. "But you've got to tell me what happened."

"He..."

"...lied."

She held my head against her chest. "I'm so sorry, sweetheart."

Hoping to find some resemblance of comfort, I pressed the side of my face against her bosom and listened to her heartbeat.

Ba-boom.

Ba-boom.

Ba-boom.

I wanted the pain to stop. My heart to heal. My soul to somehow return to its rightful place. How something that once felt so right could suddenly cripple me into a state of paralysis was hard to believe.

Nonetheless, I was incapable of something as simple as speaking.

Hoping the words came with the passing of time, I watched through the window for the next half hour as the Saturday evening sun fell against the horizon. I let out a sigh of relief, knowing sleep would come soon, during which time the day would pass.

The front door swung open. I looked up. Dressed in his normal work clothes, my father was coming in from a hard day of work in the fields.

He scanned the room and then fixed his eyes on me. "Where's Tyson?"

"At home," I murmured.

Upon realizing I was being held in my mother's arms, he shifted his focus from me to her. "What going on, Jackie?"

"She and Tyson had a fight."

"It wasn't a fight," I said. "We're done. It's over."

"What do you mean *it's over?*" His eyes narrowed. "What happened?"

"It doesn't matter."

"It sure as hell does," he snarled.

"Daddy, it's over," I explained. "It doesn't matter."

"It matters to *me*." He put his hands on his hips and gave me a look. "If you two got in a spat, that's none of my damned business. You'll have a few hundred of them before you realize they're not worth havin'. Until then, learn to like the way they taste."

He folded his arms over his broad chest and lowered his chin. "If he did something to hurt you, that's a different story. I need to know which it is, so I'll know whether to go in my bedroom and get my gun or go in the kitchen and make a sandwich."

"John!" my mother gasped.

"Well, it's the damned truth," he said. "If they had a tiff, it's not your or my business, Jackie. She needs to realize the world outside of her little bubble isn't all butterflies, bubblegum and backgammon."

I couldn't believe what he'd said. My day had been horrible, and I didn't need it to get any worse. "Don't talk about me like I'm in the other room. I'm right here, Daddy."

"Based on the fact you've said nothing," he huffed. "I'm going to make a sandwich."

After he left the room, I looked at my mother. "What's *his* problem?"

"I'm sure part of it is that he likes Tyson," she whispered. "I'm sure he'd just like to see you two work things out."

I sighed. "This isn't something we're going to be able to work out."

"Like I said, dear. When you're ready to talk, I'm ready to listen."

Enough time had passed that I was ready to talk about it, as long as I didn't have to talk to my father. He'd already expressed his belief that I was incapable of dealing with life outside my bubble of butterflies and bubblegum.

I drew a breath and leaned against the arm of the couch. "I was looking in one of his yearbooks and I found a passage written by a friend. He made a comment about Tyson being 'sweet' on someone. I assumed it was a student, but when I looked her up in the book, I found out it was the librarian. And, she looks just like me. *Just like me*. Glasses, hair, clothes, *everything*."

She looked at me as if she expected me to continue. When I didn't, she cleared her throat and placed her hand on my knee. "Sweetheart is that what you're upset about?"

"Wouldn't you be?" I asked. "He's with me because I look like *her*. His friend even said one night that I was the 'sexy librarian'. I had no idea at the time what he was talking about. It all makes sense now. It makes me sick to think about it."

"If he was sweet on the librarian when he was in school, he

must have thought she was pretty. The fact you look like her could be coincidental—"

"It's *not* coincidental."

"Maybe it's not. Tyson would have to answer that, dear."

"I'm not willing to talk to him about it."

"Do you think you might be overreacting?" she asked.

I straightened my posture. "Oh, so, you think I'm living in a bubble of bubblegum and unicorns, too?"

"Sweetheart, when your father and I were in high school, he told me I looked like Audrey Hepburn. He said my lips were better than hers, but he compared me to her. He even called me 'Audrey' sometimes." She smiled. "I saw it as a compliment.?"

I sighed. "That's not the same."

"The hell it's not!" my father bellowed from the kitchen.

I turned around. "Daddy! This is a private conversation!"

Carrying a plate with a half-eaten sandwich in it, he stepped through the threshold of the door and paused.

"No," he said. "It's not."

"Yes, it is."

"You're my daughter," he said in a stern tone. "It's my responsibility to tell you when I see that you're making a mistake. That's what parents do. And, right now, you're making a mistake."

"You're a man," I complained. "Of course, you're going to see it *his* way."

He sat on the loveseat and set his plate on the end table. "He had the hots for the high school librarian. Fifteen years later, he met you. You guys dated for a few months and you fell in love. You found out you look like the librarian. Maybe he has a thing for pretty girls with big butts and black glasses, who knows?"

"John. Wallace. Watson!" my mother screeched.

He glared. "What?"

She forced a dramatic sigh. "I can't believe you, sometimes. How could you say such a thing? She doesn't have a big butt."

His glare lingered for a moment, and then he looked away. "Sometimes I feel like a man can't win. It seems women never understand when a compliment is given. Everything's an insult."

I'd heard enough. I was exhausted, my muscles ached, my eyes were swollen, and I needed some rest.

"I need to sleep on it." I stood. "I'm going to my room."

"Your room is filled with your mother's crap."

"I'm going in there anyway."

"One question before you go," he said.

"What?" I huffed.

"Do you trust him?"

Before I responded, he corrected himself. "Did you trust him before this happened?"

I hated to admit it, but I did. Wholeheartedly. I nodded. "Yes, I did."

"If you trusted him, you're either gullible as hell or he's a trustworthy man. While you're laying in that mess of a bedroom tonight, why don't you ask yourself which one it is." He reached for his sandwich. "Goodnight, Kidd-o."

34

TYSON

IN MY MIND, the solution was simple.

Provide a detailed description of everything, stopping along the way to apologize any time Jo's eyebrows raised in wonder. Knowing neither life – nor women – were that easy, I opted to heed the shared advice of my brutally honest best friend and an orange-haired shopping mall jewelry clerk.

Just in case.

I drew a breath, paused, and then pressed the doorbell.

The door opened. John's mouth twisted into a smirk. "You've got your work cut out for you."

I gazed beyond him. From what I could see, the room was empty. "What do you mean?" I whispered.

"She's as stubborn as a mule, operatin' on about two hours sleep, and nuttier than a squirrel turd when it comes to understandin' men. Hell, the day's damned near shot to hell, and she's still wearin' the pajamas her mother gave her." He nodded toward my hand. "Those flowers might not hurt matters, though."

"Can I come in?"

He stepped to the side. "Sorry. I haven't got my wits about me this afternoon. It was a long night."

Jo stepped into the doorway that led into the living room. Wearing a pair of green and red plaid pajamas that were three sizes too small, she looked like utter hell. She glanced at the flowers I held, and then looked at me.

"What are you doing here?"

"Five minutes," I said. "That's all I want. Five minutes to explain. When I get done, you can either let me join you for dinner, or ask me to leave."

She twisted her wild hair into a bun and nodded toward the loveseat. "Okay."

John gestured to the couch. "Mind if I—"

"Yes, I do," she said, stepping aside as she spoke. "Go help Mother, please."

"Fine." He reached for the vase of flowers I held. "May I?"

I doubted Jo would accept them. I gave him a nod of appreciation. "Sure."

Flowers in hand, he stomped in Jo's direction, pausing as he reached her. "Man's got taste," he said, eyeing the flowers. "It's not every day you see an arrangement with hyacinth, jasmine, and lilies. A simpleton would have brought roses."

Jo's eyes followed the vase of flowers as he walked past her. After he was gone, she sat at the couch and fixed her eyes on the floor between us.

I sat across the room from her. "I saw Miss Garber as beautiful, because she *was* beautiful. Anyone that met her would agree. Every boy in school had a crush on her. It just so happened that you read one of many comments that were written in a yearbook that I made no effort to hide from you, because I have *nothing to hide from you.*" I cleared my throat. "For the sake of clarification, she and I never shared one physical moment together."

Her pursed lips parted slightly. "Okay..."

"The similarities you share with Miss Garber are merely coincidental. Did I think you looked like her when I met you? Absolutely. Is that why we're together? Absolutely not. At first, I thought you'd be like every other girl in my life. We'd hang out for a while, we'd have sex, and then we'd go our separate ways. That was my *modus operandi*. That is, until *you*."

"From the moment my father died until the moment I realized I loved you, all I've done is exist. After realizing I loved you, I opened my eyes to the world around me and began living life for the first time. I now have an unobstructed view of the world, of you, and of our future. I want different things out of life since realizing I love you."

"Like what?" she asked.

"A different job. A new pair of boots. Sunday dinners. Marriage. An opportunity to prove to my children that a relationship can last a lifetime. I guess when you get right down to it, I want to start living a life that I'm sharing with you."

She pulled a strand of hair from her bun and began twisting it around her finger. "When did you realize you loved me?"

"Remember when I said we needed to begin and end with a kiss?"

She smiled. "I do."

"It was then," I said. "At that exact minute, I think."

Her gaze fell to her feet. After a moment, she looked up. "I'm sorry about what happened. I think I may have overreacted when I saw that stuff in your yearbook."

"I'm sorry that I wasn't one hundred percent truthful with you from the start," I replied. "Am I forgiven?"

She stopped twisting her hair. "Am I?"

I nodded. "Absolutely."

"So are you." She stood and opened her arms. "Let's start over."

I stepped in her direction. "With a kiss."

We met in the middle of the room and embraced in a kiss. I closed my eyes and inhaled her sweet scent. My mind, as it did every time I kissed her, escaped me. When I held her in my arms, I had no comprehension of the passing of time or my surroundings.

Before I was satisfied that the kiss should end, a flicker of light began to flash repeatedly beyond my closed eyelids. Wondering if I, too, was becoming *nuttier than a squirrel turd*, I opened my eyes.

Behind Jo, just inside the doorframe, a weathered hand was

flipping the light switch on and off at a rapid rate. I broke our embrace and grinned.

She opened her eyes.

The lights continued to flicker on and off.

Jo sighed. "Daddy, stop it."

"We need to eat before the food's cold," John said. "You two can swap spit when we're done."

I gave Jo a quick peck and turned toward the kitchen. As we reached John, he stepped aside and allowed Jo to walk past. He then raised his hand to my shoulder. "We'll be there in a minute."

"Okay," she said.

He patted me on the back. "You did good, Son."

"Thank you."

"Two things for future reference." He draped his arm over my shoulder. "One, Jo's of the opinion that her butt ain't big, so don't ever say it is. And, two, I'm ready for grandkids whenever you are."

35

JO

WHISTLING a song that I recognized but couldn't name, Jenny walked into the store in a particularly cheery mood.

"Did you have a good weekend?" I asked.

She smiled. "I did."

I gestured toward her cut-offs. They were short enough that much more of her extremities were out than in. "I like the shorts, are they new?"

"They are."

She was wearing a white tee shirt with the album cover of Jamey Johnson's first album on it. I hadn't seen her wear it before.

"And the shirt?" I asked.

She pulled the hem away from her waist, straightening the fabric of the shirt for me to see. "New shirt, and...." She hiked her leg high in the air and pulled the crotch of her shorts to the side, revealing a pink patch of lace. "New panties, too."

"I'm guessing you went shopping?"

"That, and a bunch of other things."

"What's the song you were whistling?" I asked.

"The Andy Griffith Show."

"How'd you get that stuck in your head?"

"Shawn and I binge-watched about fifty episodes of it. Life was simple back then. You know it?"

Despite my desire to watch other things, I'd seen enough episodes of the show as a child to know what she was talking about.

"It's not simple now, that's for sure."

"Have you watched it?" she asked.

"I've seen it," I said. "With my dad when I was little. I never really paid attention to it, though."

"It's pretty cool. Each show has a lesson. In one of them, the little boy got a slingshot. He told Barney that he was going to use it to shoot tin cans. He ended up shooting it up in a tree and killing a bird. His dad made him take care of the three baby birds that were orphaned when he killed their mother. So, he took care of them until they could fly on their own. Then, he set them free. There's a crap-load of lessons to be learned from that one episode alone."

I really didn't care to discuss the Andy Griffith Show. I turned toward a box of books I was unpacking. "Sounds like you guys had fun."

"I like hanging out with him." She reached for one of the books. "So, what did you do this weekend?"

If she spent all weekend with Shawn watching TV, I found it odd that he hadn't told her what happened. I wondered if she knew but was acting as if she didn't.

"Broke up with Tyson," I said.

Her eyes shot wide. "What?"

"I broke up with him Saturday night."

"Ho-Lee-Shit," she gasped. "What happened?"

I wanted to explain the event as it unfolded and see what she thought of my reaction. Convinced I'd overreacted, but not sure to what degree I'd done so, I wanted her unbiased opinion.

"I found an old yearbook of his," I explained. "While I was flipping through it I found out there was a teacher that he was sweet on. A teacher that looked exactly like me."

"The librarian?" she asked.

"What?" I screeched. "You *knew*?"

"Knew what? That they had a smokin' hot librarian when they

were in school? Yeah, Shawn showed me a picture of her. Sorry, go back to your story, I didn't mean to interrupt."

"That *was* my story."

"*What* was your story?"

I was afraid I already had the answer to my question. "I found that picture, and a passage in his yearbook that said, 'If you get her to suck your dick with those DSLs, let me know', or something like that. I got mad and stomped out of his house."

She scrunched her nose. "We smoked a lot of pot this weekend, I'm sorry. Did I miss something? Tell me you didn't leave him over one of his high school buddies making a comment about that hot librarian sucking his dick."

I stared back at her, expressionless.

"You didn't, did you?"

I shrugged one shoulder.

"Jesus, Jo. Really?"

I felt like such an inexperienced fool. I'd never been in an actual relationship. At the time, it seemed like a natural reaction to the situation. After I had time to think about it, however, it seemed a little harsh.

I nodded.

"Overreact much?" she asked, her tone thick with sarcasm.

"I did, didn't I?"

"I'm thinking so," she said. "Not that it really matters, but did he get a BJ from the her? Did he say?"

"He did say. He didn't."

She blew out a slow, exaggerated breath. "Uhhm. Yeah, I'd say you overreacted. Like. *Yeah*."

I needed to redeem myself. For her to at least agree with part of why I got angry. "What about the guy saying Tyson should get her to wrap her DSLs around his dick, or whatever?"

"Did you see that chick's lips?" she asked. "If I had a dick, I'd have spent all my spare time during the summer trying to get her to suck it, I can tell you that much." She shook her head. "You've got to tell him you overreacted. That you're sorry. He was in high school, for Christ's sake. That was like, what? Twenty years ago?"

"Eighteen."

"You can't let that get between you guys," she said, still shaking her head in disbelief. "I'm sorry, but that's just kind of ridiculous. In a book, something like that might cause a breakup, but not in real life. Just tell him you overreacted."

"I already did."

"You already did *what?*"

"I already told him I overreacted."

"Is he still mad?"

"No. He came over to my parent's house yesterday and apologized."

"For *what?*" She laughed. "Being a horny teenager?"

Instead of redeeming myself, I was being ridiculed. My lack of relationship experience was showing, and I didn't like it.

"For not being truthful with me from the beginning." I forced a long sigh. "I'm an idiot, aren't I?"

"Not an idiot." She chuckled. "Maybe a little bit of a psycho, but not an idiot."

I'd rather be an idiot than a psycho. I regretted saying anything about anything. To anybody. Jenny included. "A psycho? Why do you say that?"

"If you've got to ask, that just makes you more psycho."

"Well, if it makes you happy, I apologized, too."

"That's good." She tugged at the nonexistent hem of her shorts "You should give him a big sloppy BJ. Maybe he'll forgive you."

I'd redeemed myself with Tyson. I was determined to do the same with Jenny, come hell or high water. I expected revealing my lack of relationship experience should suffice.

"He's only the second guy I've ever had sex with," I admitted.

"I'm sorry." She raised her cupped right hand to her ear. "I thought you just said you were two dicks away from being a virgin."

"That's what I said."

She lowered her hand and gave me a look. "You're kidding, right?"

"I wish I was."

She looked me over as if she didn't know me. "Are you seriously being serious right now?"

"Totally."

"Ho-Lee-Shit." She put her hands on her hips and looked me up and down. "It's no wonder you reacted like you did. You're basically a thirteen-year-old."

I was getting vindication for my reaction, but it was embarrassing as hell.

"The first guy was at my cousin's wedding," I said. "I was eighteen."

"Wait. How old are you now?"

"Twenty-nine."

Her eyes bulged. "You went eleven years without sex?"

"Roughly."

She tugged against the hem of her shorts. "These things feel like they're eating my twat." After getting them situated to a point that she at least appeared to be comfortable again, she let out a soft sigh. "Guys can't wait for sex like that. They need sexual maintenance. Just like regular oil changes in your car."

"What do you mean?" I asked.

"They have urges. Constant urges. Itches that need scratched. They're much different than we are. There are things you need to do, whether they ask for it, or not."

I wanted sex all the time. I couldn't imagine anyone having a greater desire. If a man's chemical makeup was such that he had sexual itches that needed scratched, I needed to know about it. Having my relationship with Tyson collapse due to me not maintaining it, it would crush me.

"You know this for a fact?"

"Listen. I had two dicks in me by the time I was thirteen. I'm ten years ahead of you." She arched an eyebrow. "It's regular maintenance, and yes, it's fact."

I'd entertain any advice that allowed me to glide through a life with Tyson without turmoil. "Okay. What do I need to do?"

"I'll do my best to explain it," she said. "Imagine your clit being, I dunno, like the size of a bratwurst. Everywhere you go, the thing is swinging around in your pants, banging against your leg, falling out of your shorts, stuff like that."

I laughed. "Okay."

"It's got, who knows, something like ten million more pleasure receptors in it, because it's so freakin' big. So, when you touch it, it sends a bajillion happy signals to your brain in an instant. When a guy sucks on it you go completely bonkers. Ape shit, or whatever. Your eyes roll back in your head, and all you can think about is him sucking it again. In fact, you're infatuated with it."

I stared blankly at her.

"You've had your clit sucked, right?"

"Uhhm." I shook my head. "No."

She wagged her index finger toward my purse. "Write it down. Make it first on the list. You've got to get him to do that."

I chuckled. "Where are you going with this story?"

"I'm almost there."

"Okay."

"So, if you had that big bratwurst clit, all you'd be able to think about would be sex, right? Especially having a dude suck your clit."

"I can't imagine a bratwurst clit. All I think about is sex, and mine's the size of my pinky finger."

"Pinky finger!?" Her eyes narrowed. "Mine's so small a guy needs a microscope and a map to find it."

"A road map?" I laughed. "That sucks. Mine's not really *that* big, it just seems like it is. It's definitely not hard to find."

"Tell me about it." She tugged the hem of her shorts and then shook her right leg as if she expected something to fall out of it. "Anyway. If you've got the sausage-clit, you'd be about even with a dude. They've got two pounds of dick swinging between their legs twenty-four-seven. Each time they see it, it's a constant dangling reminder that they're *not* fucking someone. Every hour of every day, they're trying to devise a way to get that thing busy. The easiest way to do it is to stick it in someone's mouth. I guess what I'm trying to say is that you can't blame Tyson for having thoughts about poking his dick in that sexy librarian's mouth. Or for the other guy mentioning it. It's all they think about. Have him suck your pinkie-sized clit, and you'll know what I mean."

I knew guys enjoyed blowjobs, but I had no idea just how much they liked them. I mentally added getting Tyson to suck my clit to our evening's activities, just so I'd be privy to the information.

I gave a nod. "Okay. I'll see if he will do it tonight."

"Good. And, another thing." She chuckled. "You've gotta give it up more than once every eleven years."

I laughed. "I know."

"Remember. He's got a constant reminder dangling between his legs. If he doesn't get it from you, he'll get it somewhere else."

I didn't plan on making Tyson wait any longer for sex than it took for me to get undressed when I got home at night. Nonetheless, I was fascinated. "What happens if he doesn't?"

"His balls will turn blue."

"I've heard of that. Blue Balls."

"Precisely," she said. "When it happens, they've got to go to the hospital and get a nurse to extract it."

"Extract what?"

"The cum."

"Why don't they just." I made the jerking motion with my hand. "You know."

"Too painful."

"Wouldn't it be just as painful if a nurse did it?"

"They sedate the guys before they do it. They probably get the interns to actually do the whacking." She chuckled. "How'd you like that job? Whack off nurse?"

I shrugged. "I've never done it."

"You've never whacked a dude off?"

"Nope. I've pretty much done everything else, though."

"Everything except for having a guy suck your clit and giving a hand-job." She gestured to my purse. "Hand-job. Put that on the list, too."

I grinned. "Okay."

"Hand-jobs are awesome, because you're in charge, and you can see your successes. It's not very often that you can be sure that you've pleased a man."

"Tyson has an orgasm every time we have sex," I bragged.

"That doesn't mean that *you* pleased him," she argued. "He might have pleased himself, and you were just the tool he used to do it. The only way to know if *you* please a man is to give him a handy."

"That's the *only* way?"

"He can fuck your pussy, and he can fuck your mouth, but *you* drive the hand-job, one hundred percent. It's the only way to know."

I'd never looked at it that way. It made perfect sense. "That makes sense."

"With a hand-job, you know you're in complete charge. If you can make a guy come with a handy, you're set. It's a good thing to fall back on from time to time. It builds self-esteem, too. Nothing's more satisfying than watching cum shoot out of the tip of a guy's dick."

"Thanks for all the help," I said. "I'll watch some hand-job videos this afternoon."

"It's the least I can do," she curtsied. "I was like you once. When I was twelve."

I was grateful that I had a wealth of sexual knowledge to spend my days with, even if she did occupy her idle time smoking pot and watching Andy Griffith.

"She actually believes the crap she tells you?" Tyson reached into the refrigerator and grabbed a bottle of beer. "That's the most ridiculous shit I've ever heard in my life."

I wondered if it was truly ridiculous, or if he was afraid to tell me that I'd learned the sexual secrets of what made men tick. "Nobody goes to the doctor and gets the pressure relieved?"

He tossed the lid to his beer bottle in the trash. "Nope."

"Ever?"

He shook his head. "Nope."

"How do you know?"

"Because I have a dick."

We sat down across from each other at the kitchen table. "Maybe you haven't had a massive buildup," I suggested. "How long is the longest you've gone without, you know, having an orgasm or whatever?"

"Forty-eight hours." He sipped his beer. "Maybe less. Definitely not more than two days."

I wasn't surprised. Before I met Tyson, I masturbated a few times a week, unless I was distracted by work. It seemed reasonable to think men would be the same way.

I gestured toward his crotch with my eyes. "Maybe if you went a few weeks without any relief, you'd bulk up down there."

"I'm not willing to find out." He took a long drink of his beer and then set the bottle aside. "What else did she tell you? Sperm's got protein in it?"

"Does it?" I asked excitedly.

He shook his head. "Nope."

Saddened I wasn't going to enhance my daily protein intake from sucking Tyson's dick, I lowered my head. Midway through my session of sulking, I remembered Jenny's recommendation.

"Oh," I blurted. "She said I need to get you to suck my clit. That way I'll have a good idea of what it's like to have a dick."

"How will having me suck your clit..." He shook his head. "She's insane."

Saddened that he'd let the air out of my clit-sucking sail, I slumped in my seat.

"What's wrong?" he asked.

"Nothing." A sigh escaped me, and I tried to pass it off as a yawn. "I'm fine."

"Seriously? I don't want to get in another tiff about something. About anything. Let's keep everything out in the open. You're not going to get in trouble with me for talking about *anything*. Spill it, Jo."

I took a breath and then fixed my eyes on his fruit-filled blown glass centerpiece. "I really wanted to find out about the clit-sucking. She said it was a must. I've been excited about it all day."

"That's what you're upset about?" He laughed. "Hell, I'll suck your clit until your eyes pop out. But that doesn't mean you're going to walk away with the knowledge of what it's like to have a dick. What does one have to do with the other?"

"Sensory receptors or something," I responded. "She said your dick has a million of 'em, and that's why guys like blowjobs so much. She said if a girl gets her clit sucked, she'll understand why guys have got to have sex all the time. It's like getting your oil changed in your car."

He fixed his eyes on mine, then slow-blinked. Repeatedly. "I'm not." He shook his head. "I'm not even going to comment."

"So, it's true?"

"If she said it," he said with a laugh. "It must be."

The thought of his mouth on my clit had me squirming in my seat like an antsy eight-year-old on Christmas Eve. "When do you want to do it?"

He downed his beer in one gulp. After raking his fingers through his hair, he met my gaze. "How about now?"

I smiled. "Now works for me."

His eager response sent blood rushing to my nether regions. I looked around the room. "Just tell me where you want me."

He rested his chin against the palm of his hand. "Based on your level of excitement, I'm going to guess this is a first for you."

I smiled. "Yep."

He stood and gestured to toward my knees. "Hike that dress up around your waist, pitch the panties, and kick your feet up on the table."

I swallowed heavily. "Right here?"

"Right here."

I exhaled a long, nervous breath. "Okay."

With my heels resting on the table, my bare ass resting on the edge of the kitchen chair, and my dress wadded in a ball at my waist, I gazed between my legs and waited anxiously.

After jockeying into position, Tyson looked up and smiled.

"I have no idea what to do," I said. "So, you'll need to guide me through this."

He popped his neck. "Just close your eyes and enjoy."

"Do I have to close my eyes?"

He glanced between my legs. "You can watch if you want."

I smiled guiltily. "Okay."

He wedged his shoulders between my knees and lowered his face toward my happy place. Taken by complete surprise, I sucked a breath as he inserted a finger and bit my lip when he added another. After bringing me to near climax, he slid his fingers free of my confines.

His breath against my wetness caused me to tremble with excitement.

Filled with wonder, I pushed my wadded dress to the side and gazed between my legs. His mouth encompassed the upper portion of my mound. A jolt of excitement ran through me. Other than the top of his head, there wasn't much to see, but knowing his mouth was on my cootch was enough to drive me wild with anticipation.

Then, something happened. Something of epic sexual proportion.

What in the…

It happened again.

Micro-convulsions raced through me.

My eyes shot wide.

I resisted at first, squirming each time his lips or tongue met my sensitive nub. Softly and gently, he continued. I embraced the magic, pushing my pussy hard against his mouth. Deep within me, pressure built until I feared I'd burst into a million little pieces.

It had only been a minute since he'd started, and I doubted I could last for another. A decade of exploring myself had produced numerous sensations, none of which were anything like what I was experiencing.

I closed my eyes and channeled my focus. Predictably, his tongue flicked against my clit. *Suck, flick, suck, flick, suck, flick…*

Mere seconds later, a wave of emotion engulfed me. I pressed myself hard against his mouth and prayed he continue doing exactly what it was that brought me to the pinnacle of sexual pleasure.

Blindly, my hands flailed about, searching for something to grab. After finding nothing, they landed on either side of Tyson's whiskered face.

I gripped his head in my hands and arched my back.

Like a spring storm's raindrops against a window, small sensations tapped away at the surface of my skin until everything was tingling.

My body convulsed. Muscles tensed.

My eyes opened wide, but I saw nothing. Then, the tension escaped me, leaving me as nothing but a puddle of exhausted emotion seated at a kitchen table.

I glanced between my legs.

Tyson looked up. His mouth glistened with my juices.

"Kiss me," I said.

He pushed my chair away from the table and leaned over me.

I lifted my head and pressed my lips to his.

The musky scent of my satisfaction tickled my nose. A hint of his cologne followed. He straddled my thighs. Feverishly, I kissed him, eagerly sucking my juices from his lips.

We'd made a pact to start and stop with a kiss. For most, that kiss would have marked the ending of the night's sexual adventures.

For me?

It marked the beginning.

36

TYSON

I PUSHED my hand against the pillow, paused, and then lifted it. Slowly, it took its original shape. "Seems weird," I said. "It doesn't *pop* back into shape. It's really slow."

"Yours are crappy. I don't know where you got them or how long you've had them, but we need to replace them." She nodded toward the pillow. "*That* is how a pillow is supposed to be."

It was my first pillow shopping excursion. I let out a dreadful sigh. "Okay."

"How long have you had them?"

I shrugged. "I don't know."

"They say you should replace good pillows every eighteen months. Crappy ones, every six months."

I laughed to myself. I hadn't replaced my pillows since my father passed. In fact, I hadn't changed anything since his death. I still had the same dishes, the same furniture, the same bedding, and the same *everything*.

Fearing repercussion if I admitted it, I gestured to the pillows in question. "Let's get these, then."

We'd spent the last several weeks alternating nights at each other's homes. Most of Jo's nights in my home were spent sleeping without a pillow. After her first complaint, I agreed to replace the old pillows with new ones. If it took pillows for her to feel comfortable in my home, I'd fill it with them.

"It's probably why you pop your neck all the time," she said.

"What is?"

"Sleeping on those awful pillows."

"They're not awful."

"They're polyester, and they feel like they're a million years old. Your shoulder's more comfortable."

"Should we get bedding, too?"

"Can you afford to?" she asked. "I can pitch in. I don't mind."

I didn't make it known, but the wrongful death settlement I'd received from the Sherriff's department set me up for life. Inheriting my father's investments were icing on the financial cake.

I'd taken the job at FedEx for one reason only – because it exposed me to horny housewives. Horny housewives minimized the chances of someone falling in love with me. Servicing the women on my route left my evenings and weekends free. The decision to take the job was a no-brainer.

I now felt like a douchebag for ever thinking it was a good idea.

"I can afford it," I said. "Let's pick some out."

An hour of paisley prints, chevron patterns, and floral designs later, and we still hadn't made a decision. Shopping was definitely a girl's passion, but I couldn't imagine Jo doing it without me. One of the many sacrifices I expected I'd make to spend a lifetime with her at my side.

"I can't decide," she said. "I like them all."

"Maybe pick two," I suggested. "And we can rotate them."

Her eyes beamed with excitement. "Can we?"

I wanted the home to be *ours*. It was my first step in that direction. "Sure."

My commitment to buy pillows and bedding somehow morphed into bed sets that included big pillows, small pillows, overstuffed pillows, slender pillows, round pillows, and pillows that were actually *pillows*. In fact, we'd purchased so much bedding that taking it home in my car wasn't an option.

Four hours later, as the delivery truck backed into the driveway, Jo jumped from her position on the couch and ran across the living room.

Brimming with excitement, she stood in the doorway with her hands covering her mouth. "I can't believe it's here."

"They said they'd bring it before six," I said. "How can you not believe they're here?"

"It's so exciting," she exclaimed.

Being with Jo was a constant reminder that excluding sex, I knew nothing of what it took to make a woman happy. Seeing her elated over something as simple as bedding hinted at who she truly was. Her desires didn't venture beyond life's necessities. She was a modest woman with minimal needs, most of which I could satisfy by simply providing her with my love and affection.

We spent the evening washing the new bedding, stripping the bed, re-making it, and arranging the pillows. When we were done, she stood in the corner of the room and admired her handiwork.

"Now *I* want new bedding," she said.

I stared at the mountain of pillows, confused. "You have new bedding."

"I mean for me," she replied. "This stuff is yours."

"It's *ours*."

"It just seems weird. There's *your* house, and there's *my* house," she argued. "I don't feel like I live in either one of them. It's like I'm in limbo, or whatever."

Strangely, I felt the same way. Early in our relationship, I liked the separation. Knowing at the end of the day that I could retire to the comfort and solitude of my own home. I now had no desire to spend so much as a single night without her.

"We need to think about consolidation," I said.

"What do you mean?"

We'd silently made the decision to sleep at each other's homes. A few nights here and a few nights there was getting old. It was time we discussed taking our relationship one step further.

"This is, I don't know, kind of silly," I said. "We sleep at your house for a few days, sleep here for a few days. We need to get our

257

heads together and decide what we're going to do. We need to pick a place and live there."

She gasped. "Move in together?"

I looked at the pillow pile. In the past few minutes, it seemed to have multiplied. "Yeah. Like normal people."

"My home is perfect," she said excitedly. "It's older, but the bedrooms are much bigger. The kitchen's just been redone, too."

I hadn't given moving into her home any consideration, whatsoever. Moving away from the home my father raised me in seemed like an impossible task.

"I was thinking we'd live here," I said.

"Oh." Her eyes searched the room before meeting mine. "We can talk about it."

I nodded toward the pillow pile. "Maybe sleep on it."

She smiled. "With our new pillows?"

"*Our* new pillows," I said. "I like the way that sounds."

37

JO

ONE OF MY fondest memories of my parent's home was the smell of breakfast being cooked. Nothing made me get out of bed on a weekend morning quicker than a hint of my mother's cooking.

I opened the oven and wafted the odor of the bacon toward the bedroom. A few minutes later, while I was contemplating waking him up, Tyson stumbled into the kitchen.

"Those new pillows are amazing," he said. "I slept like a baby."

"Well, after sleeping on them at the other house, I only thought it was fitting that we get them here."

"Is that bacon?" He stepped up behind me and peered over my shoulder. "Smells good."

"Until you give me a kiss, it's off-limits," I said.

He rested his hands on my waist and gave me a light peck on the cheek. "You cooked it in a cookie sheet?"

"It cooks evenly that way. Four hundred degrees for sixteen minutes, and it's perfect," I said. "You can cook a bunch of it at once, too."

He reached around me and snatched up two pieces. "I love bacon."

"Everyone loves bacon."

Before meeting Tyson, I never understood the satisfaction my mother seemed to get from cooking. Now, everything made sense. Short of sex, nothing equaled the feeling of preparing a meal for a man and having him express satisfaction while devouring it.

I placed the skillet on the burner. "Over medium?"

"It's the way God eats his eggs," he said with a laugh. "That's what my dad told me when I was little. In my dreams, I envisioned a man with a big gold robe, long gray hair, and a scruffy beard mopping up the yolks with dry whole wheat toast."

"God eats dry whole wheat toast?"

"I thought so."

"That's funny. He wears a gold robe, too?"

"When I was a kid, I had this image of him conjured up. Gray hair, salt and pepper beard, weathered skin. Tan. Actually, I think the robe was burgundy with gold trim. And, he wore sandals. No pants."

I tossed a slice of butter in the skillet and glanced over my shoulder. "God goes commando?"

"I didn't give that much thought. He didn't wear pants, though. Not in my mind."

"Shorts?"

"Nope," he said. "Just a robe."

"Sitting around in his robe eating eggs over medium?"

"It's funny. I ate scrambled eggs until dad told me that. He always ate them over medium, and I thought they looked like big yellow eyes. I asked him why he ate them that way, and he said, 'that's the way God eats them'. After that, I couldn't eat a scrambled egg, knowing God ate his over medium. I've eaten them over medium since."

"Sitting around in his robe," I said with a laugh. "What kind of chair does God sit in? Or, what did he sit in when you conjured up this childhood image?"

"Throne," he said matter-of-factly. "Carved of the finest wood. The legs were like a lion's leg."

"He sat in a fine wood throne and wore a robe. Did he drink milk?"

"Wine."

"With breakfast?"

"With everything," he said. "He got it at the liquor store, right inside the pearly gates"

"What was his mode of transportation?" I asked. "A chariot?"

He smiled. "Of sorts."

"Let me guess." I tapped the tip of my index finger against my lip and gazed at the ceiling. After a moment of phony contemplation, I met Tyson's gaze. "He drove a Cobra?"

"Back then he drove a Mustang GT. He didn't start driving a Cobra until I got a little older."

Loving Tyson came easily. In many respects, he was still the child his father abandoned. He was thirty-five years old and hadn't been given an opportunity to share his life, his stories, or his beliefs with anyone.

I liked that I had become that person.

"I love you," I said.

He kissed me again, this time for real. "I love you, too."

After cooking our breakfast, I placed the plates at the breakfast nook table. "You better hurry, or you're going to be late for work, mister."

"I've reached a point that I'm kind of ready for them to fire me."

I looked up. "What?"

He sat down. "I'm over it."

"Over what? Working there?"

He cut through the edge of one of his eggs. "Yeah."

I was shocked. I suspected he'd retire from FedEx. I couldn't imagine him doing anything else. "I had no idea you were dissatisfied with them."

He poked the egg in his mouth and bit the corner off his toast. "It's a stupid job."

"You've worked there since high school."

"Doesn't make it any better of a job."

"You must have liked it at one point or another."

He gave me a lingering look. "Not anymore."

"What will you do?"

"I don't know." He looked away. "I'm thinking about it."

"So, there's change on the horizon?"

He mopped the yolk from his plate with what remained of his toast. "I'm thinking so."

The thought of Tyson making changes was exciting. I desperately wanted him to find a way to see my home as inviting, eventually sell his home, and then move in with me. Until that moment came, I couldn't see it as anything but a pipe dream.

As I nibbled at my bacon I began to wonder if it might someday become reality.

He pushed his plate to the side and took a drink of milk. "That breakfast was spot-on. Just like Pop used to make it."

"Thank you."

"It's difficult as hell to get eggs just the way I like 'em, but you sure do a good job of it."

I smiled. "I'm glad you enjoy them. I think it's that new stove more than anything. They put it in when they re-did the kitchen. Cooking on it is easy."

"Well, whatever you're doing, don't change anything." He finished his milk. "They're just the way I like them."

I swelled with pride. "It's ninety percent appliance, and ten percent cook. Sometimes, I think that new stove could cook things by itself."

"I have my doubts." He stood and reached for his plate. "I'm going to hop in the shower."

"I'll clean up," I said with a dismissive wave of my hand. "You're going to be late if you're not careful."

He came around the edge of the table and kissed me on the neck. "I love you, sweetheart."

"I love you, too."

While he showered, I nibbled my bacon and dreamed.

Not of God driving a Mustang Cobra or eating over medium eggs in his gold-clad robe, but of the day Tyson and I could share a home and eat God's choice of eggs in our very own kitchen.

38

TYSON

JOHN PLUCKED a football from the trough, looked it over, and then let it dangle at his side. "Can't say I know if it really matters. Six months. Twelve months. Eighteen months. Hard sayin' what's *normal*. When the time comes, I 'spect you'll know it."

"I feel like it's already here, and I'm just too set in my ways to accept it."

"Been livin' on your own for half as long as you been on this earth," he said. "Makes sense that you'd be kind of cantankerous when it comes time to make change."

"You aren't opposed to us living together?" I asked. "When the time does come?"

"When the time comes?" He belted out a long belly laugh. "Need I remind you that the two of you have been 'living together' for some time now? Remember, Jo tells her mother *everything*. Then, that woman tells *me* everything." He hoisted the ball, hesitated, and then threw it through the center of the tire. "That chain of events makes me kind of all-knowing."

"I was meaning actually living in *one* home," I explained. "Right now, I feel like I'm sleeping in a hotel half the time."

"Jackie and I moved here when my father fell ill. Hell, we lived here when we got married. At first it seemed strange, living with my wife in the very same home I grew up in."

"Did it?"

"Damned sure did. Making babies in the bedroom you grew up in as a kid ain't an easy task to do, let me tell you. My father had been buried for near a decade by then, and every time we get to feeling a little hanky-panky was a good idea, I could hear him bitchin' at me to keep 'er quiet."

"That's funny."

"Wasn't funny back then," he said with a laugh. "Creepy is what it was."

I certainly didn't have any qualms about making love to Jo in the home I grew up in, but I couldn't help but wonder if she'd feel better living elsewhere. The thought of selling the home scared the hell out of me.

If I did, I feared I'd come to regret it later.

I picked up a football. "Do you ever regret making this place your home?"

He gazed beyond the tire, toward the fields. For a moment, he seemed to get lost in thought. "Only home I've ever known. Personally, I couldn't imagine living anywhere else."

I threw the football, missing the tire entirely.

"That little toss looked like a dying quail." He faced me. "What's on your mind, Son?"

"I think I'm scared."

His eyes narrowed. "Of change?"

"I don't know that it's fear of change, in general," I said. "I think it's a fear of certain changes. Specific things."

"Care to enlighten me a little more?"

"I'm not sure I can bring myself to sell my house."

He shrugged. "Don't."

"Jo loves her home. She goes on and on about how she saved money for her first two years of working so she could afford to remodel the kitchen."

He chuckled. "After she graduated college, she'd spend her

Sundays here lookin' at them damned architectural magazines, circling the pictures of the kitchens she liked. She modeled that kitchen after the ones in those books. Hell, them magazines are still back there, in that old room of hers."

I shook my head. "Asking her to walk away from that seems like a cruel thing to do."

"Her home's too damned small to raise a family in," he said.

"It sure seems like it's what she wants."

"Let me tell you something about women," he said. "Women like a man to make decisions for 'em as opposed to making them on their own. They'll act like they know what they want, but half the time, if a man made a decision for 'em, they'd be much happier. If I told Jackie we were goin' out to eat at a place that fried up dog turds and served 'em on a plate of beansprouts, the only thing she'd ask me is 'what time are were leavin'?' Jo might like that kitchen she has, and she might even have a little attachment to it, but if you told her you were goin' to live in a big cardboard box on the side of seventy-five, right under the bypass, she'd ask you when the move in date was. Women are awfully strange creatures."

I laughed. "You're not going to get any argument from me on that."

He took a seat on the edge of the trough and rested his hands against his knees "My only advice is to be sure and consider Jo's feelings when you're making decisions. No one likes havin' a beansprout covered turd for dinner."

The sound of the dinner bell caused him to stand from his relaxed position.

I turned toward the house, still uneasy regarding my decision, but knowing I needed to make one. John took his normal place at my side and draped his arm over my shoulder.

"Chicken fried steak is back on the rotation tonight," he said. "Man can't complain about a meal like that, can he?"

"No, Sir."

On our walk to the house, I did as John suggested on the first day I'd heard the dinner bell ring.

I thanked the good Lord for what I had. In doing so, I came to realize just how fortunate of a man I was.

By the time we reached the front porch, my decision was made.

39

JO

AFTER ALTERNATING BACK and forth between homes for months, Tyson got sick. So sick that he had to take a week off work. His home was later found to have radon gas leaking into it, which was determined to be the cause of his sickness.

He still couldn't bring himself to sell the home. I feared his attachment to his father's memories would cause us to live in limbo for a lifetime.

My father speared a new potato half and pointed it at Tyson. "I drove by that SOB yesterday. They had it so wrapped up in plastic that you couldn't see what the hell they were doin'. A big white air-up bubble surrounded it, like one of them bouncy houses they have at the fair. Damned thing was as big as a hay barn. Bet them fellas workin' in there are wearing the same suits Neil Armstrong wore when he went to the moon."

I reserved hope that as soon as they declared the home worthy of being occupied that Tyson would clear out his things, bid farewell, and sell it.

"That's what scares me," I said. "I bet they *are* wearing those suits. Radon is radioactive gas. That house could have been built over an old nuclear waste site or something. It makes me sick to think about it."

Tyson raised his fork in protest. "They said radon is emitted from the natural breakdown of uranium in soil, rocks, and ground water. I'm sure it's just coincidental. They'll get it fixed."

"The thought of you sleeping there makes me cringe," I said.

"*Me?*" His eyes narrowed. "After they get it resolved, we'll both be staying there until we figure out what we're doing on a permanent basis."

My heart sank into my bowels. I doubted I couldn't bring myself to ever sleep there again. Making that declaration would crush Tyson, but at some point, I'd have to tell him.

"Bad idea," Jarod argued. "I Googled it. Radon's a killer. I wouldn't stay there no matter what they say. I'd sell it as soon as they wave the green flag."

My mother cleared her throat. "I'm thankful you're doing well, Tyson. I'm sure you'll make the right decision when the time presents itself."

"There's only one decision that's *right*," I argued, nearly bringing myself to tears.

We had made huge strides toward taking the next step in our relationship. At the time Tyson got sick, I was strongly considering selling my home and moving in with him. My house was now our only refuge from the cancer-causing gas that had hospitalized the man I loved.

Tyson nonchalantly poked at his roast, and then lifted a chunk to his mouth. "We'll just have to take a look at it when they're done." He glanced around the table. "We'll make a decision at that time."

There was no value in arguing about it. I didn't want to fight with Tyson, nor did I want to belittle his attachment to his father's home. Recovering from the loss of both parents wasn't something I could imagine. Clinging to the home, and to his father's memories, had been the only resemblance of a family he'd had since his junior year in high school.

Frustrated that I couldn't fix matters, I poked at my food while everyone else ate. For some reason, the Andy Griffith episode Jenny had spoken of many weeks prior came to mind.

Opie had killed the mother of three small birds with his slingshot. Despite the loss of their only caregiver, they survived. Their survival required the love and affection of an outsider, the little boy.

I looked up from my meal. My family was before me, eating their meals, talking, and telling stories as if nothing mattered. Knowing that Tyson was loved by everyone at the table brought a smile to my face.

Through his newfound family, he could survive the loss of his father's home, no differently than the little birds survived the loss of theirs.

The recovery from that loss would simply take time.

Time that I was more than willing to give.

40

TYSON

MY HOME WAS STILL in repair. It had become a matter of contention between Jo and me, often bringing our discussions to near fights. Unwilling to fight with the woman I loved, but equally unwilling to walk away from the home I was raised in, I decided Jo and I needed some time away.

"I think a vacation is exactly what we needed," Jo said.

Standing at the edge of the condo's balcony with the Gulf of Mexico as her backdrop, she looked remarkable.

"Don't move," I said. "I want to take a picture."

"You know I don't like having my——"

"I know, but it's one picture. Just one. Having the sun behind you makes your hair look darker. Just let me take it, and you can decide if you like it."

She sighed. "Okay."

I retrieved my phone from the room, activated the camera, and positioned her in the center of the screen.

While she wetted her full lips and tossed her hair, I snapped a dozen or so pictures.

"Tell me when you're ready," she said.

"I will," I said as I snapped a dozen more. "Just trying to get you centered."

The bikini she wore was flattering, accentuating each and every curve of her amazing body. After taking a few more successive pictures, I told her to smile.

I took a few while she posed for them, knowing I'd prefer the first photos to the latter.

"Done?" she asked.

I nodded, opening the photo gallery as she walked toward me. When she stepped to my side, I offered her the photo I'd selected.

Her fingers were in her hair, her eyes were looking off in the distance, and the tip of her tongue was touching her upper lip. Her glasses, as always, were halfway down the bridge of her nose.

Despite our position on the second floor of the beachfront tower, the only background that could be seen was the sunlit beach.

The photo was worthy of publication.

"Snapped that one by accident when you were getting ready."

She reached for the phone. "Oh, wow. I like that one."

After studying the picture for some time, she shot me a glare.

"What?" I asked.

She pointed the phone's screen at me and thumbed through the three dozen or so photos I'd taken. "Snapped it by accident, huh?"

"*That* one? Yeah. The others were on purpose."

She scrunched her nose. "Fucker."

"I love you, too."

She handed me the phone. "I like that one. You can delete the others."

I accepted the phone, knowing I wouldn't delete any of them. I'd saved every photo of her that I'd taken. Each one marked a place in time during our relationship. In reviewing the photos, I recalled each event, scene, or occasion. With those recollections came memories of the progress we'd made as a couple.

I gave a nod. "Okay."

"What are we going to do tonight?" she asked. "It's our last night here."

We'd been to the aquarium, swam, sunbathed, parasailed, and

gone on two deep sea fishing expeditions. Our days had been filled with so many activities that we hadn't taken so much as one moment to relax.

"We came here to unwind," I said. "All we've done so far is run, run, run. I thought we'd get take-out food and just hang out."

"We should have sex," she said with a smile. "Out here on the balcony."

It was exactly what I had hoped for. "You'll get no argument from me on that offer."

I didn't *need* to have sex with Jo. Each time we made love, however, I was reminded of the magic we created *as a couple*. In her absence, I was simplistic and satisfied with my existence. In her presence, I strived each and every day to become a better man.

A better man for her.

"It's almost time to eat," I said. "Decide what you want, and I'll order it."

She shrugged. "I don't care."

"Fine," I said. "I'll order calamari. Hell, maybe one of the places will have fresh crayfish."

She reached for her mouth and feigned vomiting. "Tyson…"

"Mexican?"

Her nose twitched.

"Mediterranean?"

She swallowed heavily.

"Chinese?"

The corner of her mouth curled upward a little. "I really don't care."

"Well, I'm thinking Chinese," I said.

She kissed me on the cheek. "That sounds good."

"Beef and broccoli with extra broccoli, and pot-stickers?"

"Get that sauce for the dumplings," she said with a nod.

"I always do."

Half an hour later, we were sitting at the same balcony, eating Chinese food out of cardboard containers and drinking wine out of plastic Solo cups.

She lifted her chopsticks to her mouth and bit a pot-sticker in two. With the other half suspended by the sticks, she let out a long breath. "Oh. My. God. This food is so good. I wish we didn't have to drive six hours to get it."

With Jo, food tasted better. Wine was sweeter. Life's darkest moments were more manageable. The sun was brighter. My future was clearer.

I leaned over the side of my chair and kissed her. "I love you."

She poked the other half of the pot-sticker in her mouth and kissed me. "I wub ew too."

"Dork."

She swallowed the food. "Asshole."

"Geek."

She looked me over. "FedEx dude."

I laughed. "That's the best you've got?"

She shrugged. "I don't have many complaints."

"*Dork* and *geek* weren't complaints," I said. "They were compliments."

She smiled. "You know what?"

"What?"

"I think I want to change the name of my book."

"What book?"

"The one you asked me about on our first date. Remember? Erotica or Romance?"

"Oh. Yeah." I chuckled at the thought of that conversation, and of my early desire to fuck her and walk away. "What are you going to call it now?"

She picked up another wonton and paused. "*The Geek, the Jock, and the Ten-Inch Cock.*"

I burst out laughing. "I like it. So, what's the category, or whatever? Erotica?"

She bit the wonton and shook her head. "Romance."

"You can't name a book like that and put it in romance, can you?"

"You can name it whatever you want. Content is what matters."

I grinned. "Our content is romance?"

"Sex drives the story, or the story drives the sex? With us, our story is awesome, and it drives the sex." She nibbled at the wonton, and then looked up. "We've got good character arc, too. Our progress. Look at how much you've blossomed. And, I went from being scared of you to being comfortable enough to fart."

I gestured toward her with the tip of my chopsticks. "Fart, then."

"Girls don't fart," she said flatly. "But, I could if I needed to."

"I like it that we've migrated from erotica to romance."

She lifted her chopsticks in agreement. "For me, that's been a lifelong goal."

We finished our food, cleaned up the mess, and sat side by side with our cups of wine. Gazing at the western sky, I gave thanks for Jo, my adopted family, our progress as a couple, and for the ability to make, and to accept, change.

Long before the sun set against the horizon, Jo gulped down what was left of her wine and stood.

"Get me some more, if you don't mind," I said, handing her my empty glass.

She straddled my thighs. "I wasn't going for more wine."

"Oh."

She reached inside my swim trunks and pulled the string, untying it. "I was planning on something else."

"I see."

She stood.

I hooked the sides of her bikini with my thumbs and pushed it down her thighs. As she kicked it to the side, I stood and removed my shorts. After taking my position in the chair, she sat on my lap, facing me.

She pressed her full lips to mine.

Kissing her took my mind places I never knew existed. It seemed we were always kissing, but then again, we always started and stopped with a kiss. Given our love for one another – and our inability to squelch our sexual desires – kissing was always just around the corner.

That night we made love in each other's arms while seated on the balcony.

It wasn't a cliché moment of love-making while the sun set.

There was no voyeurism.

It was Jo and I expressing our love for one another. Nothing more, and certainly nothing less. We didn't need gimmicks, onlookers, or toys to make things exciting between us. All we needed was our love for one another.

A love that was undeniably everlasting.

41

JO

I CROSSED my arms over my chest and let out a huff. "Why can't we just follow you?" I pleaded. "You know I hate riding in this car. It reminds me of when I was a kid."

My father opened the driver's door and paused. "We're all going together. In *one* car. We can't all ride in that damned race car of Tyson's, so we're going in this."

I opened the door and nearly barfed.

"It smells funny," I complained. "How about we just follow you?"

"We're all going *together*," my father growled.

"Since when do we go out to eat on Sunday?" Jarod asked. "We always eat here."

"Yeah," I chimed. "And since when do we eat at four o'clock?"

"Since right now." He climbed inside. "Get in the damned car, Jo."

"I like this car," Tyson said. "Is it a sixty-nine?"

"Seventy," Daddy shouted out the window. "Graduation gift. Never could bring myself to get rid of it."

I looked at Tyson and rolled my eyes. "One of the many reasons you remind me of him."

"In the car, Jo," my father bellowed.

"Josephine," my mother said softly. "Get in, please."

"Fine," I breathed.

My bare skin skipped along the plastic seat covers until I took my position at the center of the rear seat. The covers had preserved the seats for forty-eight years, keeping them in likenew condition. The trade-off was a horrific smell and ridiculous hard plastic to sit on.

"Wherever we're going, just hurry," I said. "Before I get sick."

My father lifted the ancient fedora from the car's dash, placed it on his head, and checked himself in the mirror. "The good thing about a Coupe De Ville is that no matter how long it takes to get there, you make the trip knowing you're going in style."

He started the car. "Get in, Jarod, or I'll leave your ass standing there with that dumb look on your face."

After Jarod got in, my father backed out of the garage. I was certain our week-long vacation memories were going to be replaced by the recollection of a family outing in a car from plastic seat cover hell.

As we merged onto the highway, my father reached for the dash-mounted tissue holder and let out a laugh. "Anyone need a Kleenex?"

"No," I snapped. "I don't need a fifty-year-old tissue."

"That's awesome," Tyson said. "I need to get one of those for my car."

"You better not," I insisted.

As the car floated down the highway, memories of my childhood drifted through my mind. Wiping ice cream off the seat covers with the edge of my thumb, fearful that my father would see that I'd come close to getting it on the floor.

Going to the drive-in theater.

Getting in street races at stoplights with high school kids while my mother yelled for him to *slow down*.

Jarod slapping me with the spare seat belt strap while we waited in line at the Carl's Junior drive-thru.

My father's constant threats to rid himself of the car each time he filled it with gas, only to be followed up with a wash, wax job, and polish when we returned home.

My incessant complaining that the air conditioner was cold, but never *cold enough*.

I looked up and smiled. "Turn it up!" I said, reciting the phrase I'd said every time it was hot in the car.

My father tilted his hat back with the brush of his hand. "It doesn't go any higher, Kidd-o."

"Where are we going?" I asked.

"You'll know when we get there," Jarod whispered.

"You'll know when we get there," my half-deaf father repeated.

I paid little attention to anything, other than the car-related memories that came rushing to the forefront of my mind.

My father exited the highway, drove along a frontage road for what seemed like forever, and eventually took a side street into a residential neighborhood.

"Are we going to dinner?" I asked.

"Just out for a little Sunday drive," he responded. "Sit back and enjoy the luxury."

My mother glanced over her shoulder and smiled. I smiled in return.

After driving deep into a neighborhood that I didn't recognize, we turned around and began driving right back out of it. My father's fascination with all things Texas wasn't satisfied with historical sites like the Alamo or the Moody Mansion.

It seemed he got more satisfaction from driving around looking at everyone else's homes. We did it often when I was a child, and I always wondered if one day he was simply going to buy one of the homes he was driving by ogling.

I later learned that the drives were nothing but a way for him to relax.

I now wondered if it was him dreaming a *what if things were different?*

I leaned toward Tyson. "He used to do this all the time. We'd drive for hours, just looking at other people's houses."

Tyson smiled. "I'm enjoying it."

The car slowed to a roll. I looked up. The neighborhood looked familiar, but not so much that I could determine where we were. The Dallas metro area was just too damned big.

Outside my father's window, amidst the older homes, a newly constructed white brick home sat atop a lushly landscaped hill. A wrap-around porch surrounded the home, inviting the occupants to spend their evenings enjoying the beautiful Autumn Texas evenings outdoors with a glass of sweet tea.

A For Sale sign sat askew beside the driveway. "Daddy, stop!" I looked at Tyson. "That house is just like mine, only bigger!"

His focus was in the opposite direction. "What house?"

I pointed toward Jarod's open window. "That one. It's…" I swallowed my excitement. "For sale."

"Well," my father said. "Let me park this SOB and we can take a look."

The neighborhood was eerily familiar, but all Texas neighborhoods looked the same once a person was inside one of them.

After my father parked the car across the street from the home, we all got out. Half the distance to the home, a chill ran along my spine. There was something about the home's front door that was all too familiar.

I glanced up and down the block.

I looked at my father, and then at Tyson. "This isn't." I swallowed heavily. "You didn't…"

"It is." Tyson smiled. "And, I did."

I took another look at the home. My hands began to shake. "It's…it's impossible."

"Without the help of a few loved ones," Tyson said. "It would have been."

The *newly constructed* home was sitting on Tyson's lot. At minimum, his home had received an extensive remodel, including the addition of a second story, a wrap-around porch, brick façade, and what looked to be an extra bedroom or two.

I swallowed hard once again, and then looked at Tyson. "What about. What about the radon gas?"

My father chuckled. "You might be overly cautious on some things, but you were gullible as hell on that one, Kidd-o."

My eyes shot to my father. "What are you—"

He smiled. "There was no radon gas."

"But Tyson got sick," I said. "You drove to the hospital and picked him up."

"Tyson got sick of listening to you whine." He chuckled. "That's the only sickness he had. I picked him up from meeting the contractors, not at the damned hospital."

I looked at my mother. "Did *you* know?"

"Sweetheart, I'm afraid I did."

"Mother!"

"Well," Jarod said. "I feel like the odd man out. I didn't know anything."

"How come there's a For Sale sign in the yard?" I asked.

Tyson raised his hand to his chin. "Can't decide whether to sell the thing or keep it."

I reached into my purse, pulled out my keys, and marched up the drive. After reaching the front door, I poked my key into a very familiar tarnished brass lock. After turning it, I let out a sigh and pushed open the door.

Nothing about the home was the same.

Nothing.

The beiges and browns were gone.

Grays and whites had replaced them. The kitchen's oak cabinets had been replaced by a long line of tall white ones.

Formica countertops had been replaced by white quartz.

Carpet had been replaced by wide planks of gray hardwood.

The home looked like something out of the magazines I spent hours studying before I remodeled my own home. The only thing I could see that I didn't like was that the kitchen had no stove.

Tyson stepped to my side. "Well?"

"Why doesn't the kitchen have a stove?"

"I thought if you decided you liked this place, we'd bring yours over. It makes the best breakfast in the entire state of Texas."

I pointed over my shoulder. "Go get that sign out of my yard, kind Sir."

I arched an eyebrow. "*Your* yard?"

"My apologies." She smiled and gave me a kiss. "*Our* yard."

42

TYSON

"SEEMS WEIRDER'N HELL EATIN' Sunday dinner at a house other'n my own," John complained. "I guess with life, comes change."

"Be nice, John," Jackie said.

"I was bein' nice, woman."

"You could be nicer."

John looked at Jo. "Steak's mighty fine, Kidd-o."

She smiled. "It's Tyson's family recipe. He found his father's cook book when they were remodeling the home."

"Family secret," I said. "Marinate the meat in buttermilk overnight."

Jackie grinned. "I'll have to remember that."

Having everyone in our home for Sunday dinner was a dream come true. Although I knew my father was absent, I felt like a part of him was always present in our home.

"The gravy's damned fine," John said.

"Credit to the magic stove," Jo said. "That, and my cast-iron skillet."

"That skillet was your grandmother's," Jackie said. "It's prepared many a meal."

"It's going to prepare many more," Jo replied.

Thoughts of evening meals at home, making our own memories, and feeling like I hadn't forfeited my father's legacy had me floating on cloud nine.

After we finished our meal, John retrieved the ice cream maker from the trunk of his Cadillac. Together, we made ice cream in the kitchen. Doing so reminded me of the day I repaired the machine in his garage.

We served the ice cream in special dishes that Jo had picked out during one of our many trips to *Restoration Hardware*.

I glanced around the table. Surrounded by my new family, I was exactly where I needed to be. I'd undoubtedly started living life late, but I was making up for it in quality.

I clanked my spoon against the side of my dish. "I've got two announcements."

Jackie pushed her ice cream to the side and clasped her hands together. "Pay attention, John."

"I can eat and listen at the same time," John mumbled.

Jackie cleared her throat. "Jarod."

"I'm listening."

Jo looked up. "I have no idea what this is about."

"Change," I said.

"Oh, Lord." Jo shook her head. "You are not making any changes to this home. Not one!"

"I quit my job," I said.

Jo's eyes went wide. "You *what?*"

"Quit."

Jo's eyes shot from her ice cream to me. "You quit your job?"

I nodded. "Yep."

"What are you going to do?"

I glanced at John, and then at her. "I've got a few ideas."

"Like what?"

"Right now, they're not important."

"When are they important?" she asked.

"I'll let you know when they become so. I just wanted everyone to know I'm currently amongst the unemployed."

John slapped his hand against my shoulder. "Proud of you, Son."

Jo gave him a cross look, and then gave me one. "I'm afraid to ask what the second announcement is."

I stood and turned to face her. With her hair pinned in a tight bun, she looked like she did on the night of our first date. The recollection of her vomiting on my car caused me to cough out a laugh.

"Are you going to tell a joke?" she asked.

I shook my head. "No."

She wrinkled her nose. "What are you doing? Sit down."

After nervously reaching into my pocket, I lowered myself to one knee. "Josephine Annabelle Watson—"

"Oh my God," she cried. "Tyson…"

"Josephine Annabelle Watson—"

Tears welled in her eyes. She glanced at John.

"Don't look at him," I said. "I already asked his permission. I'm trying to ask yours."

She met my gaze.

I'd spent a lifetime armed with the belief that the moment that was upon me would never happen. Josephine had spent a lifetime reading romance novels, praying that one day the moment would arrive.

The moment had arrived.

It was time for me to propose marriage to the most beautiful woman in the state of Texas.

"Josephine Annabelle Watson. You changed my life with one kiss. I'd like to change yours with a lifetime of kisses." I raised the ring and held it between us. "Will you marry me?"

She wiped her eyes with the heels of her palms and nodded. "I will."

"Hot damn!" John howled. "Now get busy making me a grandbaby!"

I looked at John and winked. "That's next on the list, Sir."

"Call me Dad," he said. "If you care to, that is. We're family now, pretty much."

I glanced at the ceiling.

You'll always be my Pop, Pop.

He's not a replacement, he's just my Dad.

I swallowed a mouthful of emotion and grinned. "That's next on the list, Dad."

EPILOGUE

THE FLUORESCENT LIGHTS surrounding the field cut through the winter evening darkness, illuminating the freshly planted sod to a near daylight-like luster. Laser-straight lines in ten-yard increments clearly marked the yardage of the three-hundred-and-sixty by one-hundred-and-sixty-foot regulation-sized field.

Rows of bleachers sat on either side of the well-lighted stadium, which had been built at the edge of iron-rich farm ground. Beyond it, fields of corn stretched for as far as the eye could see.

The road leading to the stadium was peppered with cars and trucks driven by parents of the children that had come from miles around, all clinging to the hope of their child becoming as noteworthy as the man who built the field with his labor, sweat, and love for the game.

Beneath the stadium's grand entrance, an elderly man leaned against a lamppost. He ran his hand over his crew cut. Beside him, a young woman clutched a quilted blanket and watched intently as the children tossed footballs through rubber-tired targets.

"Elbows tucked," the instructor barked. "Shoulder back. Backs straight. Keep your eyes on the prize."

The children did as they were instructed, each tossing the ball with the hope of one day becoming as talented as the man who instructed them.

Beyond the lights of the stadium and past the rows of corn, an elderly woman opened her front door. She reached for a weathered rope that hung from beneath the overhang of the porch.

Three times she tugged the rope, each as sharply as the first. The clapper swung against the century-old mouth of the brass bell, sending three pleasant tones to all those within earshot.

Upon hearing the familiar sound, the elderly man straightened his posture. He leaned away from the lamppost and turned toward his daughter. She pushed her glasses up her nose with the tip of her finger and met his pride-filled gaze.

"If that bell's a ringin'," he said. "You can bet it's ready to eat."

The young woman lifted her chin and prepared to signal her husband, warning of the meal that lay in wait.

"You all know what that means," the instructor shouted. "This session's over."

He glanced at the eldest child on the field, a thirteen-year-old boy from Austin, Texas. The boy had promise of being the next great high school standout athlete, and the instructor recognized the talent.

"Get everything locked up, Byron," the instructor said.

"Yes, Sir," the boy responded with a smile. "See you on Wednesday."

"Ice on that elbow," the instructor warned. "You don't want it to swell."

The boy gave a sharp nod. "Yes, Sir, Mister Neese."

"Tyson," the instructor said. "Or you can call me TJ."

The boy smiled. "Yes, Sir, Mister TJ."

The instructor, a young man thirty-seven years of age, smiled and strode toward the elderly man and young woman who anxiously waited to turn toward the distant farmhouse.

Upon reaching them, he kissed the woman on the cheek.

The young woman pulled the quilted blanket she was clutching to the side. "Be careful," she insisted. "You'll squash him."

The elderly man chuckled. "C'mon, Jo, my grandson's tougher

than that. You're holding a future quarterback of the Dallas Cowboys, Kidd-o."

The young woman smiled but didn't respond. Silently, she hoped her father was correct. Nothing would please her more than to see her son succeed in such endeavors.

Side by side, they walked toward the farmhouse. Their place settings, loaded with generous portions of country fried steaks, mashed potatoes, gravy, and green beans, lay steaming in wait of their arrival.

Half the distance to the farmhouse, the stadium lights behind them went dark.

The instructor glanced over his shoulder and bid a silent farewell to the man who oversaw each and every football practice, while seated in the stands.

See you Wednesday, Pop.

ALSO BY SCOTT HILDRETH

Baby Girl Series

Baby Girl - Ruined: http://amzn.to/2FAxe6G

Baby Girl - Owned: http://amzn.to/2FCVxku

Baby Girl - Loved: http://amzn.to/2peR1yw

The UN Series (Boxing Romance)

Undefeated - Book One: http://amzn.to/2pbBsHW

Unstoppable - Book Two: http://amzn.to/2pjrsv8

Unleashed - Book Three: http://amzn.to/2pfgIPh

Unbroken - Book Four: http://amzn.to/2FCnbOs

Selected Sinners Series (MC)

Making the Cut - Book One: http://amzn.to/2v2D5fS

Taking the Heat - Book Two: http://amzn.to/2vVAcwo

Otis - Book Three: http://amzn.to/2vUJ9G4

Hung - Book Four: http://amzn.to/2wuUvC9

Ex-Con - Book Five: http://amzn.to/2wkgVWf

Money Shot - Book Six: http://amzn.to/2x9nwQK

Hard Corps - Book Seven: http://amzn.to/2wuJpNH

Filthy Fucker's Series (MC)

Hard - Book One: http://amzn.to/2jNSCpZ

Rough - Book Two: http://amzn.to/2iAYjcJ

Dirty - Book Three: http://amzn.to/2jUWqpd

Rigid - Book Four: http://amzn.to/2n3js02

Nuts - Book Five: http://amzn.to/2rI1IMw

Thick - Book Six: http://amzn.to/2AZeLxa

His Rules (spin off): http://amzn.to/2FYFcG6

Devil's Disciples Series (MC)

Baker - Book One: http://amzn.to/2EgT9iH

Cash - Book Two: http://amzn.to/2DwaL4Q

Ghost - Book Three: https://amzn.to/2wgRBhM

Bodies, Ink and Steel Series

Blurred Lines: http://amzn.to/2pexYEo

Pretty in Ink: http://amzn.to/2peziad

Stand Alone Books

Lover Come Back: https://amzn.to/2BvxSAN

Broken People: http://amzn.to/2FO1189

Threefold: http://amzn.to/2pe7Aub

Karter: http://amzn.to/2HBvxTc

Snatch: http://amzn.to/2FTq2Cb

Fuck Buddy: http://amzn.to/2pffofr

Dick: http://amzn.to/2phAXMn

Brawler: http://amzn.to/2FDaOld

The Alpha-Bet: http://amzn.to/2FKnUJx

Finding Parker: http://amzn.to/2pbyzXx

Made in the USA
Coppell, TX
12 May 2022

77696102R00173